YOUR SCARRED HEART

Ladies of the Order - Book 4

ADELE CLEE

Your Scarred Heart
Copyright © 2022 Adele Clee
All rights reserved.
ISBN-13: 978-1-8383839-8-5

Cover by Dar Albert at Wicked Smart Designs

Of Love: A Sonnet

How love came in I do not know,
Whether by the eye, or ear, or no;
Or whether with the soul it came
(At first) infused with the same;
Whether in part 'tis here or there,
Or, like the soul, whole every where.
This troubles me; but I as well
As any other, this can tell;
That when from hence she does depart,
The outlet then is from the heart.

Robert Herrick, 1591 - 1674

CHAPTER 1

Miss Honora Wild thrust the shillings into the jarvey's outstretched hand, tipping him an extra coin. Being charitable reaped its own rewards, though her father would insist that was how Lucifer saw benevolence.

"Thank you, Mr Hirst. I shan't need a ride home."

Mr Hirst often parked his hackney cab a short walk from her residence on Howland Street, a property owned by her employer, and her temporary abode. When Mr Daventry discovered she lacked the skills needed to catch criminals, she would soon find herself in want of a new home and position.

Bidding Mr Hirst good day, Nora took a moment to gather her composure. Meeting a potential new client should be an exciting prospect for any enquiry agent. Meeting a man with a horrid scar on his cheek, a man believed to have murdered members of his own family, proved more than unnerving.

She noticed Mr Daventry waiting at the entrance to the auction house. The master of the Order was a handsome man of thirty, a hard taskmaster, and ruthless in his cause to see justice served. Indeed, he must be convinced of Lord Deville's innocence, else he would have refused to take his case.

"Good afternoon, Miss Wild. I trust all is well." Mr Daventry scanned her with an inscrutable eye. "You've not had second thoughts about meeting Lord Deville?"

Nora lifted her chin. "Not at all, sir." It was a dreadful lie. She had woken from a nightmare in the early hours, one where the scarred baron lunged from the shadows, wielding a blood-soaked blade. "You trust Lord Deville, and you're never wrong about a gentleman's character."

Indeed, she prayed Lord Deville wasn't the exception.

"Your safety is paramount," Mr Daventry said, ushering her into the entrance hall, which was surprisingly quiet considering the rooms were full of people fighting over antiquities. "I would never place you in a precarious position."

Nora forced a smile. "I trust your judgement, sir, and would like to discern Lord Deville's character for myself. I am not one to place faith in cruel gossip." Although when people accused a man of murder, it was hard not to sit up and take notice.

"I thought we would attend the auction. It's surprising what you can learn about a man when you watch how he interacts with others."

Being an amateur sleuth, Nora merely nodded.

Mr Daventry escorted her past the sweeping oak staircase to a door on the left. Before entering the auction room, he reminded her to remain silent and avoid any sudden movements lest she wished to find herself the owner of an ugly figurine by Gouyn.

They slipped into the oak-panelled room and stood at the back, near the clerk's imposing desk, to better observe the proceedings.

People had crammed onto the benches, though she was surprised to see as many bonnets as top hats. Odd that the ladies occupied the uppermost seats. None sat in the first two rows.

The reason became apparent when her gaze fell to the

impressive figure of a man being given a wide berth at the front.

"Deville is sitting near the rostrum," Mr Daventry muttered, pointing inconspicuously. "He's here to purchase the harpsichord."

Nora glanced at the beautiful cypress instrument on the dais and then at the striking gentleman people wished to avoid. He didn't seem the sort to appreciate a charming tune, and so she made the obvious assumption. It must be a gift for his mistress, or perhaps his betrothed.

"Sir, you said Lord Deville had no close relatives." She noted the lord's stern profile, wondering if loneliness was the reason for his disdainful disposition. "Is he making plans to marry?"

Amusement played in Mr Daventry's eyes. "I tell you Deville is here to purchase a harpsichord, and you assume he's in want of a wife."

"I based my assumption on the fact he has rather large hands. Nowhere near nimble enough to play proficiently. Therefore, the harpsichord must be a gift."

"And where have you seen Lord Deville's hands?"

"At Monroe's bookshop on the Strand." And in her nightmares, although she would not declare that. "He was purchasing an old leather-bound tome. No other gentleman bears such a scar, and so it had to be Lord Deville."

"If you hope to solve this case, Miss Wild, you must look beyond what is obvious." Mr Daventry's tone carried a hint of reproach. "Deville's brother lived a frivolous life. He was declared bankrupt and sold many family heirlooms to pay his debts. Now Deville has inherited, he's made it his life's mission to reclaim those items. That's why he wants the harpsichord. It belonged to his great-grandmother."

"Oh," she said, taking the mild reprimand on the chin. The information went some way to banishing her fears. Such an act spoke of a responsible man, a loyal man, not a beast with a dreadful scar who growled at everyone in sight.

Nora might have asked about Lord Deville's need to restore his home to its former glory, but the white-haired auctioneer banged his hammer loudly on the rostrum, commanding everyone's attention.

"Now for something rather s-spectacular," he said, swallowing nervously as he read from his script. "An opportunity to own a rare item crafted by the famous Italian instrument maker Girolamo Zenti."

Lord Deville groaned. "Get on with it, Fathers."

Mr Fathers fought to maintain his composure. He proceeded to follow his notes, describing the harpsichord in great detail, including the black-stained hardwood accidentals, whatever they might be.

"I am not leaving without the harpsichord." Lord Deville's baritone voice carried a menacing undertone. "Name your price. Let's save everyone the trouble of bidding."

Lord Deville glowered at the crowd, daring them to raise an objection. He met Nora's gaze and held it for a few heart-stopping seconds. She waited for his sneer of disappointment when he noticed Mr Daventry and realised she was his agent.

It didn't come.

Nerves fluttered in her chest, but she straightened her spectacles, for they were a shield strong enough to ward off a French invasion.

"My lord, we m-must adhere to the rules," Mr Fathers stuttered. "Everyone must be allowed to place a bid."

Lord Deville dragged his gaze back to the trembling man behind the rostrum. Then he rose to an intimidating height of over six feet and addressed the throng. "Does anyone wish to purchase this old harpsichord? I suppose the real question is, does anyone have the courage to bid against me?"

No one dared look at him.

No one made a murmur.

"There you have it, Fathers. Mine shall be the only tender. Put an end to this ridiculous charade and name your damn price."

A few ladies gasped at the lord's coarse language, but he made no apology. Instead, he stepped up to the rostrum, folded his muscular arms across his chest and tapped his foot impatiently.

Mr Fathers' hands shook as he shuffled his papers. "The opening b-bid is a thousand p-pounds, my lord. That is the reserve."

"A thousand pounds!" Lord Deville's mocking laugh echoed through the room. "The Carters purchased it from my brother for three hundred."

Mr Fathers shifted uncomfortably. "Estate auctions lend towards lower bids, my lord, and one must not forget that the company's commission stands at ten per cent."

"Ten! The usual rate is seven."

"I do not make the rules, my lord." The auctioneer went on to complain about the rising cost of rent and insurance.

"Stop waffling, Fathers. I bid a thousand pounds for the harpsichord. Now strike your damn hammer so you may move to the next lot."

Mr Fathers paled and looked like he might swoon. "But Mr Carter placed a stipulation on the sale."

"What stipulation?"

"Y-you cannot purchase the item, my lord."

The crowd gasped. People looked at the door, perhaps deciding whether to make a quick escape. The air thrummed with tension. Perhaps everyone feared Lord Deville would summon his minions and raze the house to the ground.

"I demand to see a record of this stipulation." A determined Lord Deville rounded the rostrum and refused to move until Mr Fathers found proof of Mr Carter's request.

"I cannot overrule a client's instruction."

Nora watched with morbid fascination.

How would Lord Deville react? He appeared as dangerous as the devil, yet she admired his strength and tenacity. She had shown similar qualities when confronting her father, though she had not expected to find herself alone and destitute in a sprawling swine of a city.

But then the lord, who from his flawless side might be considered the most handsome man she had ever laid eyes upon, did something that left her heart pounding.

Lord Deville lowered his gaze. She saw the fight leave his body like a demon exorcised by yet another injustice. He was powerless to act, and she knew that feeling only too well.

Without thinking, Nora stepped forward and raised her hand. "I bid a thousand pounds for the harpsichord." She glanced at the crowd but imagined her father's angry face glaring back. It gave her the confidence to be bold. "Woe betide anyone who bids against me. Strike your hammer, Mr Fathers, before Lord Deville curses us all to the fiery pits of hell."

She sounded much like the Reverend Wild, the wolf in sheep's clothing who lectured his congregation on benevolence but could not show a modicum of kindness to his kin.

Lord Deville met Nora's gaze and did something else to make her heart gallop—he smiled. Yes, it was just a slight curl of his lips, but it was probably the closest he came to looking pleased.

Mr Fathers seemed confounded by this new development until Lord Deville said, "Strike your hammer. Miss Wild has met the reserve. I shall personally flog the man who bids against her."

No one dared breathe, let alone raise an objection, though the lack of air in Nora's lungs stemmed from the fact Lord Deville knew her name.

Eager to bring the matter to a swift end, Mr Fathers declared Nora the new owner of the harpsichord and directed her to his clerk's desk at the back of the room.

But the crowd had no interest in the next lot: a painting of a pug wearing a silver crown. All heads turned in Nora's direction. Everyone stared at the tall, brooding figure of Lord Deville striding towards her.

The devil's disciple came to a halt a mere arm's length away. His dark eyes scanned her dull brown pelisse, then her spectacles, while she tried to avoid looking at his ugly scar.

"You find yourself in a predicament, Miss Wild." He spoke in a low, teasing voice that stirred the hairs on her nape, though she couldn't decide if it was from nerves or something more shocking. "One suspects you do not have a thousand pounds to pay for the harpsichord."

Be brave! Don't let him intimidate you!

"And why is that, my lord?" Nora said politely. "Please tell me you haven't looked at my plain clothes and made the usual assumption."

He arched a brow. "Come now. A lady forced to work as an enquiry agent does not have a thousand pounds to waste on a musical instrument she cannot play."

Somewhat shaken by Lord Deville's direct manner, she focused on the only point she could contest. "I choose to work. My desire to punish dishonest men is the reason I accepted the position at the Order." And to give her the strength to face her tormentor again.

The lord lowered his head, his hot breath whispering over her cheek. "Admit it, Miss Wild. You don't have a hundred pounds, let alone a thousand."

"My lord, your only concern should be what I plan to do with your great-grandmother's harpsichord, not whether I have access to funds."

His arrogant sneer drew attention to his disfigurement. "We both know you purchased the instrument for me, your client."

"Prospective client. I haven't accepted your case." Tired of wrangling with this man, Nora was about to admit she had barely ten pounds to her name, when Mr Daventry appeared and said the oddest thing.

"I have settled your account, Miss Wild, and told the clerk to have the harpsichord delivered to Howland Street."

"Howland Street! Why in Lucifer's name would you do that?" Lord Deville firmed his jaw. "Miss Wild placed the bid on my behalf because of Carter's ridiculous stipulation."

Mr Daventry shrugged. "Call it a means of ensuring Miss Wild receives your full attention while working on the case. I expect you to assist her where necessary. Particularly if she's to visit Whitstable."

Nora froze.

She was to work with Lord Deville! In Whitstable!

If the lord was capable of finding his brother's killer, why did he need to hire an enquiry agent? And, as his brother died a year ago, why wait until now?

Lord Deville narrowed his gaze. "You're bribing me?"

"No, merely ensuring you consider Miss Wild's safety when employing her to find your brother's murderer."

"Keep your voice down." Lord Deville glanced briefly over his shoulder. "I'll not have all of London knowing my business."

Mr Daventry grinned. "You arranged to meet us in a coffeehouse. News will spread. The *ton* will soon learn you've hired an enquiry agent. Even a simple man will draw the obvious conclusion."

"I hired a private room at McGinty's," the lord countered, drawing them towards the door, away from the pricked ears of the gossips huddled together on the benches. "I hadn't planned on sitting in the bay window, waving to every passerby."

Surely most people noticed a man with such a prominent scar, even if he was just walking through a coffeehouse on a dreary April afternoon.

"Perhaps we should continue this conversation at McGinty's," Nora said, eager to learn why people presumed the lord was a murderer. Moreover, a frustrated Mr Fathers repeatedly banged his hammer to signal the next lot.

Both gentlemen agreed, although neither spoke again until they were inside the coffeehouse and seated at the crude wooden table in the sparsely furnished parlour.

"While Mr Daventry knows why you want to hire an agent, my lord," Nora began, trying not to stammer, "I would like to understand your motive before agreeing to take your case."

Seated opposite, the lord studied her with a critical eye. "I wonder if there has been a mistake, Miss Wild."

"A mistake?"

Lord Deville directed his next comment to Mr Daventry. "She's a mere slip of a girl. Hardly experienced enough to find a woman as conniving as Johanna. Perhaps I should pay you for the harpsichord and leave you to your business."

A slip of a girl?

How dare he!

Weeks ago, Nora would have sat silently, head bowed, ashamed of being considered weak and insignificant, believing the terrible things her father had said were true. But Mr Daventry had seen to her education. While she had a lot to learn about being forthright and self-assured, she had gained the confidence to voice her opinion.

"I am a woman of four and twenty," she informed Lord Deville. "I have seen things you've only read about in your high-priced tomes." The month spent at Madame Matisse's Pleasure Parlour had given her an insight into a man's baser needs. "Maybe Mr Daventry *has* made a mistake. His mistake is thinking you have the skill to assist me when you failed the simple task of purchasing the harpsichord."

Lord Deville's handsome eyes widened.

"Miss Wild has a point," Mr Daventry said with a chuckle as he poured himself coffee from the pot. "Without her, some other fellow would own your heirloom. Besides, I have every faith she has the skills to succeed."

Nora declined Mr Daventry's offer of coffee, though was flattered by his praise. "Let us begin again, my lord. Why do you want to hire an enquiry agent?"

The lord relaxed back in the seat. "Because unless I prove I did not murder my brother and his wife, I fear circumstantial evidence may lead to my arrest."

Nora recalled what little she knew of the couple's demise —albeit second-hand information from a reliable source. "Your brother died a year ago. If the authorities had evidence, would they not have questioned you at the time? And surely they would need damning proof to arrest a peer."

Lord Deville reached into his coat pocket, removed a letter and offered it to Nora. "I have received a similar letter every month since November. Read it. Make of it what you will."

Nora took the missive and examined the broken seal. "Were all the letters sealed with dark green wax?" It wasn't a common choice.

"Yes. Why do you ask?"

"Some consider green a symbol of greed and jealousy."

"That is exactly what the letter implies," the lord said, looking mildly impressed by her observation. "Strange you noticed. Most ladies would say green signifies hope and rebirth."

"Then be assured I'm the right agent for your case."

Nora peeled back the folds, noted the letter was dated a week ago and that it carried a faint hint of jasmine. She read the elegant feminine script written by someone who professed to be more than a friend.

My love,
I found another of your lost heirlooms in Monroe's bookshop on the Strand—that old tome of Greek tales your mother read to you

when you were a boy. If I strive to ensure your beloved treasures are returned, will you promise to stop this bitter vendetta? Felix is dead, and you have what you wanted. Lord of Highcliffe. Who would have thought you capable of achieving your ambition? Don't make me give them proof you killed the devil.

Pursue me at your peril!

Nora raised her gaze, only to meet Lord Deville's hard stare. "Are all the letters similar?" she said, struggling to imagine this cold, austere man engaged in an intimate relationship. Did they all bear the same endearment?

"The threat is always the same. Each letter points to a different item sold by my brother to pay his debts, though the book of Greek tales wasn't included in the sale. It's been missing since I inherited." Lord Deville snatched his coffee cup and downed the beverage as if it were a soothing elixir, though it failed to cool his temper. "That's how I know they were written by my sister-in-law, Johanna."

He seemed convinced the woman was alive!

In truth, it was the most obvious assumption.

"I was told she died alongside your brother. According to my source, they both fell from a cliff. They found his battered body on the beach, but say hers was washed out to sea, lost forever." Though Nora would need to study the crime scene to know if that was plausible.

The lord gritted his teeth. "The evidence to support that claim is weak. A fisherman supposedly saw them arguing on the clifftop and swears my brother pushed Johanna over the edge before jumping. Felix was a selfish bast—" He stopped abruptly and modified his tone. "Felix would not have taken his own life. I've searched for the fisherman, but he's cast his net elsewhere."

Nora glanced at the letter again. It was impolite to ask a gentleman about his affairs, but she needed to know if this man could feel something other than anger.

"You say Johanna wrote the letter, my lord. It reads as if you were in an intimate relationship. Were you in love with your sister-in-law?"

Lord Deville found the question amusing. "In love with Johanna? Miss Wild, I despise her to the depths of my being. She uses the endearment to torment me. The woman won't rest until I'm carted off to an asylum or hanged from the gallows."

"My advice is to have an open mind," Mr Daventry interjected. "I've seen many cases where the villain is the person one least expects. The focus now is where to begin the investigation."

Lord Deville resumed his usual resentful expression. "First, I must decide whether to hire Miss Wild."

Nora fought to remain indifferent. Lord Deville shared characteristics with the mystery letter writer: both enjoyed provoking a reaction.

"Don't waste our time, Deville." Mr Daventry spoke calmly and did not use the harpsichord to persuade the lord to hire her. "Another client has requested Miss Wild's assistance. But you may ask her one question if it will satisfy your curiosity and help you come to a swift decision."

The news came as a surprise to Nora. She studied the lord, who possessed such a rugged appeal, wondering if another client might be less demanding. The flicker of impatience in Lord Deville's eyes served as a warning. The determined set of his jaw and the angry scar running the length of his cheek said the man was obstinate—too headstrong to follow a woman's advice.

Indeed, she was inclined to stand and tell Lord Deville she found his lack of forbearance a problem. But she owed Mr Daventry a debt she had to repay, and so she sat patiently waiting for the lord to ask his probing question.

She expected him to ask how she planned to tackle the case or request a list of her credentials. Mentally, she planned her reply but would not mention learning to defend herself after the terrifying incident at the Pleasure Parlour.

Instead, the lord asked a question that threatened her fragile composure. "What tragedy led to you becoming an enquiry agent, Miss Wild?"

CHAPTER 2

Sylvester watched Miss Wild with keen interest. He could have asked several questions, but she was hiding something beneath her crooked spectacles and confident facade. And he was determined to discover her secret before hiring her as his agent.

"I found myself destitute," came the four words that failed to reveal the true nature of her dilemma.

"You have the manner and eloquence of a gentleman's daughter, Miss Wild." Unlike Johanna, who was as coarse as a Covent Garden harlot. "How did you find yourself impoverished on London's perilous streets?"

"You were permitted one question, Deville," Lucius Daventry admonished, "and Miss Wild has answered."

Daventry was not usually so brusque, which only added to the intrigue surrounding Miss Wild's curious past.

Sylvester raised a brow. "I am merely repeating the same question because the answer proved unsatisfactory." He decided to explain why the lack of information was a problem for him. "Deceitful women have been the bane of my existence." Indeed, he wore a permanent scar as proof. "Forgive me if I seek to clarify the nature of your agent's character."

Daventry opened his mouth to speak, but Miss Wild raised a silencing hand. "Sir, I would like to answer Lord Deville's question, if I may."

The master of the Order gestured for her to continue.

Miss Wild fixed Sylvester with her intense brown gaze, leaving him itching to remove her spectacles and test her mettle. "I shall give you a brief overview of events on condition you pry no further."

Reluctantly, he agreed.

"My mother left when I was ten, and I have not seen her since. I have no notion whether she is alive or dead, though I think about her often."

A sudden wave of grief swept over him, forcing him to press his hand to his chest to ease the infernal ache. "My mother died while I was away in Italy. Living with the uncertainty must be difficult."

Her understanding smile helped to ease his physical discomfort. "I left my father's home seven months ago. He's a vicar and undoubtedly one of the cruellest men walking the earth. I understand why my mother ran away. If I consider my own experience, he probably cast her out."

Although she tried to mask her distress, she gripped the coffee pot with a shaky hand. The beverage splashed onto the table as she filled her cup. The coffee must be cold, but she drank as if it were laudanum to numb her pain.

Sylvester waited for her to continue. Unsure why he found her fascinating when he was usually guarded in a woman's presence. But then his father had been equally wicked, and it seemed they had things in common.

"On my first night in London, a thief stole what little money I had." Miss Wild lowered her gaze briefly, a clear sign the tale was more complicated than that. "One of Madame Matisse's girls found me sobbing in an alley and took me back to the Pleasure Parlour. I worked there as a maid until Mr Daventry offered me a position." She glanced at the gentleman in question. "I have never known such kindness. While every instinct urges me to refuse this case, I owe him a great debt. A debt that must be repaid."

"You owe me nothing, Miss Wild." Daventry sat forward and pinned Sylvester with his unforgiving stare. "My agent will conduct a thorough investigation. If your great-grandmother's harpsichord is to grace your drawing room again, you will assist her in solving the case."

Sylvester couldn't help but laugh. He admired Daventry's effrontery and his faith in his agent. "Then I have no choice but to hire Miss Wild to find Johanna and discover what devious game she's playing. I must know exactly how my brother died."

He had not based his decision on securing the return of a precious heirloom. He wished to hire Miss Wild because he believed every word of her story, and because, contrary to appearance and public opinion, he had some compassion for her plight.

The lady nibbled her plump bottom lip—a nervous habit, though he found it rather becoming. She cast Mr Daventry a sidelong glance before saying with some reluctance, "Very well. I shall take your case, my lord. I shall attempt to determine if your sister-in-law is alive."

"Excellent." Daventry drained his coffee cup and pushed out of the chair. "You can start immediately, Miss Wild. You'll keep me abreast of your progress. Send word to Hart Street should you encounter any problems."

Was that to be the extent of Daventry's input? With only a few words of encouragement, did he intend to leave this woman to solve a murder case alone?

"Sir, a visit to Whitstable is necessary. I must question Lord Deville's staff and attempt to understand what happened in the days leading up to the unexplained deaths."

The deaths were not unexplained. Johanna had murdered Felix and bribed a fisherman to lie. When questioned, Whittle, Mrs Egan and the rest of the staff had given identical accounts of a volatile relationship where one might have easily murdered the other.

"Bower will accompany you to Whitstable. He will be on hand should you require assistance." Daventry turned to Sylvester. "I trust Miss Wild may travel with you."

"Indeed."

Daventry spoke only to make the arrangements before bidding them both good day. He left them in the shabby parlour, taking Miss Wild's confidence with him.

The lady sat rigid in the chair, her mouth drawn thin. If anything, she should put his mind at ease, yet he found himself searching for a way to break down her barriers.

When she looked at the open letter on the table, he was suddenly struck by a startling inconsistency.

"We seem to have a problem, Miss Wild." He reached across the table to remove her spectacles. "May I?"

Miss Wild recoiled in horror. "No, you may not!"

"Forgive me. I merely wish to examine the glass." He noted the flash of fear in her eyes. Surely she didn't think he might strike her! "I wish to assess the quality of your eyesight. Should an enquiry agent not have excellent vision? Else, how might you note the finer details?"

"I assure you, I can see perfectly well."

"Hence why I'm confused you're wearing spectacles. You watched the auction from the back of the room and read Johanna's letter. Not once did you remove them or peer over the rim."

She paled but offered no explanation.

"Do you want to look scholarly? A client might have more faith in a woman who's well read."

"Of course not." A blush stained her cheeks. "I do not need a ruse to prove my worth."

"Then why wear spectacles you don't need?" What sort of trickery was this? "As I have already explained, I cannot abide devious women. State your reason for this deception, Miss Wild, or I shall seek another agent."

Miss Wild opened her mouth but struggled to answer.

Old feelings of mistrust surfaced.

Sylvester stood abruptly, the chair scrapping on the boards. "Good day, Miss Wild. When you next see Lucius Daventry, please explain my reason for not hiring you."

He was at the door when she cried, "Wait! Please!"

Hearing her desperate plea, he faced her.

Her shoulders sagged. "I'm hiding."

"Hiding?"

"Hiding from my father. Hiding from myself."

Sylvester jerked his head. A disguise made perfect sense if her father was as evil as she claimed. "Yes, you're running from a man who controlled you. Why would you want to hide from yourself?"

She waved impatiently for him to sit. "Because I'm a coward. A coward needs armour to enter the fray."

"I was under the impression I'd hired an intelligent woman whose compassionate heart often leads her astray." He flicked his coattails and sat. "I have yet to see evidence of any other weakness."

Indeed, he was the one who had developed a weakness. Why was he prompting her for an answer? Why was he complimenting her character when he should simply leave and deal with Johanna himself?

"My compassionate heart?" she said. "You speak of me purchasing the harpsichord?"

"Did Daventry tell you to make the bid?" Instinct said no. He had seen the glint of surprise in her eyes when Daventry said he'd settled her account. "Did he know of Carter's stipulation? Did you know he planned to hold me to ransom?"

"Truthfully, I acted without thought. I presumed you would give me the money to pay for the instrument."

"What prompted you to act?" A coward would have

remained silent, would have lacked the strength to stand before a crowd and help a man marred by an ugly scar.

She shrugged. "Because I know what it's like to feel helpless. And I couldn't bear the thought of you losing something so precious just because people have invented a story about you."

No one had ever shown him such kindness. He had been shunned long before gaining his scar. The injury merely prevented people from slandering him to his face.

"How can you be sure it is a story? I had every reason to kill my brother. We were at war for years." Sylvester turned his face to better show the evidence of their hatred. "He's the one who sliced open my cheek."

Miss Wild inhaled sharply as she considered the ugly mark running from his temple to his jaw. "From my own experience, the Devil chose the guise of a godly man to do his work. He would not choose a man with a terrible disfigurement. Furthermore, Mr Daventry likes you, and he is never wrong about a gentleman's character."

Sylvester considered her for a moment. He could see why Daventry had hired her. The master of the Order fought against injustice, and Miss Wild looked like a woman who had suffered unfairly.

"Shall we begin again, Miss Wild? What say you remove your disguise and we consider the best way to approach my case?" He was rarely so benevolent.

Miss Wild pushed her spectacles firmly onto her nose. "I would prefer to wear them when in London, my lord. Perhaps when we reach Whitstable, I may consider your request."

Sylvester inclined his head. "Would you be free to journey to Kent tomorrow? On the way, you can read the other letters Johanna sent, and I'll explain something of the history that caused the dreadful rift in my family."

He was reluctant to speak about his mother's amorous antics, to lay the blame at the door of the deceased, but then

Miss Wild had secrets of her own. Indeed, numerous questions flitted through Sylvester's mind. The most prominent being why an intelligent woman thought it prudent to reside at the Pleasure Parlour?

"We don't know Johanna sent the letters." Miss Wild set about tidying the coffee cups. Perhaps it was an old habit from her time playing maid at a bawdyhouse. "I must assume she is dead until I find evidence to prove otherwise."

Sylvester grasped Miss Wild's hand, desperate to prove he wasn't mad. "Johanna's alive! I know it!" He felt it to the marrow of his bones. Good God, surely she sensed it, too.

Miss Wild stared wide-eyed, her face a mask of unease. "My lord, if we're to work together, you must refrain from these sudden outbursts." She snatched back her dainty hand.

"Forgive me." A lady did not want to be mauled by a monster. Yet he had forgotten that the touch of another could be so comforting. "I shall restrain myself lest you feel inclined to hit me with the coffee pot."

He'd hoped a little light-hearted banter might relieve the tension, but Miss Wild's brows shot up in horror. "What did Mr Daventry tell you?"

Confused, Sylvester shrugged.

"What did he tell you about my time at the Pleasure Parlour?" she pressed. "He told you something, else you wouldn't have made that terrible joke at my expense."

"I assure you, Daventry told me nothing about you other than he believed you were the perfect person to solve my case." But by God, he was keen to know what had caused such an intense reaction.

She studied him for a few uncomfortable seconds before sighing. "Tell me about Johanna. Tell me what you know of her character."

"I'll struggle to do that without cursing her to Hades." He despised the shrew and hoped to persuade Miss Wild his brother hadn't murdered the strumpet. "Johanna is the devil's spawn." He had purposely spoken in the present tense. "As you will soon discover."

"When did she marry your brother?"

"Three years ago while I was in Italy. She was his mistress for a year before that." During which time she had poisoned Felix's mind, enough for him to make her an offer. "The prestigious Lady Deville was once a courtesan."

"A courtesan!" Miss Wild frowned as if unsure whether to reveal the next question forming in her mind. "Was Johanna ever your mistress? Is that why you and your brother were at war?"

His brief encounter with the naked harpy flashed into his mind. "I'm offended you think I would stoop so low. When I returned to Whitstable fourteen months ago, she attempted to dazzle me with her womanly wiles. Hence the provoking endearment in her missive."

Johanna had made the mistake of thinking him as baseless as his brother.

Miss Wild winced before gesturing to the maimed side of his face. "Is that why your brother attacked you? Out of jealousy?"

Felix had been waiting for an excuse to mount an attack.

"He accused me of seducing his wife. As a matter of honour, I called him out for the insult. And because he was intent on ruining our family name." The reprobate had wasted funds on trips abroad, frivolous parties, diamond tiaras and a stable of costly Arabian stallions. "My brother's extravagant tastes led to bankruptcy. I returned home reluctantly in the hope I might persuade him to change his wasteful ways."

"You earned your scar in a sword fight?"

"Yes, Felix threw salt in my eyes before swiping his rapier across my cheek." Though the wound had healed, Sylvester often woke at night clutching his face, frantically trying to stem the imagined flow of blood.

"No one would have blamed you if you had pushed him off the cliff," came the comment he found alarming.

Sylvester straightened. "You do believe I'm innocent? For this partnership to work, you must trust me, Miss Wild."

"Trust must be earned, and I hardly know you. But a man who calls out his brother for the reasons you did would not kill him in a cowardly fashion."

A sudden knock on the parlour door brought the waiter, who asked if they required a fresh pot of coffee.

Miss Wild declined. She refolded the letter and handed it back to Sylvester. "You heard Mr Daventry. I'm to start work immediately, and it seems prudent to call at Monroe's book-shop before we leave London."

"But I questioned the shopkeeper at length mere days ago." The elderly gentleman had looked terrified and had struggled to form two words, let alone offer a detailed description of the person who sold him the tome. "He recalled nothing of interest."

"Mr Daventry will expect me to visit the shopkeeper. He will see it as an oversight if I fail to take a statement."

Being equally keen to solve his problem quickly, Sylvester asked for the bill, only to find Lucius Daventry had already paid.

He escorted Miss Wild through the coffeehouse—ignoring the patrons' shocked gasps and sly mutterings—and led her to his carriage parked on Great Russell Street.

They spent the journey discussing the volume he'd purchased, the weather in Naples and the fact Miss Wild had never seen the sea.

"Plato said the sea can cure all man's ailments," she said with some curiosity, "but one wonders how water acts as a restorative."

Sylvester found himself smiling, a rare occurrence these days. "Seawater contains an abundance of minerals and has the propensity to heal. Somehow, it calms the mind and the body."

"Can you see the sea from your castle's battlements?"

He nodded. "And from the upper windows, though one cannot consider the sea a restorative when a gale blows across the water and rattles the panes at night." He made no mention of phantoms or that they blamed the wind for the occasional ghostly wails echoing from the dungeons.

She glanced outside at the bustling crowds and the street vendors hawking their wares. "If I lived by the sea, I would never leave."

"Once I have purchased all the heirlooms sold in the bankruptcy auction, I shall remain at Highcliffe indefinitely." Yet the thought filled him with dread.

"How many more heirlooms are there?"

"Six, if I include my mother's diamond parure." The thought he'd been duped out of his inheritance roused his ire. "The jewels belonged to my maternal grandmother and were promised to me should I be inclined to take a bride."

Felix had sold them. They were not at Highcliffe or stored at the bank, though they had not been included in the sale catalogue, either.

Miss Wild looked at his scar as if he had more chance of scaling St Paul's without a rope than finding someone who would tolerate his defect.

"You should speak about the sea more often," she said randomly. "You don't look so stern when discussing the things you love."

Love?

Love was a word missing from his vocabulary.

Yes, he had loved his mother, but she had sadly died. He had loved his work abroad until he was forced to return home and deal with an ingrate. There, people had judged him on his merits, not his inadequate lineage. But he did love standing on the shore, looking out to sea, imagining a different life.

"No doubt you will find my moods disagreeable, Miss Wild. But if you feel discussing the sea improves my countenance, I shall endeavour to do so daily."

"I shall hold you to your vow."

The carriage rattled to a stop outside Monroe's bookshop on the Strand. Sylvester alighted and assisted Miss Wild to the pavement. She had such delicate hands. Hands made for soothing a man's tired muscles, not for wielding daggers and chasing rogues through the rookeries.

"Perhaps I should wait outside." He did not wish to scare the poor fellow serving behind the counter. "My appearance can be unnerving."

"I'm sure it won't be such a shock. Military men often have worse disfigurements," Miss Wild was kind enough to point out, yet had jerked in fear the first time she had laid eyes upon him. "Besides, Mr Daventry said a good agent should find a way to unsettle the suspects. You'll make my job much easier."

"I'm glad I can be of some use to you." Sylvester opened the door to the bookshop and gestured for Miss Wild to enter.

The few men perusing the volumes on the shelves cast him a sidelong glance. A group of young ladies tittered to each other while admiring his masculine form, though when he turned, one gasped, snatched a vinaigrette from her reticule and pressed the tiny box to her flaring nostrils.

Miss Wild marched over to the long oak counter. "Good day. May I speak to the proprietor or whoever deals with the purchase of second-hand books?"

The apprentice, a lad of fifteen with tight curly hair, tried to give Miss Wild his full attention, though he couldn't help but stare at Sylvester's scar.

"You'll b-be wanting Mr Monroe. I'll see if he's available, ma'am. Might I ask w-what it's concerning?"

"Yes, it's about the stolen tome he purchased," Miss Wild

24

said, though her confident tone belied the nervous shuffle of her feet. "It might be best if we speak to him privately, perhaps outside or in his office."

The lad nodded, then cast a nervous eye over Sylvester before disappearing through a door behind a bookshelf. He returned moments later, accompanied by the man Sylvester had questioned when he'd purchased the tome.

"Good afternoon. I am Monroe," said the fellow sporting bushy grey side-whiskers. He glanced at Sylvester and had to clutch the counter as recognition dawned. "L-Lord Deville. Heavens. Good heavens. I didn't expect to see you again."

"I may own the tome, but the matter is not closed."

"I—I assure you, I purchased the book in good faith. How was I to know it was stolen?" Noticing they were the focus of those browsing in the shop, Monroe begged them to step through to his office.

They obliged.

Miss Wild introduced herself before glancing around the poky room that was cold and smelled of dust and musty old books. She sat in the proffered seat while Monroe scurried to the chair behind his cluttered desk. Sylvester remained standing. He might need to drag Monroe from his seat and throttle the devil.

"As the person hired to find the thief responsible for stealing valuable items from Highcliffe," Miss Wild said like a Bow Street constable, "I must ask to see all documentation relating to your purchase."

Monroe appeared agitated. "You must understand, I buy many old books. Rarely does someone have proof of ownership."

"Then we require a name and a description of the person who sold you the volume." Miss Wild was determined in her quest for answers. "We're not leaving without the necessary information."

"But I purchased many books last week."

Sylvester gripped the top rail of Miss Wild's chair to calm his temper. "The tome is rare, unique. You know damn well who sold it, but for some reason, wish to refrain from revealing *her* identity."

Miss Wild looked up at him and raised a reprimanding brow. "We wouldn't want to put ideas into Mr Monroe's head. I'm sure he can recall the person but does not wish to betray a client."

"Yes!" Monroe confirmed. "Records are confidential."

"Describe the woman. Else I shall rip this place apart."

"My lord, I don't—"

"Now!" Sylvester moved.

"It wasn't a woman!" Monroe said, panicked.

The revelation stole Sylvester's thunder. He considered the weasel seated behind the desk, debating whether this was another lie, a means to throw them off the scent. Hell, Johanna could bribe most men to do her bidding. Why not this fool?

Sylvester might have grabbed Monroe by his crumpled cravat and strangled the truth from his lips, but Miss Wild pushed to her feet and took control of the situation.

"Sir, you will show me your ledger and confirm the name of the man who sold you the tome. Else I will return with a constable. Be warned, I shall ensure he questions you about the theft while in a shop full of customers."

Monroe practically jumped from his chair. "Mr Gifford! Gifford sold me the tome. Sold it for the bargain price of three pounds."

"Three pounds!" Sylvester gritted his teeth. "You sold it to me for ten."

Being fleeced was a reoccurring theme today.

"Yes, but Gifford said he would reduce the price if I agreed to his odd demands. He's an unsavoury fellow. On pain of death, I couldn't refuse him."

"Demands?" Sylvester snapped. It seemed everyone but

Miss Wild was out to make his life difficult. "What demands?"

"I—I was told to keep the book locked in my office. Mr Gifford was most insistent. If I failed to oblige him, he implied I might become the victim of an accident, a terrible fire." Monroe coughed as if the smoke choked his lungs. "That's why I made no mention of him before."

"You said demands, sir, in the plural." Miss Wild laid a hand on Sylvester's arm, urging him to remain calm. "What else did Mr Gifford ask you to do?"

Monroe winced. "He said when you came in and asked for the book, I was to pretend to have misplaced it. He was convinced you would move mountains to get your hands on the copy. He said I was to ensure you came back every day until the month's end."

"But you sold it to me within minutes of me asking?"

Monroe looked at Sylvester's scar and visibly shivered. "You're more intimidating than Mr Gifford, my lord. Indeed, when you demanded to see the book, I found I could not refuse you."

CHAPTER 3

"None of this makes sense," Lord Deville said, assisting Nora into his carriage. "Carter refuses to sell me the harpsichord, yet Gifford went to great lengths to ensure I purchased the tome."

"Have you had a disagreement with Mr Carter?" Nora spoke in a professional tone to disguise the fact her heart fluttered whenever Lord Deville touched her hand.

Hiding behind her enquiry agent persona helped stem her nerves. In truth, she should ignore her colleagues' teasing, but they insisted on reminding her that all Mr Daventry's agents had married their clients.

"I met the man once, at the races." Lord Deville slammed the carriage door shut and dropped into the seat opposite. "We barely said two words to each other. It's confounding."

"We should call on Mr Carter after we have questioned Mr Gifford." Nora unfolded the note written by the book-shop owner and glanced at the scribbled address. "Will it take long to reach Shoe Lane?" Despite arriving in town months ago, she often struggled to find her bearings.

"Fifteen minutes, depending on traffic."

She reached for the overhead strap as the carriage lurched

forward. "Might we use the time to discuss matters relating to the case? Namely, where were you when your brother died? I assume you have an alibi."

Lord Deville snorted. "You wait until we're alone in a closed carriage to ask if I can prove I'm not a murderer?"

"It's a routine question. I wouldn't be here with you if I doubted your innocence." Even though she didn't entirely trust this stranger, she trusted her employer to make sensible decisions.

Lord Deville's dark gaze swept slowly over her. "After arguing with Felix, I left the house and went to visit someone in Canterbury."

"Your mistress?" she blurted, though Lord knows why she'd asked or why it mattered. "Forgive me. Your personal affairs are none of my concern. Unless they relate specifically to the case."

He studied her through intense brown eyes. "Even a woman paid to show affection would think twice about entertaining a man like me, Miss Wild."

"Because of your short temper," she teased, desperate to banish the awkwardness, else it would be an uncomfortable few days. "Ladies often overlook a handsome man if he struggles to control his emotions."

He raised a brow. "Women dislike men who draw negative attention. Even courtesans strive to avoid embarrassment." Lord Deville raised his hands in mock surrender. "And I warned you I could be a grouch."

"Yes, you were not wrong."

Amusement danced briefly in his eyes. "I'll not endure liars or fools. I can be abrupt, impatient, but I will always speak the truth." He paused. "I went to visit a friend to ask if he had filled my position at the Foreign Office. Realising I would probably kill my brother if I remained in England, I thought to return to Italy."

"Your friend provided an alibi?"

"Yes, though there is an hour unaccounted for, during which time I visited the private chapel and strolled alone through the garden. No one saw me, and my coachman can only testify to my movements from eight o'clock that evening."

"Thankfully, the fisherman's testimony proved your innocence." So it seemed odd he wanted to challenge the man's statement. But then, hadn't he said the truth mattered most?

"Yes, but the fisherman lied."

"You have a habit of making assumptions, my lord."

Nora thought for a moment. Had Felix been so angry after their argument he acted on impulse? Perhaps he pushed his wife off the cliff and then lost his balance and slipped. That would account for the fisherman's version. Although a man peering through a telescope while miles out at sea was hardly a reliable witness.

"Has anyone ever accused you of your brother's murder?" She considered the man seated opposite, knowing how the body burned for vengeance when one found themselves a victim of slander. It explained why he struggled to contain his blistering rage.

"There isn't a man in the *ton* brave enough."

They spoke no more on the matter. The carriage turned into Shoe Lane and Nora pressed her nose to the window, wondering about Mr Gifford's connection to the case. If he had threatened Mr Monroe, what would he do when confronted by Lord Deville? Maybe Mr Daventry was right to insist she carry a weapon in her reticule.

The vehicle stopped outside a four-storey terraced house with a boarded bow window and paint-chipped door. Lord Deville alighted and spoke to his coachman before handing Nora down to the pavement.

"This is the address Monroe gave us." The lord scanned the rundown facade then turned his attention to the other houses and shops on the street. "Though on appearances, it's fair to assume no one lives here."

Nora sighed. "There's only one way to know for sure."

She knocked loudly. No one came. Lord Deville took to hammering the door so hard he was in danger of forcing it off its hinges.

A woman cradling a sleeping babe appeared on the doorstep of the house next door. "There ain't no one living there," she whispered. "Ain't been anyone there since old Mr Hodges died last June. They shut up his printin' shop, but there's another further along the lane."

Nora stepped forward. "We're looking for Mr Gifford and were given this address. Might he be a friend or relative of Mr Hodges?"

The woman rocked her babe. "Old Hodges had no friends or family. These walls are as thin as paper. I'd have heard if someone had come knockin'."

"Perhaps we have the wrong number." Nora had watched Mr Monroe scribble the address straight from his ledger. "Might Mr Gifford live somewhere else on this street?" Or was it merely a case of giving a false address?

The woman shook her head. "I've lived here all my life. There ain't no Mr Gifford on this street."

Frustrated, Lord Deville asked the same questions only to receive the same answers. "Hellfire! This has to be the right address."

The babe stirred and let out a whimper.

Nora apologised for disturbing the woman, quickly bid her good day, then ushered Lord Deville towards his carriage.

"We will resume our enquiries into Mr Gifford when we return from Whitstable. Perhaps then we may have information that will make our task easier."

The lord glanced at the shabby front door. "We could force the lock. Take a look inside."

Oh, the man was incorrigible. "I am employed to catch

criminals, not break the law." Having previously committed the worst crime possible, she had no intention of making matters worse.

With no option but to leave Shoe Lane, the lord helped Nora into his carriage before instructing his coachman to visit Howland Street. She could climb the steps herself, yet he insisted on playing the chivalrous gentleman.

"I suppose we should attempt to locate Carter. But I have no intention of venturing to his club, for I'll likely murder the first man who utters a sly remark. No. I shall take you home, Miss Wild. So you may pack for the short trip to Whitstable."

"Short trip? It won't take long to reach the coast?"

"I mean, there's nothing much to see or do around Whitstable. Sadly, that will soon change. There's talk of building a railway."

She smiled to herself. Boredom was not the problem. Lord Deville disliked company and did not want to entertain a guest at his coastal home.

"Yet you plan to remain in Whitstable permanently."

"Highcliffe is some miles east of Whitstable," he said as if it made a difference. "And I have a responsibility to my tenants, to those families who work my land. They might have lost their livelihoods had my brother continued squandering his inheritance."

Nora knew nothing about running a vast estate, but she knew of something more damaging to a family's legacy than the heir being a spendthrift.

"You have no family, my lord, and so must marry. A bachelor is more a blight to his tenants than a wastrel."

Lord Deville shifted uncomfortably. "As a man of thirty, I have time to consider the daunting prospect of matrimony." He gestured to his scar. "When I take a bride, choosing one with poor eyesight will be a priority."

His attempt at amusement failed to make her smile. Pain lingered beneath his bravado. It was plain to see.

"Rather than choose a bride who is happy to look upon your face, is it not better to choose one who admires your character? Someone who brings joy to your life, not someone who accepts your disfigurement?"

Lord Deville's problem was not the wound to his cheek but the wound to his heart. Bitterness oozed from his pores, contaminating his countenance, clouding his judgement. He had every right to feel aggrieved, but he was in jeopardy of losing more than his handsome looks.

"You make life sound easy, Miss Wild, when we both know it's difficult, often tragic."

"Miss Trimble says a good dose of gratitude can cure all ailments." The lady's insight was surely why Mr Daventry had hired her to manage the house in Howland Street. "Perhaps if you learn to love yourself, someone might grow to love you in return."

"I don't need a lady to love me, just to give me an heir," he snapped, though his tone lacked conviction. "And no doubt Miss Trimble has never found herself in a life-threatening situation."

Miss Trimble had suffered greatly, Nora feared. Why else would she refuse to speak about her past? Why else would she hide in the shadows when she had the education and grace of a duchess?

"On the contrary, I suspect her story would put both of ours to shame." Nora sought to return to the original topic before he asked probing questions about her life at the vicarage. "Besides, as someone who has never seen the sea, I imagine there is a lot to do around Whitstable."

"Can you swim?"

"My lord, I am a vicar's daughter." Correction. She was the devil's daughter. "He believes breathing is a sin. Do you imagine he permitted me to strip to my shift in public and take a dip in the lake?"

Indoors, he had made her bathe in a robe.

Lord Deville's gaze softened. "Would you like to learn?"

"To swim?"

"Yes."

"In the sea?"

"Yes. I'm afraid I don't have a bathtub big enough."

"Is it not dangerous?"

"Extremely, though I happen to be an excellent tutor."

A vision flashed into her mind. Her standing on a deserted beach, damp sand squelching between her toes, a gentle breeze whispering against her loose hair and thin shift. Lord Deville would be in nothing but his breeches, water dripping from his bronzed skin as he lured her deep into the water.

"You would teach me?" she croaked.

"If you promise to do as you're told." He removed his hat and brushed his hand through his coal-black hair as if it were already wet and in need of taming.

After the terrifying incident at the Pleasure Parlour, Madame Matisse had urged Nora to live every day like it was her last. However, Mr Daventry had been quick to reassure her that she would never feel the hangman's noose chaffing her nape.

What if Mr Daventry was wrong?

Had he given her this case to keep her out of town?

"Then I shall bring spare clothes, my lord."

"Spare undergarments will suffice." His warm gaze slipped over her, and he smiled as if privy to a secret.

The air between them sparked with nervous energy, tightening her abdomen muscles and raising her temperature a notch.

Thankfully, the vehicle slowed to a stop on Howland

Street, and the conversation turned to tomorrow's travel plans.

"It's sixty miles to Whitstable. I would prefer to make an early start. Might you arrange for Mr Bower to arrive at Howland Street at eight?"

Nora couldn't help but laugh. "The Reverend Wild says only lazy louts sleep past dawn. The soul of the sluggard be damned," she added in her stern preacher's voice.

"The Reverend Wild sounds like a pitiless fool."

"He is cold and callous and wields his bible like a weapon of destruction, not a guide to salvation."

"You must be relieved to be away from there."

"Yes," was all she managed to say as the memory of her father's final threat invaded her mind. "I shall ensure we are ready and waiting promptly at eight."

He moved to open the door, but she shuffled to the edge of the seat and grabbed the handle. "My lord, I am in your employ. You do not need to play the courteous gentleman."

Lord Deville laughed.

Sweet heaven.

The sound did strange things to her insides.

"You should mind your phrasing, Miss Wild. I'm sure you do not wish to spend hours alone in a carriage with a man who forgets his manners."

Heat rose to her cheeks, but she quickly recovered. "And you should think twice before teasing a woman who carries a weapon." She opened the door. "Good day, my lord."

"Until tomorrow, Miss Wild."

Nora climbed down to the pavement and closed the carriage door. Taking a minute to gather her composure, she stood watching the vehicle until it turned out of Howland Street.

While every instinct had warned against meeting the man, he wasn't as intimidating as she had expected. Yes, his scar was as unattractive as his stern temperament, but she had glimpsed a playful side to his character. One that made him seem much more appealing.

Upon entering the house, she found Miss Trimble seated at the escritoire in the drawing room, writing a letter, which must be for Mr Daventry because she professed to know no one in town, nor did she have any friends or family.

The lady jumped in shock. "Honora! I did not hear you come in." She opened the drawer, shoved the letter inside, and closed it quickly. "How was your meeting with Lord Deville?"

"The gentleman is now officially my client."

"Are you sure you want to take his case?" Miss Trimble gripped the chair rail and rose unsteadily to her feet. "If Lord Deville is suspected of murdering his brother, should Mr Daventry not give the case to a male agent?"

Nora might have explained why she believed the lord was innocent, but Miss Trimble's fragile countenance proved worrying.

"Are you well?"

"What? Yes. Quite well." Like her smile, the lie was a veil to hide her sadness.

Nora glanced at the escritoire. "Have you received distressing news?"

Miss Trimble closed the gap between them and clasped Nora's gloved hands. "I am paid to care for you, Honora. You've no need to worry about me."

As always, the lady diverted all attention away from herself. She avoided questions about her past. Yet her distinct distrust of men spoke of a wicked betrayal.

"Have you asked Mr Daventry if he plans to hire more female agents?" The house was empty now Nora's colleagues had married. Having spent many childhood hours alone, locked in her room for days on end, she found the constant hum of silence deafening.

"No. Not yet." Miss Trimble gave a light laugh, though her

blue eyes remained dull. "Perhaps he hopes you will marry your client and has other plans for the house."

"Good heavens, no! He knows I have no intention of marrying." She would never bind herself to a man, and certainly not one who overreacted to every situation.

Was that the cause of Miss Trimble's discontent?

Did she fear being left alone, too?

If so, there was a solution to the problem.

"I'm leaving London in the morning to conduct an investigation. Mr Bower is joining me. Ask Mr Daventry if you can come too."

"Leaving London?" Her countenance brightened.

"Yes. Come with me to Whitstable to visit Lord Deville's home and question his staff. I shall be gone for a few days. A week at most. It will mean a trip to Canterbury." To check the lord's alibi. "But it's not far from Lord Deville's clifftop estate."

Miss Trimble's smile died. "C-Canterbury?"

"Yes, we might visit the cathedral if we have time."

She brought a shaky hand to her throat, covered by the high collar of her serviceable grey dress. "I cannot go to Canterbury or to Whitstable."

Nora frowned. A moment ago, Miss Trimble had seemed excited at the prospect of leaving town. "Why ever not? There's little to do here. I shall ask Mr Daventry if you can assist me with the investigation."

"No!" she suddenly blurted before moderating her tone. "No. Thank you for thinking of me, Honora. I'm sure Mr Daventry has tasks to occupy me here until he hires more ladies. And you need to solve this case yourself, need to prove you're capable. I will serve as a distraction and would hate to be the one responsible should you lose your position."

How strange.

With her distrust of men, and being the person paid to

oversee the welfare of Mr Daventry's female agents, one would think she would be keen to act as chaperone.

In what seemed like a desperate bid to prevent further discussion on the matter, Miss Trimble set about tidying the desk. "You never mentioned why Lord Deville wants to hire you."

Nora gave Miss Trimble a summary of the afternoon's events. Except for where she was to strip to her shift and let the lord lure her into dangerous waters.

"I'm hoping the servants will know something of what went on before Lord Deville's brother and sister-in-law were murdered."

Miss Trimble's brow furrowed. "I am inclined to believe Lord Deville's version. Johanna is alive and takes pleasure tormenting him."

If Johanna was alive, why had she remained in England? A murderess would likely take the first ship to anywhere to avoid the noose. And why write letters? Why send Lord Deville on a hunt for his precious heirlooms?

"I know one thing for certain," Nora said, drawing on all she had learned from her colleagues' cases. "Nothing is as it seems."

CHAPTER 4

"Forgive me for not calling yesterday, Miss Wild." Sylvester studied her from the seat opposite as his carriage stopped at the Green Man turnpike and his coachman paid the toll. Her lips were drawn thin, her shoulders tense. "I trust you received my note informing you of the delay."

"I did." She sat with her hands clasped in her lap.

Perhaps she would have preferred Daventry's man to sit inside the vehicle, not atop the box.

"My coachman took ill." Sylvester had warned Sykes to avoid the beef stew, but the man's belly was bigger than his brain. "As I've no house in town and had no desire to hire another coachman, I preferred to wait until he recovered. However, be warned. During the journey, he may have cause to stop abruptly."

"Pay it no mind." She managed a smile which was a vast improvement. "The day was not a complete waste. Mr Daventry's man found Mr Carter. I met with him at the Hart Street office last night."

"You met with Carter?" It was Sylvester's turn to show his frustration. "Had you sent word to the Musgrove, I would have joined the interrogation." He had spent a mundane evening at the hotel, dining alone, pondering Miss Wild's secrets.

"You did not state the reason for delaying our departure. I presumed you had pressing business elsewhere." She pushed her fake spectacles past the bridge of her nose. "I am your enquiry agent. You're paying me to find answers, not cling to your coattails."

Sylvester glanced at the verdant fields in the distance, relieved to be leaving London, and took a calming breath. "Then I beg your forgiveness again, Miss Wild. I shall take great pains to ensure my tone is not so demanding."

"You're forgiven." The corners of her mouth curled in mild amusement. "Mr Carter was most apologetic. He said your brother sold him the harpsichord at a ridiculously low price on condition he promised never to sell it to you."

What the devil?

Sylvester silently damned Felix to the infernal pits of hell. As a child, he had sat for hours watching his mother play. She had been her happiest when lost in a cheerful tune. It was perhaps the only time she had ever felt free.

"My brother's spite knew no bounds, Miss Wild."

"Is there a reason for his animosity towards you?"

Bitterness pumped poison through his veins. "I suppose it's better you hear it from me than a servant." The venom took control of his tongue. "One of us is a bastard, born to my mother by a lover she had years ago. She told my father during an argument—to torment him for his coldness towards her—though she refused to name which child."

It had been her only weapon in a war with a heartless man. As in any wretched conflict, there were innocent casualties.

Miss Wild coughed to clear her throat but said nothing.

"Felix convinced himself he was the rightful heir, and I

was the devil's spawn." Spoken in the heat of the moment, one hurtful comment had torn the family apart. "Because I inherited my mother's dark hair, my father believed I must be the other lord's by-blow."

Sylvester fell silent—a means of coping with the damnable ache in his chest. Words were deadly. A knife to the heart caused pain that lasted mere seconds. An angry comment caused pain that lasted a lifetime.

"I don't blame my mother. She did not mean to hurt me."

"I understand your plight. I know how cruel words affect the mind." Miss Wild's sympathetic smile warmed him like a blanket on a cold winter's morn. "It wasn't what your mother said that hurt you. What hurt was that your brother and father believed her. That they singled you out."

Sylvester leant back against the squab, the last twenty years flashing before his eyes. He had been abandoned yet still lived with the family he loved. He had been neglected yet was afforded every luxury.

"Is that why you went to Italy?"

The comment served to banish the ghosts of the past. "My godfather said a man is not the sum of his lineage, but of the mark he has made on the world. I focused on my allegiance to the King and served my country in the Foreign Office."

And he'd have feared for his life had he stayed in England.

Miss Wild's eyes narrowed. "My father gave me advice. He said a woman's ability to obey orders was the true measure of her worth. He needed to control me, whereas your godfather wished to set you free."

Something passed between them.

A sense they were on the same path for a reason.

Unused to feeling anything other than hatred, Sylvester sought to fill the silence. "Consequently, I consider Sir George my friend as well as my godfather. He's the one who wrote and told me about the bankruptcy auction. He's also my alibi for the night of my brother's murder. So you see why it may become a problem if Johanna tries to implicate me in Felix's death."

"Yes," Miss Wild mused. "Although one would expect the magistrate to believe a distinguished gentleman's word." She paused and eyed him suspiciously. "Unless Johanna has a means of proving you intended to kill your brother."

Sylvester inwardly groaned. He had something to confess yet did not want Miss Wild thinking him a maniac, a man who lost control of his mind at every given opportunity.

"Johanna may have a letter I wrote, informing Felix I would throttle him with my bare hands if he sold another of our family's heirlooms." He had also said he would toss his brother's lifeless body into the sea. "And the servants heard me cursing him to the devil in the days before he died."

Miss Wild thought for a moment. "But no one gave a statement to that effect? No one gave the magistrate your incriminating letter?"

"No." Sylvester sat forward. "Which is why I know Johanna is out there, biding her time, waiting for an opportunity to frame me for murder."

A story formed in his head, Johanna being found in a remote fishing village, having spent a year recovering from her injuries. She would produce an heir born to her during her convalescence. A son—her lover's child—whom she would present as the rightful master of Highcliffe.

Sylvester relayed his fears to Miss Wild. "During their three-year marriage, Johanna failed to conceive. Yet I'm persuaded she will appear with a child to oust me out of Highcliffe."

Miss Wild sighed. "You must consider the facts. Concocting a story based on your emotions will only hinder our progress. Johanna cannot have sent the letter alerting you to the book of Greek tales and be recovering from her injuries in a remote fishing village. It's not plausible. There-fore, one of your theories is incorrect."

The lady had a point, but how might he convince her there was some truth to his premise?

"Should a man not trust his heart?" He clutched his chest as if swearing an oath of allegiance. "Should he ignore his instincts?"

Miss Wild tore off her spectacles and looked him keenly in the eye. "After what you have told me about your family, how can you trust your heart? Is it not equally scarred?"

Sylvester stared at her, realising two things.

For a young woman, she was incredibly insightful. And when she spoke to him, when her bewitching brown eyes journeyed over his face, she did not flinch or falter. In that moment, he felt normal, so normal he experienced a sudden flicker of tenderness in his chest.

"Then I shall place my faith in your heart, Miss Wild. I shall keep my stories for bedtime." Hell, another image came into his mind. One involving Miss Wild and an impressive Jacobean bed in a clifftop castle.

Her empty laugh took him by surprise. "My heart is equally damaged. Thankfully, I have been taught to detach from all emotions when working on a case. As you're assisting me, I suggest you do the same. It's the only way to guarantee your sanity."

Before hiring her, he hadn't planned on playing her assistant. Yet the thought of spending time with a woman who did not tremble when he turned his head had distinct appeal.

"Then let us focus on the evidence, Miss Wild, not my overactive imagination. Is that not what Lucius Daventry would suggest?"

Sylvester reached for his leather portfolio. He delved inside and offered Miss Wild five letters. They were tatty at the corners because he had read them a hundred times, looking for clues to Johanna's whereabouts.

She took the letters, sorted them into date order but did not peruse the contents. Instead, she examined the size and texture of the paper, held them all up to the window to better study them in the light.

He watched intently as she read the first letter, received last November, reciting it verbatim in his mind. Johanna—or the mystery author—had drawn his attention to his mother's Jacobean writing desk, sold to Captain Armstrong's wife in the bankruptcy auction.

"The desk is now back in my mother's boudoir," he informed her. "Indeed, I was able to purchase all the items mentioned in the letters."

Miss Wild flicked through the missives, pursing her rosy lips. Seconds passed before she spoke, though he was happy to watch her. "We must ask ourselves what the mystery writer wishes to achieve by sending these. Why would the person care if you found your heirlooms?"

He shrugged. Being permanently angry, he'd not considered other motives, only Johanna's need to torment him.

"Also, the letters are all dated the seventeenth day of each month." Miss Wild returned his letters and encouraged him to study them himself. "Do you always do what the sender suggests?"

Sylvester nodded. "Nothing is more important than returning the items to their rightful home." He had journeyed hundreds of miles to ensure he recovered the prized possessions.

"Since November, you have been away from Highcliffe for days on end. Does it not seem odd that the writer encourages you to leave home on a specific date each month?"

Foolishly, he had not considered it important.

"Equally, the items themselves are relevant," she said, offering him another example of her sharp wit. "A lady's writing desk, mother-of-pearl opera glasses, an emerald cluster ring. Did they all belong to your mother?"

"Yes." Hence why he had been so determined to reclaim them. He glanced at the letter sent in January. "As did the painting of two pipers in a gilt frame."

Miss Wild became lost in thought. She ran her finger over her lips as she considered the information, then rubbed her eyes. Sylvester preferred her without spectacles. Not because it dramatically altered her countenance, but because she seemed more relaxed, more herself.

"My lord, I believe the writer's motive is to send you miles from home. The person knows of your deep connection to your mother and so uses those items as bait."

"Bait?" How had he missed something so obvious? "Felix despised our mother and sold her belongings before her death. It's rather ironic considering I was the one who suffered for her mistake."

"Then the sender knows how important her possessions are to you. We must discover why this person wants you to leave Highcliffe, though that may mean waiting until you receive the next letter in mid-May."

Since being maimed, Sylvester had avoided female company. When a man took a woman in his arms, he wanted her to shiver from delight, not fright. And yet, the thought of working closely with Miss Wild for three weeks seemed oddly appealing.

"Let's hope the letters aren't our only line of enquiry," she said, sounding less pleased at the prospect of spending time with him.

They fell silent while she removed a small black notebook from her reticule and scribbled away with her pencil. He examined the letters once more, then flicked through the book of Greek tales but found nothing unusual.

The carriage turned into the yard of the Hare and Hound

coaching inn, and she looked up from her notebook entries. "We're stopping to change the horses?"

"And stretch our legs."

She scanned him from hip to ankle and nodded.

"Are you hungry, Miss Wild?" Wanting to reach Highcliffe before nightfall, he had insisted they left promptly at eight and feared she'd not had time to take breakfast. "Though I can do little about you missing the church service this morning, perhaps I might have the innkeeper prepare a basket."

The lady swallowed, her cheeks turning a pretty shade of pink. "Did Mr Daventry mention my healthy appetite?"

"No, he did not." Sylvester scanned her figure, noted the tempting curve of her breasts pushing against her faded brown pelisse. Hmm. There were many things her employer failed to mention. "Only that I'm to ensure all your needs are met during the course of this investigation."

He referred to food and lodgings, yet erotic images entered his head. Having forgone the pleasure of a woman's company for so long, surely it was normal for a man to have amorous thoughts.

"Miss Trimble insisted I ate a hearty meal before leaving this morning. Unlike my father, who often punished me by withdrawing food. As for missing church," she said, her voice turning brittle, "I have begged the Lord for forgiveness so many times I am guaranteed a place in heaven."

They had much in common. He had been treated like a sinner. As if he had committed his mother's transgression. As if his presence tainted the air and his blood was a blight on the Deville legacy.

"One might say life is a school for the soul," he said stoically. "The hard lessons make us stronger. Without such an education, we would wander about like witless fools."

When Miss Wild smiled, the day seemed brighter. "Suddenly, you sound grateful for your plight, not angry."

It was easy to appear objective when tending to a

stranger's wounds. One did not wince in pain or feel a sharp stab of rejection. One's only consideration was cleaning the cut, not allowing it to fester.

"A grateful mind is a great mind," he said, quoting Plato.

Miss Wild grinned. "My lord, I shall remind you of that the next time you lose your temper."

Highcliffe stood on a clifftop overlooking the North Sea, a monstrous Norman fortification that had replaced the ruined Saxon burg destroyed by the Danes months after the Siege of Canterbury.

The first Lord Deville built a modest castle, though talk of a Norse seeress cursing the land led his predecessors to add towers and battlements, to dig deep into the earth and build escape tunnels and dungeons.

As a boy, Sylvester had prepared for an imminent Viking invasion. He'd raced through the cold corridors, shouting a war cry. He'd dared to venture into the dank tunnels to lay traps. Armed with his homemade bow and arrows, he'd climbed to the highest point and peered over the parapet, waiting to sight the sails of a ship in the distance.

Highcliffe had been his beloved playground.

The home he wished to protect.

Until one flippant comment made him the enemy.

"Is it usually so dull and dreary here?" Miss Wild's question drew him back to the present. She had left her spectacles on the carriage seat, for the shaped glass misted whenever she pressed her nose to the window. She pointed to the loathsome structure. "It's as if black clouds linger above your home to make it look more menacing."

He dared to glance at the place he longed to conquer, yet bitter memories always left him sighing in defeat. "The inclement weather is a godsend during times of war. As a child, I used to stand on the battlements and summon the storm." He explained something of the castle's long history. "Although I wasn't expected to inherit, I thought it my duty to protect my home from foreign invaders."

Miss Wild dragged her gaze from the window, seemingly finding him more interesting than a centuries-old fortress. "Is that why you seek your mother's lost heirlooms? Because you have a duty to protect your inheritance?"

"Not entirely." The carriage rattled over the stone bridge, and his stomach lurched as it always did when he neared home. "I do not see why they should erase my mother from history because of one mistake."

Miss Wild fell silent for a time. "May I ask how your mother died?"

Sylvester's chest tightened. It took him a moment to draw breath. "Her heart gave out. Her maid rushed to Highcliffe to raise the alarm, but it was too late. Mother lived in a cottage on the estate, some two miles south. Felix waited until I sailed for Italy before banishing her. He said a whore did not deserve to live in splendour, though I suspect it was an excuse to sell her treasures."

His mother's death was a poignant reminder of the price one paid for fleeing one's problems. That said, had Sylvester stayed, it would be his body buried beneath the flagstone in the chapel.

"I'm glad I waited until now to ask," Miss Wild said softly.

"Why? Because you wouldn't want to sit for hours with a man in a morbid mood?"

"No. Because I've longed to punish my father for driving my mother away. I can only imagine how badly your mother's death affected you. Had you told me before, I would have presumed you were guilty of murder."

Part of him wished he'd dared to end his brother's life, but

Sylvester was the last Deville, a responsibility that weighed heavily on his shoulders. "Though I'd dreamed of squeezing the last breath from Felix's lungs, on my word, I am innocent of the crime."

"I know," she said with such faith in his character, his heart thumped faster. "I would not be here otherwise."

Immense gratitude filled his chest. "Then let me take this opportunity to thank you, Miss Wild. No other woman would brave this place willingly."

She craned her neck and peered up at the cold grey walls that seemed to stretch as high as the clouds. "You live here, so it must have some merits."

He struggled to think of one and was thankful when the carriage slowed to a halt in the courtyard. Embarrassment soon replaced relief when no one rushed to greet them.

"I should warn you. I run the house on minimal staff. Some servants left when I inherited." Disappeared more to the point. No one wanted to work for a man deemed the wrongful heir. So they had gathered their meagre belongings in the dead of night and fled. "Doubtless they lacked your faith in my character, Miss Wild."

"The lack of hired help matters not. I can fend for myself, my lord." She gripped the overhead strap as Mr Bower hauled his burly frame down from the box seat, sending the carriage rocking on its axis. "While I have no need of a maid, I pray you have a cook. As Mr Daventry undoubtedly warned you, I have a voracious appetite."

"As do I, Miss Wild." He hadn't meant to deepen his voice or for the comment to sound seductive, yet something about this woman stirred his blood. "A castle of this magnitude should have fifty servants. I have fifteen, including my coachman and groom."

He noticed Bower waiting for permission to open the carriage door and gestured for him to continue. Daventry's man would keep a careful eye on proceedings and had probably been instructed to intervene when necessary.

Bower handed Miss Wild down to the courtyard. The lady shivered as she considered the sheer scale of the building. That or she had sensed the malevolent spirit sent to remind Sylvester he was not a Deville but a bastard who did not belong here.

The longer he remained at Highcliffe, the more he believed he was destined for a life of misery. The curse had torn his family apart and would do so again if he dared to grasp a chance of happiness.

Indeed, a violent gust howled through the gatehouse to remind him an otherworldly presence was lord of these lands.

Miss Wild hugged herself as her teeth chattered. "May we go inside? It's so bitterly cold, much colder than one expects of a late April evening."

Despite feeling the devil's gaze boring into his back, he shook off his trepidation and offered Miss Wild his arm. To his surprise, she slipped her dainty hand into the crook and let him lead her up the flight of stone steps.

Bower opened the studded oak door and stepped aside. "Mr Sykes said there's room for me in the coach house, ma'am. I'll bid you good night and take supper there. I'll report to you in the morning."

A look passed between Miss Wild and the man with a deep scar cutting through his brow. Sylvester concluded that she had already given him a list of tasks. Befriending the servants was surely Bower's primary goal, though Daventry's man would struggle to get more than a passing pleasantry from anyone but Sykes.

"Very well." Miss Wild nodded. "Good night, Mr Bower."

Bower turned his attention to Sylvester, and though he inclined his head respectfully, his gaze held a flash of warning. Indeed, it was more intimidating than if he'd waved his mallet-sized fists.

"Good night, Bower. Rest assured, Miss Wild will be perfectly safe in my care."

Sylvester escorted Miss Wild into the dim entrance hall, illuminated by a single candle lamp burning on the console table. A chill settled over his shoulders, for no one had prepared or lit the fire.

"Mrs Egan is not expecting me until Friday," he said, feeling decidedly colder when Miss Wild removed her hand from his arm. "No doubt the staff are taking supper in the servants' hall."

By his estimation, it was seven o'clock. A journey that usually took eight to nine hours, depending on the day and the weather, had taken much longer. Mainly due to the lengthy conversations he'd had with Miss Wild during their stops at various coaching inns en route, and her insistence on eating a hearty luncheon.

The lady crossed to the two portraits hanging next to the fireplace. She gestured to the one of a man sporting a grey periwig. "Is this your father?"

"That's a point of contention," Sylvester mocked, "but it is the man whose title I bear."

She studied the likeness amid the muted light, tilting her head while peering through her pointless spectacles. "You have his proud chin and strong patrician nose."

"If only it were enough to negate any doubt over my bloodline."

"You're Lord Deville now. No one saw fit to dispute your claim."

"There's no one to dispute it besides the King, and he believes most of the *ton* are bastards." His gaze moved to the other painting. "My mother's portrait hung there until she made her damning revelation. Now it's my paternal grandfather, though he died before I was born."

"After the way you were treated, I'm surprised you've not relegated your father's portrait to the attic."

The answers came to him almost immediately, whispers from his heart, not logical statements forming in his head.

"I keep it there for two reasons. Because I like to look upon my father when I curse him to the devil." He paused, nausea roiling in his stomach when he acknowledged the second reason. "And because I'm waiting for the day when our gazes meet, and I feel like I belong."

CHAPTER 5

Through her spectacles, Nora observed the man she had spoken to at length during the eleven-hour journey to Whitstable. The black cloud hanging over Highcliffe had a profound effect on its occupants. Since crossing the threshold of the formidable castle Lord Deville called home, his mood had darkened.

The cold seeping through the stone walls had stolen the warmth from his gaze. His teasing grin had disappeared along with any glimpse of the sun. His velvet voice was now as grim as the forbidding fortress.

Perhaps her solving the case might bring him a modicum of peace. Though why she found herself concerned with Lord Deville's welfare was anyone's guess. She should remain impartial. Yet any attempt seemed impossible when the lord looked at her through dark, troubled eyes.

"You cannot gain acceptance from the departed," she said, closing the gap between them. "The dead cannot give you their blessing. You must find other ways to achieve a sense of belonging."

Since joining the Order she had found a purpose. A means to prove her worth and fend for herself. If Lord Deville focused on being a good master to his tenants, they would accept him regardless of his dubious parentage.

"Are you always so direct, Miss Wild?"

"Having spent years biting my tongue, it is something I'm resolved to do." And Mr Daventry had insisted a good agent must voice her opinion. "As my client, you are within your rights to tell me to keep to my own affairs."

"I'm hoping the same insight will lead you to Johanna."

The sudden bang of a door preceded the clip of hurried footsteps. A thin middle-aged woman burst into the hall, and it took her a moment to catch her breath. Indeed, she was in such a rush to greet the master she had not brushed the dust from her plain grey dress.

"My lord! You're home. We were not expecting you until Friday." She smoothed loose strands of brown hair back into the tight knot before stealing a glance at Nora. "I shall have Thomson fetch your luggage."

"You'll be pleased to know I found and purchased the missing tome of Greek tales." Lord Deville's friendly tone carried a faint hint of mistrust. Did he think Mrs Egan had stolen the book? "Have Thomson leave it in my bedchamber."

"That is good news, my lord." The woman's strained smile said otherwise.

Perhaps the nervous edge to her tone stemmed from being caught unawares. Or did she believe Lord Deville was not the rightful heir, and so her mild hostility tainted every interaction?

When the woman looked at Nora again, Lord Deville said, "Have a room prepared for my guest. Miss Wild is an enquiry agent from London and is here to conduct an investigation."

Mrs Egan's brows shot up in alarm. "An investigation?"

"Yes, into my brother's death." The lord gave a nonchalant

wave. "I need answers, Mrs Egan. And Miss Wild is considered the best in her field."

It was Nora's turn to raise a brow. The best in her field? No doubt it was a ruse to intimidate Mrs Egan. But why?

"She will remain at Highcliffe until she can shed light on the tragedy." Lord Deville's gaze met Nora's and lingered for far too long.

Theirs was a mere business arrangement. So why did her pulse thump wildly in her throat whenever their eyes met? Why did she experience a wave of excitement at the prospect of spending time alone with him? Evidently, her heart was impervious to his bad moods and terrible scar.

"Miss Wild is to stay at Highcliffe, my lord? While you're in residence?" Mrs Egan evidently found the prospect distressing. The word *harlot* was probably uppermost in her mind.

"Mrs Egan," his lordship began with a huff of frustration, "Miss Wild is here to find clues, not cavort with the master. She is in my employ. Unlike my brother, I am not a man who abuses his position."

The information failed to improve Mrs Egan's mood. "You mean Miss Wild is to have a room below stairs?"

"Miss Wild is to have Lady Deville's room for the duration of her stay. Now, might you arrange for refreshment and a light repast? Having spent hours rattling through the open countryside, we shall take our meal in the comfort of the drawing room."

Mrs Egan was surely appalled by the arrangement, but she dipped a curtsy, informed them she would send Blanche to light the fire, and retreated through the door from whence she came.

Nora waited until Mrs Egan was out of earshot before relaying her own concerns. "You mean to put me in Lady Deville's room? My lord, you cannot—"

"Not you as well, Miss Wild? Let me assure you, the

choice is a practical one. The room is comfortable and close to mine should you uncover something unsavoury and need my protection. I vowed you would be safe here, and I mean to keep my word."

Nora stepped closer and lowered her voice to a whisper. "My lord, the staff will presume we are ..." She gave a discreet cough.

"Lovers, Miss Wild?"

"Indeed," she said, mildly embarrassed.

"Doubtless, Mrs Egan thinks you're my mistress, and we invented the story of you being an enquiry agent." His appreciative gaze slipped over her body. "I don't see why you're concerned. You spent time at the Pleasure Parlour and must have tolerated many disapproving comments."

Hardly. She'd kept to the shadows for nigh on a month.

"Life at the vicarage prepared me for unjust criticism." She had been called every evil name known to man. Like the lash of a whip, the words stung for a while until eventually she felt no pain. Nonetheless, she was often aware of the wounds weeping, particularly at night.

"Then I fail to see the problem."

No, he couldn't possibly know that Mr Daventry intended for them to marry. That the master of the Order hoped to right any injustice they had suffered. He was surely unaware that Mr Daventry was as much a devious matchmaker as he was a ruthless seeker of the truth.

Of course, this time, her employer had made a mistake.

Still, it did not prevent Nora from imagining what it would be like to be loved by such a captivating gentleman.

"Is there an adjoining door?"

Lord Deville smiled. "I shall give you the key."

Something about his tone suggested he had a spare.

Thankfully, a maid arrived to light the fire, bringing the conversation about adjacent bedchambers to an abrupt end.

The next two hours passed quickly. They sat in the

elegant drawing room, discussing the case and Lord Deville's staffing issues while eating a collation of cold meats, bread and cheese.

Any concerns she'd had upon her arrival disappeared. The lord was in good humour. Conversation flowed easily when he was not in a dour mood.

A knock on the door brought the glum-faced Mrs Egan, who looked at Nora sipping sherry and frowned. "Your room is ready, Miss Wild. Send for me when you wish to retire, and I shall give you a brief tour of the house."

"Thank you, Mrs Egan, but there's no need." Lord Deville straightened from his relaxed position in the chair. "I shall give Miss Wild a full tour in the morning. She will want to question the staff. Please warn them to co-operate fully while she makes her enquiries."

Mrs Egan's faint smile failed to hide the slight tremble of her chin. "Perhaps it might be easier to summon them to your bedchamber one at a time, Miss Wild. Save you scouring the warren of cold corridors." The woman fixed Nora with her beady gaze. "Some places aren't safe to wander alone."

"What an excellent idea, Mrs Egan," Nora said, using flattery as a shield against the woman's resentment. "We can make the arrangements after breakfast."

Mrs Egan gave a curt nod then faced her master. "Mr Babbage warned of another storm, my lord, more violent than the last. We can expect it to batter our shores sometime tomorrow afternoon."

"Babbage is usually quite precise in his premonitions. Miss Wild will need to draw the bed hangings and plug her ears." He looked at Nora. "The wind howls through the dungeons and underground tunnels like a horde of screaming banshees. We bolt all doors in the basement as a precaution. When Mrs Egan rings the handbell, you'll refrain from venturing downstairs."

The hairs on Nora's nape bristled with apprehension. The

thought of being accidentally locked in the dungeon squeezed the breath from her lungs. "I shall be sure to keep to my room until the storm has passed."

Mrs Egan seemed appeased and withdrew.

Nora pushed to her feet, overcome with a desire to escape to her bedchamber and bolt the door. "It's late, my lord. I must make an early start in the morning if I'm to examine the beach before the storm."

When alone with Lord Deville, she felt oddly at ease. But the tense atmosphere in the house, coupled with Mrs Egan's veiled warning, played havoc with Nora's imagination.

Some places aren't safe to wander alone.

Doubtless, Mrs Egan meant the tunnels or the clifftop, but Nora sensed the woman's enmity and saw it as a threat not to pry.

Lord Deville stood. "If I'm to accompany you during your investigation, I should retire, too. Let me show you to your room." He reached for the candelabrum to light their way. "Felix sold the silver to pay his gambling debts, and I had to find replacements. He had stripped this room bare. I purchased the furniture at another estate auction."

Nora noted the elegant chinoiserie bureau and the walnut occasional tables. Lord Deville's scar might make him appear brutish and uncouth, yet his tastes spoke of sophistication.

"Your mother would be proud of your achievements," she said, forgetting to mind her tongue. It was not her place to comment on his personal affairs. She looked at the empty space near the window and imagined his great-grandmother's instrument standing proudly there. "The return of the harpsichord will complete the room."

His gaze turned sad, reflective. "My mother always said I had the makings of an honourable man. It seems it's quite a rarity amongst the Devilles."

"Then you're the exception to the rule."

He gave a half-smile in response, though remained silent

as he escorted her out into the hall, past the dusty suit of armour and up the dark, winding staircase. His slow steps were almost hesitant. Perhaps he was tired of carrying this burden. Perhaps he did not relish the prospect of sleeping alone tonight.

She had jumped to the last conclusion because of her own issues sleeping. While her bedchamber had been her haven, a place of peace away from her father's endless preaching, it was also where her mind ran amok.

Nora cast Lord Deville a sidelong glance as they navigated the dim corridors. Candlelight cast shadows over his handsome profile. It occurred to her that he always walked on her right, always presented the side that would make any maiden's heart flutter.

He stopped outside an arched wooden door. "This will be your chamber for the duration of your stay," he said quietly, opening the door wide and stepping back for her to enter. "Before I leave, you must give me your word you won't explore these corridors at night. I know you have a case to solve, but this is not the sort of place one wanders alone."

His warning rang with concern, while Mrs Egan's carried a prickle of animosity.

"I have no intention of going anywhere in the dark."

He inclined his head. "Then I bid you good night, Miss Wild. If you wish to take your first glimpse of the sea, your window offers an excellent view."

"The sea!" Excitement bubbled in her chest. "I had almost forgotten we were on the coast." An enquiry agent should be mindful of her surroundings. Always observant. "I shall be sure to look at once. Good night, Lord Deville."

He hesitated as if he couldn't find the strength to leave before turning on his heel and retreating along the gloomy passageway. A sad shadow of the arrogant man she had witnessed in the auction room.

The desperate urge to soothe him sprang from nowhere.

Lord Deville was right. Her compassionate heart often led her astray, yet it was imperative she remained objective.

Pushing thoughts of Lord Deville aside, Nora entered the room and closed the door, grateful someone had lit the fire and the lamps. A longing to look upon the sea had her hastening to the window.

She pulled aside the heavy brocade curtains and peered through the tiny leaded panes.

Disappointment had her heart sinking like a brick in a well. The sea was nothing but a never-ending blackness, nothing like the magical vista Lord Deville described. At night, with grey clouds looming, it was a dark stream of emptiness. Desolate. Bleak. A vast abyss that failed to comfort her anxious soul.

Quickly drawing the curtains, she focused on examining the bedchamber that had been Johanna's room before her mysterious death. Or her mysterious disappearance, if one believed Lord Deville's theory.

It was not the lavish courtesan's boudoir she had expected. The oak furnishings were sturdy and practical. The thick red bed hangings served to keep out the cold, not give an air of extravagance. Even the detailed wall tapestry depicting the changing seasons was a means to keep the chill from seeping through the stonework.

Nora crossed the room and came to stand before the door leading to Lord Deville's chamber. Her thoughts turned to his mother and the many nights she must have stood in the same place, staring at the frosty barricade.

The key was not in the lock.

She rapped on the door.

The heavy pad of footsteps preceded the clink of a key turning. Lord Deville appeared. Having removed his waist-coat and cravat, he stood in his shirtsleeves, his stance relaxed, the glint in his eyes playful.

After her time at the Pleasure Parlour, she should be used

to seeing a man partly dressed, but her traitorous gaze swept over the breadth of his chest and heat flooded her cheeks.

"Miss Wild. Missing my company already?"

Nora offered her palm. "May I have the key, my lord?"

"Certainly." He removed it from the lock and placed it into her palm, the tips of his fingers grazing lightly over her skin in the process.

Nora shivered. "It's not that I don't trust you."

He smiled. "Of course not."

"It's that my father often locked me in my room, and ..."

"You feel more comfortable when in control."

She nodded. "I can be pedantic about such things."

"Understandably."

She apologised for disturbing him and bid him good night. Despite closing the door and slipping the key into the lock, she sensed him waiting on the other side.

Something about the pull of his magnetic presence kept her rooted to the spot. Indeed, Nora waited to hear his retreating footsteps before changing into her nightgown and venturing to the washstand. Plunging her hands into the cold water failed to draw her thoughts away from the man sleeping next door.

Lord Deville was a contradiction in terms. His horrid scar should leave her trembling to her toes, yet it added a certain vulnerability to his character that she found quite charming. Oddly, his angry outbursts did not frighten her. Why would they when she knew quiet men were the ones to fear? That said, when they conversed as they had done moments ago, when he spoke in a soft, tender tone, she found herself drawn to him in inexplicable ways.

Nora shook her head. She had not ventured to Highcliffe to examine her client's confounding character. With a case as complicated as this one, she should avoid all distractions.

On that sobering thought, she climbed into bed and settled her head on the pillow, happy in the knowledge the candle in the lamp would remain lit for at least an hour. After the incident at the Pleasure Parlour, she struggled to fall asleep in the dark.

And yet, just like the night she had woken to creaking boards and knew someone had stolen into her room, her heart crashed against her ribcage. For there, carved into the wooden canopy above, was a word that stole her breath and chilled her blood.

Just one word.

One silent plea.

Help!

"Help? You're certain?" Lord Deville stood in the corridor outside her chamber door, a stream of morning light catching the dark lock of hair falling over his brow. He looked more puzzled than shocked to learn of the strange carving.

Nora had thought about little else all night. Whenever she'd tried to sleep, the wind howled across the battlements and rattled the windowpanes. Twice she had heard foot-steps padding along the corridor and coming to a halt outside her door, but was certain Lord Deville had not left his room.

All in all, she had hardly slept a wink.

"Pray come inside and see for yourself." Nora stepped back and beckoned the lord to cross the threshold.

Lord Deville hesitated. Through mischievous eyes, he scanned her loosely tied hair and mauve dress as if she were tempting him to sin. "Inviting a gentleman into your bedchamber, Miss Wild? What would Mrs Egan say?"

Nora sighed. "Come through the adjoining door. Then no one will know we have broken the bounds of propriety."

Not that it mattered. As a working woman who'd slept in

a castle with an unmarried lord and no chaperone, her reputation was on par with that of a bawdyhouse mistress.

He glanced cautiously left and right, then stepped inside and quickly closed the door. "If I need to make a hasty retreat, I can slip into my room." His gaze met hers. "Am I the only man you've ever welcomed into your bedchamber, Miss Wild?"

A vision burst into her mind, a violent struggle with a devious lout. A memory she had tried hard to forget. "Stop being facetious and focus on the evidence." Nora hurried to the tester bed, pointing to where he would find the offending article. "It's here. Look. You can see it as clear as day."

Lord Deville closed the gap between them. He craned his neck to examine the word she had stared at for most of the night.

He squinted.

"Climb onto the bed, my lord."

The wicked glint in his eye made her regret the suggestion. "Let's hope no one heard your delightful order and jumped to the wrong conclusion." Still, he hauled his powerful frame onto the mattress and ran his finger over the letters scratched into the wood. "Who would have done such a thing?"

"Your mother or Johanna, perhaps."

"Johanna!" He scoffed. "I doubt the person who terrorised everyone thought to play the victim."

"Has no one mentioned it before?"

"No. Never." He climbed down from the high bed and straightened his blue coat. "I shall speak to Mrs Egan, although it may be a mystery we never solve."

Nora nodded yet made a mental note to question the staff about the ominous word carved into the wood. When a woman was locked in her room, denied food and a voice, she sought ways to release the pent-up anger, to alert others of her loss of liberty.

"If you're inclined to accompany me, I would like to see the clifftop and beach before we take breakfast." Before she toured the house and interviewed the staff. "Before the storm hits the shore."

Lord Deville inclined his head. "Be warned. The clifftop is unsafe. We must proceed with caution."

Was there anywhere amid this sprawling estate that wasn't considered dangerous? By rights, she should be shaking in her half-boots, terrified to venture from her room. Yet she felt remarkably calm in Lord Deville's presence when the opposite should be true.

Was it because he had suffered greatly and still battled on?

Yes, she admired him for that, even though he held so much bitterness in his heart. And she couldn't shake this sense of kinship, though she did not think of him as a brother.

Nora stole a glance at his broad shoulders and muscular thighs. No, she definitely did not think of him as a brother.

CHAPTER 6

Miss Wild had a secret. A secret that plagued her night and day. A secret that forced her to hide behind her professional facade and reveal nothing about her true self.

Sylvester found it more intriguing than why Gifford wanted him to purchase the book of Greek tales, or who the devil had scratched the word into the wooden tester bed. Though he feared the latter must have been his mother.

He cast Miss Wild a sidelong glance as they walked out of the grounds and onto the narrow coastal path. The wind whipped at the ribbons securing her straw poke bonnet, teased a silky brown lock loose. The gusts stole her breath and nipped her cheeks, leaving them a healthy shade of red. Head slightly bowed, she pushed on with steely determination.

When a man spent time with people who barely spoke his language, he learnt to study and observe every nuance. He knew to look for the slight changes in tone, note any sudden eye movement. Indeed, he had often plied his Italian counterparts with wine and brandy to lower their inhibitions. Sadly, he could not use the same tactic on Miss Wild.

As a man who despised secrets, he would find a way to

break down her barriers, to delve deep into her psyche and discover the truth.

"Stop here!" he shouted against the gale. The dark clouds in the distance warned of the impending storm, but the sun still cast golden rays where the sea lapped the shore. "According to the fisherman, this is where Felix and Johanna were seen arguing."

Miss Wild kept hold of her bonnet and gazed out over the North Sea. It was the first time she dared hold her head high and brave the weather. He expected her to bombard him with questions about the fisherman's account. Instead, she stared in awe.

"It's so beautiful," she said breathlessly. "Not at all what I expected after gazing out of my window last night."

Desperate to watch her take her first glimpse of the sea, to see excitement dance in her eyes, he had found it almost impossible to leave her.

"What is it you find so enchanting?" he said, keen to explore her character, to hear her opinion about something other than the case.

"The sea is so vast everything else seems insignificant."

"That's an observation, Miss Wild. I'm more interested in how you feel."

Accepting the challenge, she closed her eyes briefly. He took advantage of the moment to gaze upon her fine features.

The chill had drawn the colour from her lips. Yet he knew them to be the same dusky pink as the wild roses growing in his walled garden. No doubt both were silky soft to the touch. Her nose was small and delicate, unlike her courage, which might best be described as robust. Her long lashes batted against her pale cheeks like butterfly wings. Yet he saw nothing fragile in her countenance.

Miss Wild looked out towards the horizon. "I feel free."

Based on her life at the vicarage, the choice seemed apt.

"And peaceful," she quickly added. "Despite the challenges associated with solving your brother's murder, suddenly I feel able to tackle the world." She faced him. "What about you?"

Sylvester's mood turned reflective. No one had ever asked him how he felt. No one had ever cared enough to hear the answer.

"I am afraid our opinions differ. When I look out to sea, I feel trapped. Trapped by a legacy I don't deserve. Trapped in a life I detest." Trapped in this monstrous form.

She studied him through narrowed eyes. "And yet you play the brooding lord so well one might think you love the role."

He raised his hands in mock surrender. "You've found me out, madam. The moods and bad temper are merely props." If only that were true. "All used to give the impression of a bleak and miserable future."

"Your future doesn't have to be bleak."

"Marriage to a woman too terrified to look at me? People forever whispering their suspicions behind my back? It sounds depressing to me." The task was to find out more about her, not lament his own miserable fate.

"Mr Daventry said if you focus on making the best of the present, the future takes care of itself. The philosophy has helped me no end."

Good old Lucius Daventry.

"The man is a monument to wisdom," he said.

"He's not always right." She laughed as if remembering another of her employer's inspiring quotes. "In sending me here, Mr Daventry has made a grave error."

"A grave error?" Sylvester swallowed hard against the rising panic. "You doubt your ability to solve the case?"

No other woman would tolerate a man with his affliction. Daventry had refused to send a gentleman agent, even when offered an extortionate fee.

"Not at all. Failure is not an option." A blush crept up her neck. "It's ... it's a little embarrassing. But as you're a man who appreciates the truth, I may as well tell you."

"Tell me what?"

She winced. "You might insist on sending me home."

"Why would I send you home when I need your skill and expertise?" And she brought a semblance of normality to his life, which was rather ironic considering her unconventional occupation.

"Because the news will come as a shock."

He breathed deeply. "Let me assure you, nothing will change our working relationship." In such a short time, he had come to depend on her.

"Keep that thought in mind because I believe Mr Daventry sent me here so you might marry me, Lord Deville."

"Marry you!" He clutched his chest, though his heart did not pound in alarm.

"Indeed. All the ladies of the Order have married their clients. I am the last agent living in Howland Street." She snorted. "It's a ridiculous notion, I know. But forewarned is forearmed, is it not?"

It was damn ludicrous. So why did he imagine carrying her to the marital bed and consummating their union?

Sylvester shook the fantasy from his head.

"My lord, if one considers his success rate, Mr Daventry is the most proficient matchmaker in London. Which makes this whole thing confounding." She waved a dismissive hand at him. "You will only marry if forced, and I have no intention of ever taking a husband."

He considered Miss Wild and her protests. Despite his brother's attempts to bankrupt the estate, Sylvester was wealthy and could trace his lineage back to the Norman Conquest. Despite his scar, he was considered quite hand-some on his good side. And while he'd argued no one wanted

68

him, a desperate woman might use every tactic to force him to the altar.

Not Miss Wild.

She did not chase fame or fortune.

Which made her more alluring than any woman of his acquaintance.

"I'm glad you told me, Miss Wild. Now we will be prepared should Daventry try to manipulate events to his advantage."

She offered a warm smile. "Thank you, my lord. If we work together, we're sure to avoid the obvious traps. Now, let us return to the case." She turned to examine their position on the cliff edge. "Why would your brother come out here at night to argue with his wife?"

"Who can say? But they argued daily. They may have sought privacy away from the servants, and so went for a walk before dinner." His knees shook as he watched her teeter near the edge and peer down to the shore. "Merciful Lord! Step away, Miss Wild. Please. The ground can be unstable underfoot." In all likelihood, his brother had slipped and plunged to his death in much the same manner.

She shuffled back a little, but not enough to appease him. "Mr Daventry will ask to see a timeline. Can you recall when you last saw them?"

"I dined alone at six o'clock. They wished to eat later at eight, though Felix came to harass me during my meal." It had taken every ounce of restraint not to drive the bread knife through his brother's black heart.

"Harass you?"

"As I am the bastard son, he demanded I find alternative accommodation. He gave me a week to leave Highcliffe."

"What did you do?" She looked unnerved, for it did, indeed, give him a motive for murder.

"I didn't kill him," he reiterated. "I went to the chapel and for a walk in the garden. Then I rode to Canterbury to see Sir

George. Sadly, he had filled my position in Naples but agreed to find something suitable abroad."

"And when you returned to Highcliffe, did you—" She clutched her bonnet as a sudden gust almost knocked her off her feet.

Sylvester gripped her wrist and yanked her away from the cliff edge. She stumbled and tripped, but he caught her before she fell.

"I told you to move back!" he snapped, stone-cold fear taking command of his temper. "Do you want to get yourself killed?"

Miss Wild clung to him, her frantic gaze locking with his. Petrified, she couldn't quite catch her breath.

"You're safe now," he reassured her, softening his tone. How could he be angry when she felt so warm and pliant in his arms? Indeed, he couldn't quite find it within himself to release her. "I had no intention of letting you fall."

"Does the wind often catch you unawares here?"

Sylvester stared at her wide brown eyes and parted lips and couldn't, for the life of him, recall what she had just said. The sweet scent of roses breezed up to his nostrils, reminding him Miss Wild was every bit a woman, delightful and desirable in equal measure.

He cleared his throat. "I beg your pardon?"

"The wind, does it often hit the clifftop in sudden gusts?"

"Yes. The weather here is unpredictable." Recalling Lucius Daventry's matchmaking agenda, Sylvester ensured Miss Wild was steady on her feet before stepping back to a respectable distance. "We should head down to the shore while the tide is out. The path begins at that sign up ahead."

She nodded, though he could see the prospect of falling two hundred feet had left her nerves in tatters. "May I take your arm, my lord? Just until we reach the shore."

Every instinct said he shouldn't touch her again, not when loneliness clung to every cobwebbed corner of his heart.

"Certainly." He steeled himself as she slipped her gloved hand around his bicep.

"May I ask you something that's been on my mind since yesterday?" She did not wait for a reply. "Why would the fisherman lie?"

Glad to focus on something other than his newfound appreciation for Miss Wild, he said, "Who can say? But Felix was besotted with Johanna. He would never have pushed her off the cliff. The fool spent every penny trying to make her happy. Had she made him a cuckold, he would have forgiven her."

"But you said they always argued."

"Felix liked that she was volatile."

"I see."

He wondered if she did. Some men enjoyed physical domination in the bedchamber, and Miss Wild must have seen enough at the Pleasure Parlour to understand men and their vices.

"Be assured, my tastes are not the same."

"I did not for one moment think they were," she said, confirming she was more knowledgeable in the matter than her innocent smile belied. "Be assured, my role at the Pleasure Parlour involved making beds and clearing away dirty dishes, nothing more."

"I don't doubt it." Despite living in a den of iniquity, he would wager she was untouched. A virgin who, having seen the worst of men, was discouraged from ever taking a husband.

They remained silent while navigating the steep path down to the shore. Miss Wild clung to him as one would the mast of a sinking ship. He felt like a pirate, a man possessed with wicked thoughts of plundering the maiden beside him and stealing her precious treasure.

They stepped down onto the beach, the shingle crunching beneath their feet.

Miss Wild gasped. "Oh! I expected sand."

"The nearest sand beach is ten miles away in Westgate."

"Ten miles!" She sounded disappointed. "It's silly, but I've imagined the feel of sand between my toes ever since you mentioned teaching me to swim."

Why *had* he suggested playing tutor? Probably because he'd seen excitement dancing in her eyes and couldn't recall the last time a woman had looked at him without cringing.

He craved that look again. Desperately so.

"We could take a trip to Westgate."

Her eyes brightened. "When?"

"When the storm has passed."

"What reason would we have to go there? Mr Daventry will want to know how the trip relates to the investigation."

Sylvester smiled. "I am sure Daventry will understand your desire to walk barefoot in the sand."

After some consideration, she nodded. "Then I must stop dallying and use my time more effectively." She removed her hand from his arm, looked out to sea and then at the shingle. "So the tides are on a six-hour cycle."

"Thereabouts. The tide was at its lowest two hours ago. In four hours, the beach will be submerged in water again. Although at this time of year, it gets later each day, sometimes by as much as an hour."

She replied, though the wind had gathered momentum, and it was difficult to hear above the roar.

Sylvester cupped his ear.

"Can you show me where they found your brother's body?" she cried, gesturing to the beach.

"Yes!" He pointed to the mass of rocks close to the cliff face. "They found Felix there, sprawled face-down on that huge rock."

"Who found him?" She lowered her voice as the wind settled.

"Whittle and Mrs Egan. When the fisherman came

ashore, he raised the alarm. The vicar called at Highcliffe and alerted the servants. Discovering Felix and Johanna were missing, he sent for the magistrate, Lord Rutherfield, who lives in Hoath, between here and Canterbury."

Miss Wild studied the scene, shifting between the sea and cliff face while lost in thought. "Was Mrs Egan the last person to see them alive?"

"Yes, she saw them in the drawing room at seven o'clock, but when Whittle went to inform them dinner was served, the room was empty. The fisherman said he saw a man and a woman involved in a violent struggle at half-past seven, just before sunset, though he was two miles from shore at low tide, so I doubt he saw them at all."

Why would a fisherman have his telescope trained on the shore? If he had nothing to hide, why had he mysteriously disappeared days after giving his statement?

"Do you know what time the vicar arrived at Highcliffe?"

"Around eleven o'clock that evening."

"So late?"

"The fisherman gathered his nets before coming ashore. By all accounts, it took time to wake people from their beds and convince them he wasn't a drunken buffoon."

Miss Wild frowned. "And what time was high tide?"

"Midnight." The wind whipped at his hair, and he was thankful he had not worn a hat. "With the beach being on an incline, the sea doesn't completely cover the largest rocks, hence why they found Felix."

Miss Wild pursed her lips. "So, because of the fisherman's account, and the fact Johanna was missing, they assumed her body got washed out to sea."

"Yes. The servants' statements supported the fisherman's claim that the couple were often violent and abusive to one another. The magistrate agreed, although after speaking to the coroner and jury of witnesses who inspected the body, both deaths were registered as accidental."

Hence the reason most people suspected Sylvester had pushed them both from the cliff and paid the fisherman to give a false statement.

"Was the inquest held within forty-eight hours?"

"Yes. After making complaints to the local magistrate, there was a second inquest in Canterbury. Though due to a lack of new evidence, the coroner's ruling was upheld."

Those in attendance had stared at him as if he'd shuffled into the tavern wearing shackles, their suspicious gazes searing his soul, branding him the murderer.

Miss Wild wrapped her arms around her chest and shivered. "And the second inquest was when?"

"Last July." He gestured to the narrow path leading back to the clifftop. "It's bitterly cold, and you must be famished." The angry growl of his stomach proved timely. "Let's continue this conversation in the warmth of the dining room."

"No!" Raising a hand to apologise for her abruptness, she said, "By all means, let us return to the house. I'm chilled to the bone. But we must have a care when speaking about our theories. At least until we know who we can trust."

A shudder of trepidation ran the length of his spine. Had Miss Wild sensed the servants' aversion to him? Might she know he felt like the enemy in his own home?

"Are you referring to Mrs Egan?"

"To all the staff, although I get the sense Mrs Egan dislikes me immensely."

Sylvester sighed with relief. "And I thought I was the problem."

Miss Wild stepped forward and placed her dainty hand on his arm. "Something strange is afoot. Something I fear has nothing to do with your right to the lands and title. Be assured, I shan't rest until I have uncovered the truth."

Her hand was half the size of his, her touch featherlike, yet he had never felt anything so comforting.

"Despite all the mistakes I have made, the Lord saw fit to grant me a boon, Miss Wild." He covered her hand with his, gratitude flooding his chest.

"He gave you the resilience to tackle your problems?"

"No. In my darkest hour, he sent you."

CHAPTER 7

The sea air made one ravenous. Nora had two helpings of ham and eggs and demolished every morsel while Lord Deville drank his coffee.

His mouth curled into a grin as he watched her over the rim of his china cup. "Based on the amount of food you consume, you should have the girth of a packhorse, Miss Wild."

She placed a hand on her abdomen, remembering the many times it had groaned with hunger. "Thankfully, the quantity has no effect on my midriff, though I suspect my phobia of starving is a problem I should address."

"Perhaps it's as well I am not deducting board and lodgings from your fee. For your services, Daventry would receive the paltry sum of four shillings and threepence."

Nora laughed. He was quite amusing when in a relaxed mood. "If you include your fee for swimming lessons, I imagine I shall owe you a crown."

"That depends on how many lessons you need." His warm brown eyes sparkled with mischief. "On how many times you'd like me to take you in the water."

She should offer a witty retort, but the intimacy of the

moment drew her back to their brief clinch on the cliff. Yes, he had stopped her from falling, but he'd held her against his chest, his mouth hovering close to hers, his breath breezing across her lips like the whisper of a kiss.

Nora placed her cutlery down gently. "As I'm sure to need a few lessons, I shall curb my appetite lest I end up owing you a small fortune."

"Hiring you might prove profitable, madam."

"Undoubtedly."

Mrs Egan arrived to see if they required a footman to remove the breakfast plates. Her hair was scraped back into a simple knot, revealing the sharp angle of her jaw. Though she wore a brown dress today, there was still dust on the hem.

Lord Deville drew his watch from his pocket and inspected the time. "I shall give Miss Wild a quick tour of the house. Then she will conduct the interviews from the privacy of her bedchamber. Have a maid light the fire in her room."

Nora cleared her throat. "Might I conduct the interviews before the tour, my lord?" When discussing her findings with Lord Deville, she would do so away from the servants' pricked ears. "With limited staff, I'm sure Mrs Egan would prefer I deal with the matter promptly, so she may concentrate on her work."

"The interviews won't take long, Miss Wild." Mrs Egan's tone was as cold as her gaze. "The staff know nothing about what occurred here a year ago, other than what they told Lord Rutherfield and the coroner."

"Like you, I am paid to provide a service, Mrs Egan, and must do so to the best of my ability. My employer will expect a detailed report."

Nora needed the names of those servants who left when Lord Deville inherited Highcliffe. They surely knew something pertinent. The challenge would be dragging the information from his unwilling staff, hence why she chose not to mention her plan to Mrs Egan.

Indeed, as Lord Deville escorted Nora upstairs to her chamber, she made a point of asking, "Do you have a record of all the servants employed by your brother? Those who left Highcliffe without giving notice?"

"Of course. Lord Rutherfield interviewed most of them, and their statements were read out at the inquest. They all told the same tale. Felix and Johanna were violent, and it was only a matter of time before one killed the other."

"What of Johanna's lady's maid? They are usually loyal to a fault."

"Audrey returned to London. We were unable to locate her."

How strange. That said, London was a sprawling metropolis, a perfect place to hide.

"Probably because Audrey still tends to Johanna's needs at a secret location," Lord Deville sniped. He opened Nora's bedchamber door but remained in the hallway. "I shall find the information you seek and wait for you in my room. Knock the adjoining door once you've finished speaking to the servants, and I shall give you a tour of the house."

Not just the house. She needed to see the tunnels and dungeons, too.

"Have Mrs Egan send Mr Bower up first." Hopefully, Mr Daventry's man had plied the coachman with gin and dragged a tale or two from his lips.

"Certainly. Good Luck, Miss Wild." Lord Deville touched her gently on the upper arm before turning on his heel and striding away.

The scent of his cologne lingered, an exotic mix of Mediterranean herbs and cypress that roused images of rugged Italian landscapes.

The alluring aroma stayed with her long after she entered the room and set about positioning the chairs for the interviews. Indeed, Lord Deville occupied her thoughts a great deal of late. He was unlike any man she had ever known. He did not seek to control her or force his opinion. She sensed something familiar in him, a need to shake off the shackles, a longing to break free.

She was still thinking about the lord when a knock on the door broke her reverie. Mr Bower entered when summoned. She urged him to close the door quickly and beckoned him to the window.

"Have you learnt anything from Mr Sykes?" Nora kept her voice low. Mrs Egan might be listening at the door. Should Mr Bower reveal anything damning, Nora would break the news gently to Lord Deville to prevent him flying into a rage.

"Only that he's made to feel as unwelcome as his master, ma'am. Sykes came to Highcliffe a year ago. The previous coachman left the day they found Felix Deville's body on the beach."

"Did Mr Sykes say why?"

Mr Bower shrugged. "To save his neck from the hangman's noose. That's what the groom muttered when Sykes arrived but now denies he ever spoke the words."

"I see." Suspicion flared. Had the coachman feared he would be implicated in the murders? "Did Mr Sykes mention Mrs Egan?"

"Only to say that she runs a tight ship. And she accused him of theft, which is why he's forbidden from entering the house, though the matter was never reported to the master."

"How odd." Though if Nora had a shilling for every strange occurrence, she wouldn't need to work for a living. "We may be here for a week or more, Mr Bower. Do you feel comfortable staying in the coach house?"

Mr Bower grinned. "I've stayed in worse places, ma'am."

"Good. Not good that you've stayed in worse places, but I do need you to dig a little deeper. Discover what you can about Audrey, the lady's maid. She disappeared, along with her mistress. And spy on Whittle." The butler carried himself with the usual aplomb, but what was he like below stairs? "For the chief manservant, he tends to make himself scarce."

Mr Bower nodded. "I shall report with my findings tomorrow."

Nora instructed Mr Bower to send Mrs Egan upstairs and then took a moment to gather her wits before finding her notebook and pencil and settling into the chair.

Her stomach roiled like a ship in a storm as she waited. The thought of being alone in a room with the stern housekeeper had her nerves pulled tighter than a sail rope. Still, it couldn't possibly be worse than sitting opposite the Reverend Wild when he had a point to prove, though she feared that day was on the horizon.

Mrs Egan appeared at the open door, and the air turned frigid. "You wish to question me, Miss Wild?"

Nora gestured to the chair she had positioned a few feet away. "Please sit, Mrs Egan. I shall not keep you long." Not if she could help it.

With obvious reluctance, the housekeeper sat. Noticing dust on her hem, she batted the material with unnecessary vigour.

"You seem angry, Mrs Egan."

The woman inhaled sharply. "There's not enough of us to get the work done, Miss Wild. Forgive me, but I have better things to do with my time."

Nora held her nerve. "People suspect Lord Deville killed his brother. Do you not wish to see your master's mind at peace?"

"People always find a means to gossip."

"Then explain something to me." Nora hesitated. This woman had recited her story so many times it was unlikely she would reveal anything new. A different approach was needed. "Tell me about the day Lord Deville's mother died. You must have found it traumatic."

Mrs Egan's eyes widened in shock, but she gathered

herself quickly. "There isn't much to tell. Edith came to the house in a panic. By the time we reached the dowager, her heart had stopped."

"We?"

"Lady Deville summoned the coachman to take us to the cottage in the cart." *The coachman who left Highcliffe suddenly*, Mrs Egan failed to add.

"Where was Felix Deville?"

"In London on business."

Gambling away his fortune, no doubt.

"What time did Edith arrive at the house?"

Mrs Egan appeared to find the question confusing. "What time?"

"Yes."

"S-sometime in the afternoon. As you say, it was distressing, and my memory is vague."

Nora offered a sympathetic smile. "How did Lady Deville take the news of her mother-in-law's passing?"

Again, Mrs Egan struggled to form a reply. "She was upset, naturally, though they were not close."

"Why would they be close? They banished the dowager to a remote cottage two miles away?" Nora glanced at her notes. "Was Edith the dowager's maid or her companion?"

"Her maid-of-all-work."

"Then I need her direction. You must know who she went to work for after leaving Highcliffe."

"Lady Deville dismissed Edith. No one has heard from her since." Mrs Egan's tone turned defensive. "We've too much work here to concern ourselves with those who've moved on."

"Then I shall detain you no longer." Nora could stretch Mrs Egan on the rack, and the woman would still keep her tongue. "Could you send Whittle up next?"

"Yes, Miss Wild." The housekeeper stood abruptly, her

lips thinning. She mumbled something beneath her breath as she passed the adjoining door.

"All secrets come to light eventually, Mrs Egan," Nora said, stopping the housekeeper in her tracks, though the woman did not turn around. "By all accounts, Felix Deville did not deserve your loyalty, but your current master is a good, honourable man. A wise woman would bury the ghosts of the past and look to the future."

Mrs Egan straightened her spine. "And what if the ghosts refuse to stay buried?" she uttered before disappearing along the hallway.

Nora's breath caught in her throat. Was Mrs Egan offering the proverbial olive branch? Was that last comment proof Johanna had not plunged from the clifftop or been dragged out to sea in the undercurrent?

She sat, contemplating where Johanna might be, wondering if Lord Deville was correct in his assumption. Would his sister-in-law appear with the true heir to Highcliffe? Would the courts produce a document stamped with an official seal, confirming Sylvester Deville the unlawful heir, reinforcing the fact he did not belong here?

Heavy footsteps on the landing captured her attention. She expected Whittle, but Lord Deville's impressive physique filled the doorway.

"I found the ledger containing details of all employees, though some pages are missing." A deep frown marred his brow, and he growled in frustration. "Some devil tore the last ten pages from the book."

"Tore them!" Oddly, she cared more about smoothing away those worry lines than the missing evidence. "I presume the pages contained the details of those who left Highcliffe after the murder."

"Indeed."

"Then I shall interview you last, my lord. You may recall the names of those who were working here when you returned to England." As with most large estates, the employees were often local to the area. "With fourteen servants left to interview, I expect to finish later this afternoon."

He nodded. "I shall ride to Herne Bay before the storm breaks. Felix's valet had family there. I should be no more than two hours, depending on how forthcoming they are with information." His gaze softened. "Will you be all right in my absence? I don't have to leave. If you prefer, we can go together tomorrow?"

The tenderness in his voice sent her thoughts scattering. No one outside her colleagues cared if she lived or died. Yet this man considered her every comfort.

Nora mentally shook herself.

Of course, Lord Deville cared for her welfare. As an honourable man, he had made an oath to Mr Daventry, one he intended to keep.

"No, we have much to do. Go to Herne Bay and see what you can discover." She did not warn him to be careful, though repeated the plea in her mind. "A valet is privy to things other staff are not."

Whittle appeared, catching Nora by surprise. The man moved like a panther creeping up on its prey.

Lord Deville gestured for his butler to enter the bedchamber. "You may sit down, Whittle."

"Thank you, my lord." Whittle waited for his master to leave before prowling forward.

He was a man of forty, with coarse brown hair and bland features. Unlike Lord Deville's full, attractive lips, Whittle's were pale and thin, swallowed by an expressionless mouth.

Nora took hold of her notebook to stop her fingers shaking and fired a question she hoped would unnerve him. "Who do you think killed Felix Deville?"

Whittle stared through apathetic eyes. "It's not my place to comment, Miss Wild. The coroner claims it was an accident, though some believe he slipped off the cliff after murdering the mistress."

"Yet our evidence suggests Johanna Deville is alive."

"Then one wonders why the mistress has not returned home, ma'am. Doubtless, his lordship would care for her as he did before his brother tragically passed."

"Like any responsible brother-in-law would," she said, not rising to the bait.

Whittle lingered in the background for a reason. Based on her education at the vicarage and the Pleasure Parlour, she knew brash men were not the ones to fear. But what was the butler hiding?

"As you say, Miss Wild," Whittle said with deliberate sarcasm, "his lordship was just being brotherly."

This man knew how to plant a poisonous seed and watch it contaminate the earth. Now, Nora could think of little else but whether Lord Deville had ever had intimate relations with his sister-in-law.

Indeed, was guilt the reason for the lord's hatred?

"Tell me why Edith was given her notice."

"Perhaps you should ask Mrs Egan, ma'am."

"I wish to hear your opinion. On what grounds did Lady Deville dismiss the maid?"

"On the grounds, she neglected her duty, ma'am."

"How?"

"That's all I know."

Heavens! Whittle was less forthcoming than Mrs Egan. Perhaps Nora should focus on those servants who were easier to intimidate.

"Do you believe Sylvester Deville is the rightful heir to Highcliffe?"

"I do not make the laws of the land, Miss Wild. But I respect my master as I did the master before him." His gaze shifted to the window and the ominous clouds in the distance. "But the wages of sin is death," he said, reciting the

Reverend Wild's beloved biblical quote. "Some might say that's why Felix Deville perished. Some might say that's why everyone at Highcliffe is doomed."

Nora sat silently. The odd premonition weighed heavily on her shoulders. She had sensed deceit clawing the air the moment she crossed Highcliffe's threshold. Her father had filled her mind with stories of omens and curses and the horrible things that happened to sinners. It was a means of control, and Whittle meant to scare her with the wrath of God, too.

"That will be all, Whittle." She couldn't bear to spend another minute in his company. "Please send the next person upstairs."

Whittle stood. "Heed my advice, Miss Wild. Leave this place. Stay within these walls another night, and you'll not keep the devil at bay." He glanced at the adjoining door as if his master were a servant of Satan. "Leave while you can."

Had Whittle spoken with an ounce of conviction, with anything but monotone indifference, she might have flung her clothes into her valise and raced to find Mr Bower. But these veiled threats were all part of the charade, and she had more sense than to give them merit.

"Thank you for your concern, Whittle, but I have a job to do here and cannot leave until I find answers."

"Then we're all damned, ma'am."

Whittle inclined his head and left the room. She had thrown down the gauntlet, and a fight would surely ensue. Months ago, she would have fled like the other servants, but fear was merely the anticipation of evil, and she had been taught to focus on the facts.

Lord Deville appeared in the hallway, looking magnificent in tight buff breeches and black Hessians. A welcome distraction. "I shall return posthaste."

She fought the urge to beg him to stay. "Have a care, my

lord. No one knows precisely when the storm will hit these shores."

His smile was so warm she barely noticed his scar. "I appreciate your concern, Miss Wild. More than you know." And then he was gone.

The next two hours passed quickly. Between the gathering wind rattling the panes, the gusts howling down the chimney, and it growing as dark as hell's corridors, Nora interviewed most of the servants.

Their stories bore an uncanny resemblance.

Consumed by greed and jealousy, Felix and Johanna Deville murdered each other. One pushed the other off the cliff, then slipped to their doom.

No one knew who carved the word into the canopy.

No one knew why the servants left suddenly.

No one had corresponded with those who had moved on.

Nora had finished questioning the groom when Mrs Egan appeared, slinking from the shadows, to confirm everyone had given their statements.

Nora checked her notes. "I haven't interviewed Blanche."

Mrs Egan frowned. "Did she not come upstairs after you'd finished with Cook?" The sullen housekeeper did not wait for a reply. "Miss Wild, we work from dawn until dusk. If Blanche was waylaid, I cannot spare her again today."

Nora studied the woman who had just lied to prevent her from speaking to the maid. "I understand. I shall search for Blanche myself and question her while she works."

That proved a problem, too.

"A girl cannot work when there's talk of mischief and murder." Mrs Egan glanced back over her shoulder and lowered her voice. "Blanche has a nervous disposition and suffers dreadful nightmares. I would prefer you didn't make matters worse."

The sudden growl of thunder outside served as an omen. An ominous warning something was dreadfully amiss here.

Mr Daventry said an agent must know when to advance and when to retreat. There was no cowardice in the latter. A war was often won by the side with the best strategy.

"Very well. I shan't trouble Blanche today." Mrs Egan couldn't hide the maid away forever. Besides, a more important matter stole her attention. "Has Lord Deville returned from his afternoon ride?"

"Not that I'm aware, Miss Wild."

With a sense of foreboding, Nora turned to the window. Black clouds swirled ominously in a volatile sky. The first drops of rain had hit the panes half an hour ago, though the gentle *pitter-patter* suddenly became a biblical deluge pinging rapidly on the glass.

Possessed by mild panic, Mrs Egan said, "I must check everyone is indoors. Quickly. Draw the curtains. Keep away from the windows." Then the housekeeper raced from the room, slamming the door behind her.

Nora hastened to the window, her stomach roiling as she thought of Lord Deville battling the ferocious gale. Life had a way of repeating old patterns. So it was hardly surprising she found herself a prisoner in her room, fearing God's judgement.

Almost another hour passed before she heard the clip of booted footsteps echoing along the corridor. Relief surfaced. She yanked open the door and peered into the hallway to see Lord Deville, his hair and clothes wet and dishevelled, striding into his room.

Thank heavens!

Nora prayed he had been more successful in securing information than she had. She considered calling out to him, but then Blanche appeared, carrying a wicker basket of wood.

"His lordship said I'm to stoke your fire, miss, and hook the fire screen to the wall." The young woman failed to meet Nora's gaze. "The damp has a way of getting into your bones when the room is chilly, and the wind can charge down the chimney and scatter the embers."

Nora checked Mrs Egan wasn't lingering in the corridor and then motioned for the maid to enter. "Come in, Blanche. As I didn't have a chance to interview you earlier, might I ask you a few questions now?"

Blanche's nervous gaze shifted to the door. "Not here, miss. It ain't safe."

Nora's pulse thumped hard in her throat. So Mrs Egan did have something to hide. "Do you know what happened to Felix Deville?"

Blanche set down her basket and dropped to her knees. "The master was murdered, miss, but I'll not talk here."

"Where, then?"

Casting her frantic gaze at the door again, she whispered, "Meet me tonight outside the castle walls, through the gate, past the herb garden. I'll not finish my chores until eight, and then I need to take supper with the others. Come at ten."

Keen to be on her way, Blanche added more logs to the fire and secured the screen.

"Can you tell me anything in the meantime? Do you know who carved the word *help* into the bed canopy?"

Blanche gathered her basket and moved to the door. "I did, miss, but I'll explain why later. I need to fetch more wood and light the fire in his lordship's room." She gripped Nora's arm. "Don't trust anyone, miss, else you'll end up like the others."

"The others?"

A sudden crack of thunder made Blanche gasp and drop her basket. She gathered it quickly, then darted from the room and along the corridor, disappearing down the servants' staircase.

Feeling equally unnerved and seeking her confidant, Nora knocked on the adjoining door. "Lord Deville!"

Moments ago, she had heard clattering and banging and a

muffled conversation coming from the lord's chamber. Now she heard nothing.

"My lord!"

Deathly silence ensued, then Lord Deville cried, "Argh! Good God, man, do you mean to kill me?"

Nora grabbed the dagger from her reticule and unlocked the adjoining door without hesitation. All was quiet again, and so she crept through the lord's dressing room and into his bedchamber.

She stopped abruptly upon finding it deserted.

The potent scent of his cologne stole her attention. As did the imposing Jacobean poster bed dominating the masculine space. Strange sounds emanated from behind the door on the opposite side of the room.

"Lord Deville," she whispered, though received nothing but a pained groan in reply.

Armed with her dagger, Nora crossed the room and cautiously opened the door.

Merciful Mary!

The sight beyond near scorched her eyes.

Her heart hammered against her ribs.

Her chin almost hit the floor.

Lord Deville stood naked in a huge copper tub; thank goodness he faced the wall. Perched on a ladder, the footman was busy emptying the contents of a bucket into the top of a strange contraption. Water trickled like a rain shower over Lord Deville's ebony hair, over the rippling muscles in his back, over his tightly clenched buttocks and muscular thighs.

Nora covered her mouth with her hand but failed to stifle a gasp. Sweet heaven! Lord Deville was a perfect specimen of masculinity. It was wrong to look. She should make a hasty retreat, yet couldn't tear her gaze away.

Indeed, the gentleman dashed any hope she had of creeping out of the room unnoticed when he uttered, "Miss Wild, to what do I owe the pleasure?"

CHAPTER 8

Sylvester heard Miss Wild's shocked gasp but did not turn around. At the bawdyhouse, she must have seen many naked men. The fact she had not fled in a fit of hysterics left him somewhat aroused.

"I pray you're wearing spectacles, Miss Wild. Pray the steam has misted the glass and obscured your vision."

"Regrettably, I left my spectacles on the nightstand."

"And yet you've stood ogling me for a minute or more."

"Ogling you?" she said, sounding most offended. "I am merely curious about your contraption."

"My contraption?" He laughed. Was this a rare glimpse of naivety or a deliberate attempt to tease him? Was innuendo a skill gained at the Pleasure Parlour? "Are we discussing my bathing machine or something else, madam?"

He could not recall when he had last flirted shamelessly with a woman. But Miss Wild made him forget his life was a shambles. Indeed, he almost forgot his footman was standing statue-like on the ladder.

"What else would I be curious about?" she countered, yet he could feel the heat of her inquisitive gaze journeying over his back. "Now it's evident you have not been murdered by your footman, I shall leave you to your ablutions, my lord."

"Murdered by my footman?"

Thomson met Sylvester's gaze. "Miss Wild is holding a blade, my lord. I believe she heard you complaining the water was too cold and, what with her being an enquiry agent, feared something wicked was afoot."

"Then one must question the lady's observation skills," Sylvester teased. "An enquiry agent should be quick to determine if a man is dead, not gape at his naked form for minutes on end."

The lady's huff of annoyance preceded the stomp of retreating footsteps on the boards.

"Miss Wild has retired to her room, my lord."

"Then empty the bucket, Thomson, and help me dress."

Sylvester chuckled to himself. Miss Wild's boldness knew no bounds. And yet he owed her a debt of gratitude. Lust coursed like lava through veins that were usually ice-coated. Masculine pride warmed his chest for the first time in years. The lady evidently admired his muscular physique and saw him as more than a man with a hideous scar.

He dressed quickly, told a nervous-looking Blanche there was no need to light the fire, for he was to give Miss Wild a tour of the house.

"It's not safe to wander about during the storm, my lord."

"It's not safe to go down into the dungeons," he corrected. "We shall be perfectly fine above stairs."

Being a girl scared by her own shadow, Blanche glanced quickly over her shoulder before muttering, "Best have a care where you go these next few days."

He might have asked the maid to explain her cryptic comment, but she hurried into the hall, and he had more pressing business on his mind.

After brushing a hand through his damp hair, he knocked on the adjoining door and waited for Miss Wild's summons before entering her chamber. Scanning the dim room, he found her pacing by the window.

"Did Mrs Egan not warn you to keep away from the window during the storm? Flying debris can shatter the panes."

"The curtains are thick enough to act as a barrier. Like everyone else here, Mrs Egan has a tendency to cause unnecessary alarm."

Tension rippled through the air, made worse by Miss Wild's inability to remain still. "You appear at odds. Can you not shake the arousing vision of a man taking his ablutions? Are you annoyed because I caught you spying?"

"Spying?" She flew around to face him. "Do not flatter yourself. Were it not for your incessant groaning, I would have remained in my room. I feared your footman meant to murder you, for one of the servants most certainly killed your brother."

Sylvester jerked back in shock. He closed the gap between them. "Did something happen while I was away? Did a servant confess?"

"No, not exactly." Miss Wild gestured to the chairs and begged him to sit. She gave a detailed account of all that had occurred in his absence. "In short, Whittle tried to frighten me with his biblical mumblings. Mrs Egan is definitely hiding something. The other servants merely recited their scripts."

"But you think Blanche knows who murdered Felix?" Was that what Blanche meant when she warned him to have a care? Was his life in danger, too?

"She definitely knows something."

Noises in the corridor—the creak of a door and a hushed conversation—led him to tap his finger to his lips, an urgent plea for Miss Wild to remain silent.

They listened intently for a time, though the patter of footsteps outside forced him to grab her hand and draw her through the adjoining door.

"You were right, Miss Wild." Sylvester kept her at his side while scanning his bedchamber. Then he snatched the lit lamp before locking them in his dressing room.

"Right about what?"

"We must trust no one but each other."

She nodded. "My lord?"

"Yes."

"You're still holding my hand."

Sylvester glanced at their entwined fingers and reluctantly released her. "Please forgive any impropriety. These strange goings-on have me on edge, and I vowed to keep you safe."

Her gaze slid slowly up over his chest, stoking the inner fire that had been simmering since their lengthy conversations yesterday. Her eyes met his. "When working so closely together on a case, it is easy to make such an oversight."

"Yes," he agreed, though that failed to explain why it felt so natural to take her hand, or why he wanted her to admire his bare buttocks and firm thighs. "If we're to speak about my brother's murder, we'll do so in this dressing room or when alone outside."

Miss Wild nodded and repeated Blanche's cryptic request to meet beyond the castle walls. "She said to trust no one. She admitted to carving the word into the canopy, though didn't say why."

"But if Blanche knows who killed Felix, why did she not confess to Lord Rutherfield at the time?" The magistrate would have offered his protection.

"No doubt she will answer all our questions when we meet her tonight." Miss Wild pursed her lips, her expression turning coy. "Whittle made an interesting remark. He implied your relationship with Johanna was anything but hostile. That it was of an ... intimate nature."

"Intimate!" Sylvester firmed his jaw. He made a mental note to throttle his butler. Indeed, he might have replaced Whittle a year ago, but no one within a thirty-mile radius wanted to work at Highcliffe, probably because of the curse. "How many times must I tell you? I despise the harlot."

"Johanna must have been beautiful," she said with a tinge of jealousy. "And a courtesan knows how to use her wiles to charm men into bed."

"Johanna *is* beautiful, though her inner ugliness leaves a lasting impression. And she may have charmed weak men into bed, but not me." It was not from a lack of trying. Perhaps that's what Whittle meant. "During one particular storm, I entered my chamber to find Johanna sprawled naked on the counterpane. When I threw her out, she lied to her maid and gave a salacious account of how she bedded her husband's brother. It's how I earned this damnable scar."

Miss Wild looked at his marred cheek, and her pretty eyes softened. "Was it terribly painful?"

"It hurt like the devil for days. Now it only pains me when it's cold." And when others grimaced in disgust. He turned his head to let her look upon his face fully in the muted light. "Johanna ruined my life." People shrank away from him in the street. Children clutched their mother's skirts as he passed. "To everyone, I'm a monster."

"You're not a monster to me," she said softly before doing the unthinkable. She reached up and touched her fingertips to the tight skin. "I barely notice it now."

Sylvester hissed a breath and closed his eyes. A surge of emotion almost swept him off his feet. Like a parched man at an oasis, he drank in this simple act of kindness, mentally cupping his hands and devouring every last drop. Aware nothing in his entire life would prove as satisfying.

"The skin is smoother than I expected," came the sweet voice of the woman who had touched him in ways he couldn't possibly explain.

"As you rightly said, my heart took the brunt of the blow."

She cupped his cheek gently. "I may have the ability to

help solve this case, but as a fellow sufferer, I lack the skill needed to mend your scarred heart."

"Kindness is an ointment that soothes many wounds. Hence why I shall give you my helping of dessert tonight."

She stole back her hand, though the imprint would forever remain. "Who would have thought the disagreeable Lord Deville could be so benevolent?"

"Who indeed?" The difference in him could be easily explained. "Thank you, Miss Wild." He felt a strange tug in his chest.

"For what?"

"For not judging me as most people do." *For making me feel human, a man any woman would be proud to present to her family and friends*, he added silently.

"I like that your flaw is visible."

"Though I am yet to find any evidence of yours."

Her smile slipped, and he cursed himself for ruining what had been a tender moment. "I bear a mark only the Almighty can absolve." She shook her head. "In any case, we should concentrate on the matter at hand. You haven't told me what happened on your trip to Herne Bay."

Sylvester opened the adjoining door. Once confident Mrs Egan wasn't lurking in Miss Wild's bedchamber, he locked them in the dressing room again.

"I spoke to Mrs Warby, the valet's mother. She moved to Boyden Gate a year ago, hence why the trip took longer than two hours."

"Did she give you her son's direction?"

"Yes, Warby left for France the day after they found my brother's body. He told his mother he had been offered a better position. He sends her small gifts on occasion."

Miss Wild frowned. "Other servants found new positions. If you have no significant information, why check my room?"

Oh, he had significant information.

"When I questioned her, Mrs Warby struggled to keep to

her story." Thankfully, she had found Sylvester's appearance intimidating. "As it happens, her son said he'd end up dead in a shallow pit if he remained in Kent."

"Dead because he would hang for murder?"

Sylvester shrugged. "Or dead because he knew the identity of the killer. Either way, the most interesting part is he gave her thirty pounds and told her not to discuss the matter with anyone. He said, having seen what they had done to Lady Deville, they would likely hurt her too if they discovered he had given her money."

Miss Wild inhaled sharply. "Then he can confirm Johanna is dead?"

"No, he meant my mother." The sudden tightness in his throat mirrored the crushing ache in his chest. His mother would not have perished in that damn cottage had he remained in England.

"Your mother!" Miss Wild appeared stunned. "He implied she died by another's hand? That her death had nothing to do with her weak heart?"

"I'm not entirely sure, but Blanche has worked here for two years and surely knows what happened the night my mother died."

Miss Wild jerked her head. "The night! Mrs Egan said your mother died in the afternoon."

"No. Felix said she suffered an attack after supper."

"This is all so confusing." She pressed her fingers to her temple. "We should ignore everything your servants tell us. Although I am interested to hear what Blanche says when we meet her tonight."

Sylvester pulled his watch from his pocket and checked the time. "I shall inform Mrs Egan we're to dine at half past seven. We'll take a tour of the house afterwards, then no one will question why we're wandering around the grounds. Let's pray the worst of the storm is over by then."

"In the meantime, might I use your study, my lord? I must

detail all the evidence gathered so far. Mr Daventry can be quite a hard taskmaster, and I mustn't disappoint him."

Sylvester doubted Miss Wild could disappoint anyone.

Except for the father who'd mistreated her.

"I have work to do there myself, letters to read, papers to sign, but promise not to disturb you."

Sylvester caught himself. Why was he so eager to spend time with Miss Wild? He scoured his mind to find a sensible explanation, and came up with one quickly. While his brother's death remained unexplained, it was right to worry about her welfare.

Yet that didn't account for why he craved her company.

The main reason left him debating if Lucius Daventry was more than a matchmaker. For Sylvester to feel affection for his agent, Daventry must be a bloody magician.

"I want to hear more about you, Miss Wild. When we spoke at the coffeehouse, you implied your father cast you out. You did not leave of your own volition?"

Seated to his right at the formal dining table, Sylvester observed her keenly. And not for the first time today. When it came to Miss Wild, he had developed an enquiry agent's curiosity. Now he knew she nibbled her bottom lip whenever she dipped her nib in ink. Her penmanship was as elegant as her bearing. And when her gaze turned reflective, nothing but sadness lingered there.

"The Reverend Wild gave me an ultimatum." She dabbed her mouth with her napkin. "But my story is unimportant. I do not wish to bore you with the mundane details."

"I am not a selfish man, Miss Wild." Except for the one time he had chosen to escape his tormentors. "I am tired of talking about my troubles. And I would like to understand why you chose such an unconventional path."

She raised a defiant chin. "Is it unconventional to take control of one's life? Is it wrong to fight against one's oppressor? Should I have obeyed my father and married the man of his choosing?"

"He wished you to marry?" Saying the words left a bitter taste in his mouth. Still, he added, "As most fathers are wont to do."

"He didn't wish it. He demanded it."

"And you objected to the suitor?"

"Wholeheartedly." She shivered visibly as if plagued by a harrowing memory. "The Reverend Wild would have forced the union, by physical means, had I not used my bedsheets to climb out of the chamber window. I left with what little money I had managed to save and a few items of clothing stuffed into a valise."

He, too, had fled in the dead of night, only stopping to kiss his sleeping mother softly on the forehead and leave a letter on her nightstand. Yet he had been plagued by mixed emotions. Relief at being free of his brother. Guilt for being every bit a coward.

"It can't have been an easy decision."

Tears welled in her eyes, but she kept them at bay. "I have not slept properly since."

"You fear the Reverend Wild will find you?"

"I know he will find me, eventually. As an agent of the Order, I have received an education in bravery. But I doubt I have the strength to fight my father."

The need to protect her burned in his chest. The urge to throttle a man of the cloth meant he was likely in league with the Devil. And it occurred to him that Daventry was, indeed, a man of great cunning. He knew Sylvester had struggled to make his father see sense. That a man's heart might soften for a woman who had suffered the same plight.

"Daventry will do everything possible to ensure your father won't find you." Was that why he had sent her to Kent? "And you'll always be welcome here should you need a place to hide."

Miss Wild looked up in surprise, her brown eyes glistening in the candlelight. "Would you not worry what people said?"

Sylvester shrugged. "According to the locals, I'm a murdering devil who bears Satan's scar. Let the gossips have their day."

She stared, her expression revealing the depth of her gratitude. "Thank you. While I am always ready to flee at a moment's notice, I had not considered where I would go."

"The stagecoach for Canterbury leaves the White Horse in Fetter Lane most days. There is no need to signal ahead and warn Mrs Egan of your arrival."

"I am most grateful to you." Her eyes shone with warmth and appreciation. "And to think you almost didn't hire me."

He wished he could decant that look into a bottle, sip from it when the nights were long and lonely. "My frustrations affected my judgement."

"You've mellowed since then, my lord."

Yes. Tonight Sylvester had let her sit to his right, giving her an ample view of his scar. "And you seem more relaxed when away from London. There, you appear permanently on edge. Indeed, you've not worn your spectacles once today."

She fell silent, sadness falling over her like a heavy veil. He sensed there was another reason for her disguise, besides hiding from her father, who would surely recognise his own daughter if she donned a grey wig and hobbled with a walking stick.

Sylvester stood, deciding not to press her further at present. "Shall I take you on a tour of the house? We should be seen wandering the halls if we're to allay suspicion."

"Certainly."

She pushed out of the chair before he could offer his assistance. Was her enthusiasm a means of avoiding a discussion about why she was so tense in town?

Sylvester showed her the library, which had once held some of the oldest books in England, and the old chapel, where they spent a moment lamenting the loss of their mothers. He took her to Gabriel's Tower, though the studded door was bolted on the outside.

"When the storm has passed, I shall take you to the top. If you look south on a clear day, you can see the spires of Canterbury Cathedral."

Miss Wild smiled. "I would like that. On the subject of Canterbury, we must visit Sir George. I need to hear his account of what happened the night of the murder."

"You mean you want to check my alibi."

"I know you didn't kill your brother, but your godfather may know something about what happened during your time in Italy."

Sylvester had not told his godfather of his plans to hire an agent. Sir George would take one look at Miss Wild and jump to the wrong conclusion. Force him to sit through an awkward lecture about why peers should marry for love, not duty.

"Very well. We can go to Canterbury tomorrow." Once she had interviewed Sir George, there was little left to do in Kent. "That said, the road may be impassable after the storm." It was a case of wishful thinking on his part, though he couldn't keep her at the castle forever.

He concluded the tour in the long picture gallery. Purely because he would not have time to regale the names of all the Devilles who may or may not be his ancestors.

"Yes, I see a family likeness." She studied the portrait of Alexander Deville, posing in his ruff, then gazed at Sylvester's face and scrutinised every facet. "The Devilles all have square jaws and ... full lips."

"Are they characteristics you admire, Miss Wild? Do you find a man's mouth particularly attractive?" His attention fell to her luscious lips. They were soft and plump and just waiting to be kissed.

She averted her gaze briefly before finding the courage to look at him. "Madame Matisse said one should never measure a man's worth on the shape of his mouth but on what words slip between them."

Sylvester laughed. "Madame Matisse is a wise woman."

"Yes, she has been very kind to me." Her voice was tinged with sorrow, but she shook off the sudden melancholy. "Might you show me where you access the tunnels and dungeons?"

"By all means. The door is in the basement, off the servants' corridor." He gestured for her to follow him out of the gallery. "Though if you want to peek inside, we will have to wrestle Mrs Egan for the key."

He led her through a maze of draughty rooms and corridors.

In the old armoury, where one could almost hear the clang of metal, Miss Wild caught his arm and brought him to a halt. "What's through that door?" She pointed to a black door in the corner that looked to lead nowhere.

"A watchtower. It's considered unsafe and will be my next project once I have recovered my mother's possessions."

"A house this size must need constant repairs."

"Yes. It occupies my time." Time that was endlessly lonely.

They walked in companionable silence, down the flight of stone stairs to the servants' quarters. The chill air hit them like an arctic breeze when they entered the vaulted corridor.

Knocking more than once on the housekeeper's private parlour, they waited for Mrs Egan, but she failed to appear. It was then he heard a bang further along the corridor. Upon inspection, he found the iron door to the tunnels open, a lit lantern left on the floor outside.

"What in blazes? Mrs Egan is fastidious about securing the door when there's a storm. Blanche has been known to sleepwalk."

Having surveyed the tunnels when he inherited, he had no need to visit the basement. Still, that didn't stop Mrs Egan panicking about crumbling masonry and insisting no one venture down there.

"May I know the time, my lord?"

Sylvester pulled his pocket watch, took the lantern and raised it aloft to inspect the time. "A quarter to ten. If we're to meet Blanche, we need to leave now."

Yet they glanced at the open door and then at each other.

"We should check the tunnel, my lord." Miss Wild's curious mind was a match for his own. "Mrs Egan may have had an accident."

Despite his reluctance, he agreed. "We'll navigate the passageways for a few minutes. Stay behind me. Once we're down there, hold on to my coat."

"We should leave something behind to alert the servants of our intention, lest they bolt the door."

They scanned each other before Sylvester gave Miss Wild the lantern and set about untying his cravat. "When Mrs Egan sees the sapphire stick pin, there's sure to be no confusion."

Miss Wild watched him, her gaze lingering on the open neck of his shirt as he tugged his cravat free and placed it on the floor.

Taking tentative steps, he held the lantern high and led her down the narrow flight of worn stairs into the dark abyss. Miss Wild gripped his arm and shuffled slowly behind.

"Mrs Egan!" he shouted upon reaching a fork in the path.

"Mrs Egan!" Miss Wild called when they entered a large circular chamber with six possible exit routes. She released him, stepping over the stone debris to peer along the nearest tunnel.

"Is anyone down here?" Sylvester's words echoed through the chamber. He turned to Miss Wild, unable to ignore the prickle of unease between his shoulder blades. "We should return to the house."

"Yes." Miss Wild cocked her head. "What's that noise?"

Sylvester listened. "The sea crashing against the rocks. One of the tunnels leads to an escape route. To a cave less than a mile from here." That's why water dripped from the ceiling, and it was so darned cold and damp.

"Tomorrow, we should return and explore. I don't know why Mrs Egan demands the door be bolted during the storm when it seems quite peaceful down here."

Yes, Sylvester had always trusted his housekeeper's word, though his parents had discussed blocking the tunnels and bricking up the door.

Then, as if Satan wished to toy with them, a violent gust tore through the chamber though it sounded more like a ghoulish howl.

Miss Wild hurried over to him and captured his arm. "I think we've seen enough for now, my lord. Don't you?"

"Indeed." As a boy, he'd been warned never to venture below ground. Even when he disobeyed his father's instructions, he always did so with a clawing sense of unease.

They hastened through the subterranean passageways, though his blood ran cold when they reached the flight of steps and found the door to the servants' corridor closed.

"Damn the devil!" Sylvester rattled the iron handle and pushed at the door. "It's no use. It's bolted on the other side."

"Mrs Egan!" Miss Wild shouted numerous times. "Mrs Egan!"

They hammered hard and cried out.

No one came.

CHAPTER 9

They were trapped, locked in the dark tunnels, hoping a servant ventured out into the corridor and heard their panicked cries.

What if their shouts went unanswered?

What if this was Mrs Egan's plan all along? Had she been biding her time, waiting for an opportunity to murder her new master?

Nora cursed herself for being so foolish.

"Never take unnecessary risks," Mr Daventry had said many times. "Always look for a safe means of gathering information."

If she made it out of the tunnel alive, she would not write about this mistake in her report. Though it was only a matter of time before Mr Daventry realised trouble stalked her like her own shadow.

Nora hugged herself in a bid to keep warm.

"Here, take my coat. It should stave off the chill." Lord Deville shrugged out of the garment and draped it around her shoulders. His fingers brushed her nape, awakening a need to prolong every intimacy. "Someone will hear our cries soon."

Nora dared to reveal her worst fear. "There is every chance this wasn't an accident. Mrs Egan tried to prevent me from speaking to Blanche this afternoon. Perhaps she sought a means to prevent me from talking to her tonight."

Had Mrs Egan hidden in the darkness?

Had she stalked them through the house?

"Ordinarily, I would look for an innocent explanation, but when one considers my brother's fate, I find I'm inclined to agree with you."

But what possible motive could she have?

"When you said you were the last Deville, did you mean of your direct bloodline? Who inherits Highcliffe if you die?"

"No one. The patent decrees only a male can inherit and so the peerage becomes extinct." Lord Deville frowned before banging violently on the door again. "Why? Did you suspect Mrs Egan was in cahoots with the heir?"

"No, but it's a question I should have asked while at the coffeehouse." She slipped her arms into the sleeves of his coat and pulled it tighter across her chest. His intoxicating scent enveloped her, causing another inner tug that proved most confounding. "What about enemies abroad?"

"I have none. Besides, we should concentrate on escaping the tunnels before adding more lines of enquiry." He beckoned for her to step back while he kicked the door. "Cursed saints! There's no way to break it down, but you'd think someone would hear the loud racket."

"Perhaps they have chosen to ignore the banging." Nora glanced back into the gloom. Nerves knotted in her stomach, but she tried to focus on tackling the problem. "How adventurous are you, my lord?"

"How adventurous? Madam, I lived in a foreign country for years. Gathered secret information in a bid to appease our allies. I believe that makes me a man who's willing to take risks. Why do you ask?"

"It strikes me we could foil our captors by finding another way out. You said the tunnels lead to a cave. Let us find it quickly before the candle in the lantern dies." They could assess if the cave was a viable means of escape.

Lord Deville looked at the closed door and cursed. He rattled it once more and banged loud enough to wake the dead. Finally, all hope abandoned, he conceded. "Very well. It shouldn't be too difficult. We simply need to follow the sound of the sea."

They returned to the circular chamber. Lord Deville stood, stroking his jaw while establishing which way was north.

"Where are the dungeons?" she said.

"You turn right at the first fork in the path."

"What made you turn left earlier?" During their first inspection below ground, he had not stopped to ponder the decision.

Lord Deville shrugged. "What business would Mrs Egan have in a row of old cells?" He held the lantern aloft at the entrance to one tunnel before moving to another. Behind the glass, the candle guttered. "It's this way. I remember now." Lord Deville pointed to a narrow passage. "Hold on to me. Stay close."

Stay close.

When spoken in his hypnotic voice, a lady's mind conjured many romantic scenarios. Thank heavens she knew of Mr Daventry's attempt at matchmaking, else she might get swept up in these perplexing emotions.

Nora came to stand beside him. "I am quite capable of walking without support."

He looked confused. "Yet you sound frightened."

Fear did hold her in its claw-like grip. Not because of the dark or the thought of being trapped deep underground. Not because she might starve in these dank passageways. She was frightened because she liked Lord Deville much more than she ought. Doubtless Mr Daventry was clapping his hands with glee.

"Is it wrong to feel worried?"

"Not at all. But we agreed to be honest."

Was it not better to lie than admit to a mild attraction?

They navigated the maze of tunnels. The ground was damp and uneven. Water dripped from the low ceiling. She slipped but managed to right herself. One glance behind had her heart pounding against her ribs. It was so dark anyone could be hiding in the gloom, waiting to pounce.

"Mind the steps." Lord Deville clasped her arm to assist her descent and lowered the lamp so she could see where to place her feet. "Have a care."

The roar of the sea grew louder. A chill breeze whipped at Nora's hair. The wall to her right came to an abrupt end, leaving her perched on a narrow flight of stairs leading down into a cavernous chamber.

Lord Deville did not release her until her feet were firmly on the ground. "In an hour, the tide will be at its peak." He motioned to the water surging in through the cave mouth and crashing against the rocks. "We have a choice. Turn back, or wait until the morning when the tide is at its lowest ebb."

"Will I be able to touch the seabed?" Perhaps she should have had swimming lessons before accepting the case.

"Yes, if we head left towards the bay. It's too dangerous to attempt it while the tide is high. I would have to hold you while I swim."

"Hold me!" Nora scanned his physique, wondering what it would be like to have those strong arms wrapped around her, his body pressed close.

Lord Deville considered their surroundings. "If we decide to remain here until dawn, we'll need to find a way to keep warm." He gestured to the flight of steps. "Unless we head back through the tunnels and attempt to alert the servants."

Someone must have noticed the discarded cravat and

alerted the housekeeper. If Mrs Egan meant to get rid of Lord Deville, it was unlikely anyone would answer.

"Let's wait to see how deep the water is at low tide. Should it prove too difficult for me, we will have to resort to hammering on the door."

Was this to be another reckless decision?

Would Mr Daventry berate her for risking life and limb?

"Then let's make our way to the opposite side of the cave. The ground is higher and reasonably flat, and I see a few wooden barrels. Perhaps we'll find smugglers' booty."

Despite their dire circumstances, Nora smiled. "I would give anything for a nip of brandy and a blanket."

Lord Deville offered his hand.

She hesitated for a heartbeat before sliding her hand into his. Heat radiated from his palm. Was that why she suddenly felt all aglow?

They climbed carefully over the rocks. Sea spray splashed them when another wave charged in through the cave mouth. Nora should have cursed beneath her breath, for it was the final straw in a night that had gone dreadfully awry. Yet a burst of laughter escaped her.

Lord Deville shook water from his hair and laughed, too, which proved infectious because neither of them could stop.

"I'm not sure why we're laughing," Lord Deville said when they reached the stone platform. "There's every chance we'll die tomorrow."

"Die!" Another chuckle escaped her. "Yes, it's by no means a laughing matter. I should be terrified out of my wits." She clutched her aching abdomen and gasped a breath.

Lord Deville howled. "I cannot recall the last time—" He stopped abruptly, unable to continue.

"You were so afraid?" she offered.

"No, the last time my sides hurt from laughing."

"Neither can I." She dashed tears of joy from her cheeks

and licked her lips though they tasted salty. "It would be wise to conserve our energy."

Her companion found that hilarious. "Lest we drown?"

"Indeed." Nora glanced at their twined fingers. "My lord, you're still holding my hand. It's becoming rather a habit."

The lord's grin turned sinful. "It might have something to do with the fact I like you, Miss Wild." His amusement faded as he considered her through dark, untroubled eyes. "You excite me while making me feel equally at ease. It's a rare quality in a woman."

She might have laughed at his teasing but didn't. She had been called a stupid girl so many times she doubted her ability to attract a man's attention.

"Have a care, my lord. Have you forgotten Mr Daventry's secret agenda?" Was it a coincidence they were alone in a secluded cave, the sound of the sea soothing their senses? "Perhaps this is all part of his cunning plan."

A good dose of laughter was like a good dose of brandy.

It made one lose one's inhibitions.

"How could I forget? I am reminded of his machinations whenever our eyes meet, Miss Wild. Whenever I touch you and my heart lurches."

Sweet heaven!

The lack of air had affected his brain.

"No doubt this is a ploy to distract me, my lord." Indeed, his nearness had a profound effect on her pulse. "There's no need. I have every faith we will both live to see another day."

"And if this were our last night on earth," he drawled in a voice that made her stomach flip, "would you regret keeping secrets?"

Panic tightened her throat. "Secrets?"

He couldn't possibly know she had killed a man.

"If I asked you to describe my bathing contraption, I wonder if you could. Or do you have the courage to admit your attention was diverted elsewhere?"

Heat flooded her cheeks at the memory of those rivulets running down his impressive physique. She might have lied, but a man who thought himself monstrous might like to hear a compliment or two.

"What do you want me to say, my lord? That you have the body of Hercules?" Every hard muscle had made her mouth water. "That I barely noticed the contraption because I found you more than pleasing to the eye?"

"If it's the truth."

"It is."

He inhaled sharply. "Then it's fair to say our thoughts are aligned. You must have noticed the way I look at you."

Yes, she had caught his covert glances numerous times. "It's fair to say I am your agent and have no intention of ever becoming your mistress."

"And yet the curiosity is killing us both."

"Curiosity?"

"Have you ever gazed upon a delicious cake in the baker's window, only to take a bite and find it bland? Not at all to your liking?"

"Yes, but I fail to see how it's relevant." Perhaps it was fortunate they hadn't found brandy, though they were yet to inspect the barrels.

Lord Deville touched his hand to his chest. "From my experience, a kiss will confirm if two people are compatible."

Nora frowned. "My lord, we admit an attraction exists between us, but neither wishes to succumb to Mr Daventry's plan." A seed in the mind often sprouted roots.

He thought for a moment. "Logic says we will achieve one of two things. Either you will find kissing me akin to kissing a fish, and then we need never worry about Daventry's plan again."

"Or?" She knew the answer.

"It will be remarkably pleasing, and we can die satisfied. If we survive, we put certain parameters in place to prevent a reoccurrence." He shrugged as if there was nothing untoward about his suggestion.

Despite her lack of experience, she was certain love affairs did not begin with a mundane discussion about the whys and wherefores.

Surely that meant they were incompatible.

"My lord, I have never kissed a man but believe it should be a spontaneous sign of affection. Passionate, not logical. Hence, it's clear we are not at all—"

He pressed his finger gently to her lips, and his voice turned warm like winter wine. "Make no mistake. I ache to kiss you, Miss Wild. Any lack of passion stems from a fear of rejection."

Heat pooled between her thighs.

This glimpse of vulnerability was rather arousing.

She couldn't offer a reply even if she wanted to because he trailed his finger slowly along her bottom lip, his sensual gaze rendering her mute.

Nora placed her hand on his chest, aware of the hard muscle flexing beneath her fingers. Oh, she was a fool to succumb so easily. But in all likelihood, this was her one and only chance to kiss a man—one she admired, at any rate.

"One kiss," Lord Deville whispered. He seemed keen to take this perilous risk. "One kiss to test the waters."

Nora nodded, though her pulse raced, and she couldn't quite catch her breath. Doubtless he would taste her inexperience, as bland as stale sponge, and it would be over in the blink of an eye.

The lord cupped her cheek, his dark eyes drinking in her features before he lowered his head and claimed her mouth.

The touch of his lips set her body aflame. They were warm, tasted of claret and sea spray and something so potent it reached inside her and tugged deep in her core.

She had no measure with which to gauge the experience,

but it was akin to her first taste of brandy. Hot. Intoxicating. It left her breathless, her mind in a whirl.

Nora threaded her arms around his neck in case her knees buckled, but Lord Deville took it as a sign to press his advances.

The devil coaxed her lips apart and slipped his tongue into her mouth. A growl of appreciation rumbled in his throat. He wrapped his arms around her, one hand sliding down to caress her buttock, the other crushing her against his solid body.

Desire unfurled, not slow like a spring bud, but wild and fast and furious. She thrust her tongue over his with maddening urgency. She couldn't taste him deeply enough to satisfy the craving. Couldn't grip him hard enough to convey the excitement coursing through her veins.

Lord Deville tore his mouth from hers. "Curse the saints!"

"Is something wrong, my lord?" Nora panted.

"Wrong? No! Everything is so damn right." Seemingly confused, his gaze met hers, and those commanding lips devoured her mouth once more for good measure. "Hell, it seems our plan is flawed."

"I'm not sure I follow your meaning." Indeed, he was acting most peculiar. She had heard a first kiss was often a huge disappointment. Though her colleagues had been quick to suggest otherwise. "Flawed, my lord?"

He stroked his firm jaw while studying her intensely. "If I die tonight, I'll not die satisfied."

"Oh!" Both kisses had literally stolen her breath, but then she was a novice when it came to affairs of the heart. "Was it so terribly lacking?"

"Lacking?" His voice dropped low and husky. "Miss Wild, never has a kiss aroused me to such an alarming degree."

"Oh!" Pride warmed her chest. She wasn't a complete failure, after all. "Thank heavens. I thought I was the only one who found it remarkable. You're every bit a rogue when you kiss." There had been nothing gentlemanly about the way he'd ravished her mouth.

Lord Deville offered a self-assured grin. "I'm a gentleman with my clothes on, Miss Wild, not so with them off."

A vision of his firm buttocks flashed into her mind. "Who would have thought losing your cravat could turn you into a rakehell?"

"Who indeed?"

"So now we have no choice but to follow the second option." When he frowned, she added, "Put parameters in place to avoid such a thing occurring again. Being swept away in the moment, we forgot about Mr Daventry's ambitions."

"And yet if I die tonight, I shall regret never knowing what the future holds." His gaze drifted from her mouth to her hair. "Something about you leaves me captivated."

Caution reared its head. They had spent an inordinate amount of time together these last few days. During distressing situations, people rarely made sensible decisions.

"Forgive me for saying so, but perhaps your judgement is swayed by the fact I can tolerate your scar."

"You think I'm that desperate for affection?"

They were both lonely. That was plain to see. Though sharing a kiss was a step too far for a woman whose past might come to haunt her.

"The clue to Felix's murder could be hidden in there." She motioned to the barrels to distract him, though it was darker in the cave since the candle had died. "We must focus on the case and ignore this fleeting attraction." Yet she could still feel the searing heat of his lips.

Nora didn't wait for his reply but went to investigate.

There were four barrels in total. One looked reasonably new while the others were weather-worn, the staves cracked, the heads missing.

Nora peered inside. "It smells of brandy and tobacco but looks empty."

Lord Deville joined her. "They must be old smugglers' barrels. Often they have secret compartments to enable the transport of different commodities. One presumes many criminals have made use of this cave over the years." He sounded unconcerned.

Nora considered the steep flight of steps leading to the castle. "Any cargo must have been hidden in the cave, as it would be impossible to carry a barrel into the tunnels."

"I often wonder if that's why my father insisted I never come down here. Many times, I ignored his warning, but rarely ventured beyond the chamber."

"This barrel is fairly new."

Lord Deville reached into the barrel and banged the sides. "It's empty, but the inner dimensions suggest it's designed to conceal contraband. Smugglers can sell goods bought on the continent for ten times the price here in England."

"Do you think Mrs Egan knows smugglers use this cave?" It would explain her odd behaviour and why she tried to prevent anyone from entering the underground passages.

"Felix employed Mrs Egan when the last housekeeper retired, so nothing would surprise me." He braced his hands on his hips and scanned the cave. "Are you sure you wouldn't rather head back through the tunnels and attempt to alert the servants?"

It was colder in the tunnels than in the cave. They had no light to guide their way and might easily get lost. Instinct said she would rather catch Mrs Egan unawares. That said, as a non-swimmer, it might be impossible to reach the beach.

"I believe we should wait until morning to decide." She shrugged out of his coat, the chill biting into her almost immediately. "You'll need this." His fine cambric shirt would do little to keep the cold at bay.

"We'll share my coat. Use it as a blanket."

Lord Deville's chest might be broad, but the garment was

not large enough to cover two people. But then recognition dawned.

"You mean we'll need to sit closely together?"

His lips curled into a smile. "You might want to revise your calculation. If we're both to keep warm tonight, you'll need to sleep on my lap."

CHAPTER 10

Sylvester woke to the gentle *whoosh* of the sea, to a sleeping Miss Wild curled on his lap, her cheek pressed to his heart, her arms wrapped around his waist. Cold seeped through the stone wall at his back. His legs were numb, his life an utter shambles, yet he had never felt so content.

He lowered his head and inhaled the piquant scent of her hair. It wasn't the smell of soap or rosewater that made him close his eyes and breathe deeply. It was the essence of the woman herself. An intoxicating aroma that might make a man lose all sense and reason.

What the devil was Lucius Daventry about?

Had he an ulterior motive when suggesting Miss Wild was the perfect agent to solve the case? In one aspect, the master of the Order was not wrong. Miss Wild had quickly become the epitome of perfection.

The memory of her passionate mouth had kept Sylvester awake half the night. It had been a mistake, seducing her into testing his theory. Now he wasn't just longing to kiss her. He ached to know her intimately.

"Hmm." Miss Wild shuffled in his lap, her thigh rubbing against his morning erection. She yawned and stretched, and his coat slipped off her shoulders as if she meant to play the coquette.

Sylvester stifled a groan.

Upon noticing the break of dawn, a sane man should jump to his feet, keen to return to Highcliffe and punish his devious servants. Sylvester knew he was in trouble because he would give a king's ransom to spend one more hour in the cave.

Dazed from her slumber, Miss Wild sat up and rubbed her eyes.

She faced him.

His breath caught in his throat.

Merciful Lord!

She was a vision of loveliness. Her mussed hair and pouting lips stirred a hunger that would be impossible to sate.

Sadly, the inhibitions that caused her to look for other ways to keep warm last night resurfaced. "Forgive me, my lord!" She scrambled to stand, unaware every movement prolonged his agony. "You should have woken me."

"You'll need your strength for the arduous task ahead. I thought to let you sleep a while longer." And because of Daventry's machinations, he suspected she would maintain a respectable distance from now on.

Miss Wild glanced at his lap, a blush staining her cheeks, which she disguised by brushing creases from her dress. It was a pointless exercise, for they would soon take to the water.

"When might we leave? When can we expect low tide?"

Sylvester stood, pulled his watch and checked the time. "We can go now and should be able to cling to the rocks in the deeper parts." In his youth, he had swum to the cave on many occasions before being scolded by his father and warned never to be so damned foolish again.

You've got your mother's sense, boy!

"Leave your pocket watch here. Collect it later."

Sylvester shrugged. "It has no sentimental value. My brother inherited my father's gold hunter, which he sold to pay his debts."

"No doubt you would have kept it for Sunday best."

The compliment touched him. "No doubt."

She nibbled her lip as she stared at the cave mouth. "Perhaps we should get this over with. The more I think about the task ahead, the more the thought terrifies me."

"I won't let you drown," he reassured her. "But I beg your forgiveness in advance if I touch you inappropriately."

Miss Wild drew a shaky breath. "When our feet touch dry land, we should forget everything that happened here last night."

"Everything?" Did she think he could forget how soft and supple she was in his arms? How her sweet moans had fired his blood? How she made him feel desirable, every bit a virile man?

"Should I remove my half-boots?"

Only a lady who doubted her ability to abstain would avoid answering the question. "Yes, and your stockings. You may need to tread water."

While removing his own footwear, he explained how one kept afloat. She turned away from him to roll down her stockings, though he found the action so damnably arousing.

Once ready, Sylvester took hold of her hand.

It was becoming a habit.

"How long will it take to reach the shore?" She gasped as he led her into the cold water and it lapped her toes. "Oh! It's bitter. Perhaps this is a mistake."

"We'll reach the shore in minutes. Don't let go of my hand. Hold your breath if we need to duck beneath the water. Trust me to keep you safe."

She nodded, though her shoulders shook and her teeth chattered. "M-my friend survived a shipwreck. I'm sure I can cope for a few minutes."

Soon, the water was to their waists. She squealed as a wave hit them and the frigid sea splashed over her chest. Though he had never known a woman so brave in all his life. The Reverend Wild was a buffoon if he couldn't see what a gem he had for a daughter.

Sylvester stayed close to the headland and edged further out into the sea. Miss Wild coped well for a few minutes but panicked when she struggled to touch the seabed, and a rogue wave almost took her under.

"You must remain calm!" Sylvester pleaded.

"I am trying."

"Wrap your arms around my neck." He dashed water from her face, cupped her cheek. "I shall pull you to shore."

Miss Wild did not need to be told twice. She clung to him like ivy, pasting her lithe body to his. "Don't let me go." She was so close her breath breezed over his lips like a gentle kiss.

"Keep your eyes on me, Miss Wild."

Despite the weight of her skirts adding to his burden, he made for land one slow step at a time. Though he would brave the roughest sea for a chance to hold Miss Wild close again.

Thankfully, when they scrambled to shore, the beach was deserted. Sylvester collapsed onto his back and heaved in relief. Shingle made for an uncomfortable bed, but he took a moment to close his eyes and count his blessings.

Miss Wild dropped down beside him, breathless and soaked to the skin. Her delicate hand came to rest on his chest as if they were forever bound by their harrowing experience.

If life were a fairytale, he would scoop her up into his arms, board a ship to anywhere, and never look back.

"Thank you," she panted.

Sylvester squinted against the morning sun. "For what?"

"Saving me."

"You did remarkably well for your first time in the water."

And the feeling was mutual. Last night, she had given him a reason to look forward to the future. A reason to hope it might be better than bleak.

"I'm employed to help you, not make your life difficult."

She had helped him in ways she would never understand. "I'm remarkably calm considering my servant locked us in the tunnels. I have you to thank for that."

She smiled. "I think it has more to do with the healing power of the sea. It has dispelled your anger."

Sylvester sat up. "Make no mistake. The water did little to douse fury's flames. Mrs Egan and Whittle are about to feel the Devil's wrath. They will pay dearly for what they've done."

"We don't know who bolted the tunnel door. As much as I dislike them both, it would be a mistake to jump to conclusions."

"Once I've dismissed my butler and housekeeper, I guarantee the other servants will be forthcoming with information." He should have dismissed them long ago. They were hiding something, conspiring, keeping secrets.

Since his mother's confession, the house had been a hive of suspicion. And despite being the only surviving Deville, the air at Highcliffe was still tainted with deceit.

"Would it not be prudent to wait?" Miss Wild suggested.

"Wait until Mrs Egan murders me in my bed?"

"Wait until we have concluded the investigation." Miss Wild stood and offered her hand. "If you send them away now, we might never discover what they're hiding. It will hinder our progress."

Sylvester accepted her offer of assistance. He could stand without help but would not forgo an opportunity to touch her.

"You mean we continue as normal so as not to arouse their suspicions? All in the hope of uncovering their duplicity?"

"Yes, by laying a trap." Miss Wild released him and kicked at the shingle beneath her feet. "Now I wish I'd worn my boots. The walk back to Highcliffe will prove painful."

"Let me carry you."

"And what about your poor feet?" she said.

"Perhaps I would like to hold you one last time; before we put certain parameters in place." Just like the intimate moment in the cave had brought them closer together, the perilous journey back to shore had seen all barriers swept away with the waves.

"I will walk, albeit slowly. Heaven forbid we fall for Mr Daventry's cunning plan."

"Heaven forbid," Sylvester drawled.

Regardless of Miss Wild's advice to continue as if they hadn't almost perished from cold or hunger in a dark cave, Sylvester stood in Highcliffe's dreary hall, dripping water onto the Aubusson rug, and shouted for his disloyal servants.

"Mrs Egan! Whittle!" Anger surfaced. People often referred to him as the Horror of Highcliffe, so he may as well behave like a beast. "Mrs Egan! Whittle!" He strode to the bell pull and yanked hard.

Miss Wild watched him with mild disapproval. "By all means, show your displeasure, but remember what I said."

Sylvester inhaled a calming breath.

The scurry of footsteps in the corridor brought a harried Mrs Egan. His housekeeper came to a crashing halt, her wide eyes taking in their sodden clothes and bare feet.

"My lord! Good heavens!" Mrs Egan clutched her chest. "What happened? Where have you been? Myrtle came up with the warming pans last night and found both of your beds empty."

"You know damn well where we've been," he growled.

Mrs Egan looked confused. "Did you go out walking and get caught in the storm?"

"Do not play me for a fool, Mrs Egan. If you want to keep

your position, you have two minutes to gather the servants in the hall." He tapped his waistcoat pocket. "I might time you, but having spent half an hour neck-deep in water, my damn watch is useless."

Whittle appeared. Even he managed to raise a shocked brow. "Saints preserve us! I shall have Thomson draw a hot bath, my lord. Have Myrtle light the fires."

Sylvester repeated his instructions. "You both have one minute to summon the staff. Else you will be gone from this house without notice or references."

Fear filled the housekeeper's eyes. "No! My lord, I can't lose this position." She hurried away, bemoaning her fate, while Whittle snatched the handbell off the console table and rang it like a crier.

As Sylvester paced, his agitation grew. Being so preoccupied with purchasing his mother's heirlooms, he had allowed his staff too many liberties.

Things were about to change.

"Would you like me to stay?" Miss Wild asked quietly.

"Of course I'd like you to stay." He needed someone he trusted to advise him. "If I need to rein in my temper, clear your throat by way of a warning." He took one look at her blue lips, then charged into the drawing room, found a wool blanket and returned to drape it around her shoulders. "This should suffice until you bathe."

"Thank you. Might I suggest you make your health a priority?"

"Have no fear. I'll be out of these wet clothes soon."

Her gaze journeyed slowly over his chest. Was she imagining him standing naked beneath his bathing contraption?

A sudden commotion brought all the servants hurrying into the hall, herded like sheep by Mrs Egan, who stalked behind in the role of Border Collie.

Sylvester waited for his coachman and groom to arrive,

though Sykes gazed at the paintings and suit of armour as if he had never seen the grand house.

"Last night, during a tour of the house, I found the door to the tunnels open." Sylvester stared all the devils in the eye, looking for a flicker of guilt. Most bowed their heads.

"Open!" Mrs Egan looked horrified. She turned to her colleagues, suspicion marring her brow. "My lord, the staff know to leave the door bolted during a storm."

"Not only was the door wide open, but someone left a lit lantern outside. Unsure whether anyone had ventured down there, we decided to search the tunnels."

Mrs Egan clasped her hand to her throat. "You went below ground? You might have been killed, my lord."

"Perhaps that was the plan, Mrs Egan." Anger lanced through him. Did they think him a complete fool? "One of you locked the tunnel door last night, knowing we would be trapped inside."

"Why would anyone—"

He cut Mrs Egan short. "Because one of you knows who killed my brother. One of you fears Miss Wild will discover the truth." He struggled to contain his raging temper. "One of you is prepared to kill us both to keep the secret!"

Miss Wild gave a discreet cough.

"Hell, I should dismiss you all without notice!"

Panicked mutters filled the hall.

Miss Wild coughed again.

"Or perhaps someone can explain why we were forced to swim from the cave to the shore this morning." Sylvester modified his tone. "Miss Wild might have drowned."

No one spoke except Miss Wild.

"Where is Blanche?" She stepped forward and scanned the row of blank faces. "I don't see her amongst you."

"We've not seen Blanche since supper last night," Whittle said, his tone carrying nary a hint of concern. "Myrtle said Blanche went out after dark and didn't return to her room.

We've searched the house and grounds, and she's nowhere to be seen."

Myrtle stepped forward and bobbed a curtsy. "We thought Blanche might have got caught in the storm."

Mrs Egan clasped her hands together in prayer. "My lord, I have a confession. I bolted the tunnel door last night. I saw it open and thought Thomson hadn't secured it properly. We often leave a lantern in the corridor until all the staff have retired. Blanche complains of hearing voices. The light keeps her calm, helps prevent the nightmares."

Sylvester considered his housekeeper, trying to determine if she spoke in earnest. "Did you not hear us banging and shouting?" Had they not found his cravat?

"No, my lord. The wind echoes along the corridor whenever there's a storm. As you know, we've come to ignore any odd noises." She cast a nervous glance at Whittle, and something passed between them. "Mr Bower is outside now, combing the garden and clifftop."

Sylvester fell silent.

Instinct said he should throttle his lying housekeeper.

Instinct said he should take Miss Wild and leave this evil place.

"If Blanche is not found within the hour, I shall visit Lord Rutherfield en route to Canterbury." Maybe the mention of the magistrate might put the fear of God into these deceitful souls. Yet the thought of visiting the useless peer roused his ire all the more. "We had planned to carry on to London. Miss Wild must meet with her employer and update him on her progress."

It was a lie. But he, too, could play a devious game.

"We should be gone for a few days," Miss Wild said, keen to support his story. She faced him. "Though perhaps we should remain at Highcliffe until Blanche is found."

Mrs Egan stepped forward. "Blanche always gets nervous when there's a storm. Happen she will appear when she's gathered her wits. But I'll take someone with me, go into the tunnels to check she's not cowering in the darkness."

If Blanche was nervous during a storm, why would she arrange to meet Miss Wild outside the castle walls? Why would a girl afraid of her own shadow venture down into the subterranean passageways?

He considered Miss Wild's advice, chose to suppress the twist of fury in his gut and set about laying a trap.

"Very well. After our trip to Canterbury, we shall return to Highcliffe before venturing to London. Let's pray Blanche is found safe and well, and we're able to proceed as planned."

They achieved much during the next two hours. They bathed, dressed and packed for a short trip to town. During one last search for Blanche, Sylvester insisted on inspecting the dungeons but found no sign of the missing maid.

He warned Miss Wild not to speak about their suspicions until they were safely inside his carriage, although she met with Bower, who took to the box seat and joined them on their journey.

"I'm glad Bower decided to come with us." Seated opposite Miss Wild in the carriage, Sylvester observed her as she delved into the basket prepared by Cook. "Had we left him at Highcliffe, we might return to find he has mysteriously disappeared."

"We're leaving Mr Bower in Hoath." She withdrew a slice of buttered bread and licked her lips. "He will hire a horse and make his way back to Highcliffe, attempt to enter the cave and inspect the tunnels."

Sylvester was impressed by her foresight. "Then you suspect Mrs Egan is lying."

"They are all lying. Most servants were too afraid to look at you and not because you lost your temper." She gave a sad sigh. "I pray Blanche had the sense to run when we failed to meet for our scheduled appointment."

"We'll mention her disappearance to Lord Rutherfield."

She bit into the bread, relief at sating her hunger evident on her face. He had witnessed the same look of pleasure last night, and the thought stirred the damnable craving in him again.

"Yes, I must work on gathering information from other sources. Find other lines of enquiry." Clearly, she found the thought troubling because she stared absently out of the window while munching on bread.

As if the day was destined to be difficult, Lord Rutherfield was his usual obnoxious self. He waved for them to sit in the worn chairs his footman positioned some distance from his desk. Then kept them waiting for five minutes while he read a document.

Even when he apologised for his disregard, there was an air of irritability to his tone. "I have important letters to write that must reach London tomorrow. Can this matter not wait? Must you persist in being a thorn in my side, Deville?"

A man should respect his elders, but Lord Rutherfield was forty and far from wise. "If the job of magistrate is too taxing, perhaps someone else might like to carry the burden."

Miss Wild cast him a sidelong glance, no doubt wondering why he sought to provoke the magistrate. Sylvester hadn't mentioned his dislike of the man, but she surely sensed the thrum of tension.

Lord Rutherfield's mocking snort was as grating as his handsome profile. "And who would take up the gauntlet? You, Deville? Did Benson not say you've come because of a missing maid? Perhaps you should get your own house in order before criticising mine."

Having exhausted his patience today, Sylvester firmed his jaw. "We come because of your mistake, Rutherfield. Johanna Deville is alive. She murdered my brother, and my servants are too terrified to admit they know something. We come because you failed to investigate the matter properly."

Rutherfield relaxed back in his chair and steepled his

fingers. "As I said once before when you charged in here with your baseless rants, bring me evidence of murder, and I shall reopen the case."

There was no evidence, and Rutherfield damn well knew it.

"Is it not your job to find evidence?"

"Then perhaps I should consider where you were between the hours of seven and eight that night. Perhaps I should consider why you've hired this young woman and not an experienced runner from Bow Street."

Anger flared anew. Not because Rutherfield implied a monster had to purchase female company, but because he implied Miss Wild lacked intelligence and skill.

Indeed, Sylvester was about to jump to her defence, but Miss Wild stood. "Thank you for your time, my lord," she said politely, though her fists were clenched at her sides. "We have business in London and must make haste."

Rutherfield gave a mocking grin. "Enquiry agents are supposed to ask questions, madam. Yet you've sat there like a timid little mouse waiting for a nibble of cheese."

Miss Wild approached the desk. "Clearly, you are unfamiliar with modern practices. I have spent the last few minutes watching you closely. Your mannerisms say a lot about your character."

The magistrate's arrogance faltered. "Doubtless you concluded I am a man of firm opinion. A stickler for rules."

She reached into her reticule, removed a letter and opened the folds. "This is from Peel, granting me permission to examine the evidence." She offered it briefly to Rutherfield. "Would a runner receive a personal letter from the Home Secretary? And how will I explain your lack of assistance in this matter?"

Rutherfield shot out of the chair. "Madam, I assure you, I left no stone unturned. The evidence points to Felix Deville pushing his wife off the cliff. The coroner recorded accidental death because Deville was a devoted husband, and that clifftop is notoriously dangerous."

"I will be interested in reading his report." Miss Wild placed the letter back in her reticule. "Before we leave, my lord, allow me to give you some advice."

"Yes?" Rutherfield said with evident unease.

Miss Wild looked the devil keenly in the eye. "Never mistake silence for weakness. It's the quiet ones you should fear."

CHAPTER 11

"You're an enquiry agent, Miss Wild?" said Sir George Tutton —godfather to the man who had spent the entire journey to Canterbury complimenting Nora's handling of Lord Rutherfield. "What a novel way to earn a living, my dear."

Nora had braced herself for the raise of a disapproving brow. A warning no man in the land would take a wife who enjoyed such a morbid pastime. But Sir George looked upon her with warm admiration.

Despite being in his late fifties, Sir George's thick grey hair was cut in the latest style. Like Mr Daventry, he wore a fashionable black coat she knew to be from Monsieur Pavot in Oxford Street, for she recognised the signature cut of the lapels. Equally, Sir George seemed to be a modern thinker.

"It was more necessity than choice, sir," she admitted before sipping her tea and gazing about the elegant drawing room. "You've been to London recently, Sir George. Do you like the hustle and bustle of city life?"

Sir George smiled. "The smog is no good for the lungs, my dear. Hence why I prefer living close to the sea."

Lord Deville returned his teacup to the trestle table.

"Miss Wild would like to ask you a few questions. I fear they may be blunt and of a personal nature."

Sir George laughed. "You're party to most of my secrets, Sylvester. It won't hurt to discover them all. Besides, a little excitement will brighten the day. Ask what you will, Miss Wild."

Nora steeled her nerves. "I beg your pardon in advance, Sir George, but I must ask a rather delicate question." She paused, knowing she would probably cause offence. "Are you Lord Deville's father?"

Lord Deville almost choked. Had he been drinking tea, he would have dribbled the beverage down his expensive coat. "Why would you ask that?"

"Because she can tell I love you like a son," Sir George said, looking amused. "And she knows of your mother's foolish remark and wonders if I killed Felix to protect you."

"I know you did not kill Felix, sir."

"How do you know?"

"Because the finger of suspicion would have fallen on your godson. I know you would not want to cause him distress." Indeed, the lord's happiness and welfare had quickly become her main concern, too.

Sir George's eyes brightened. "How astute you are, Miss Wild. To answer your question, Sylvester is the legitimate son of Frederick Deville, as was his brother. I only wish Sylvester were my son. He is a good, honourable man, but you know that, too."

Nora glanced at Lord Deville, a glow of admiration filling her chest. He did not deserve the gossips' condemnation. He did not deserve to carry the burden of his brother's failures or to wear a permanent scar.

"Lord Deville is exactly as you describe, sir." Except when his mouth covered hers. When principles gave way to passion and the need to be wicked proved overwhelming. "He tells me you never married but were a frequent visitor to High-cliffe in his youth."

Sir George looked to the hearth, lost in a memory that marred his cheerful countenance, but he shook it off quickly like rain from his umbrella.

"In marriage, love should be the only consideration. Hence why I remain unwed." Sir George glanced briefly at Lord Deville. "But I see what you're insinuating, Miss Wild. A man goes where his heart leads him."

"Perhaps not consciously." While she should consider why Sir George had felt the need to visit Highcliffe frequently, she wondered if Lord Deville's heart would eventually call him back to Italy. "Can you tell me what happened the night Felix Deville died?"

Sir George repeated the story she had heard from Lord Deville before adding, "I planned to visit my colleague in the Foreign Office the next day, determined to have Sylvester on the next ship to Italy. I failed Elisabeth and would not see my godson fall foul of that useless ingrate."

"You did not fail my mother." Lord Deville's eyes swam with compassion. He, too, carried the burden of guilt for his mother's tragic demise. "You were not to know she had a weak heart."

"But I knew your brother's reckless ways would drive her to an early grave. I begged her to move out of that damned cottage, to move here, but she refused."

Nora pieced together the information. Lord Deville said his father had forbidden male visitors after Elisabeth's damning declaration. And yet Sir George had rekindled his friendship with Elisabeth Deville after her husband's death.

"Elisabeth wished to protect her son," Nora said because she also felt compelled to show the world they were wrong about this man. "Moving here would have fuelled the rumour that Sylvester was the illegitimate child."

Lord Deville inhaled sharply. Perhaps because Nora had

used his given name. Perhaps because he knew his mother had suffered to protect him.

"Elisabeth was selfless to a fault," Sir George said solemnly. And yet she had made a mistake that had hurt her family deeply.

For the third time in as many minutes, Sir George touched his hand to his chest. Mr Bower performed the same action when talking about his beloved mother, whom he lost three years ago.

"May I ask what you carry in your coat pocket, sir?"

Sir George looked surprised by the request but answered honestly. "Yes, I carry a miniature."

"Of Elisabeth Deville?"

"Indeed."

Lord Deville jerked his head, his eyes widening. "What?"

"Don't look so shocked, my boy. We cannot help who we love. I assure you, Elisabeth was never unfaithful to your father."

When Lord Deville found his voice, he bombarded his godfather with questions. "Was my father suspicious? Is that why you stopped visiting? Did my mother know how you felt?"

"Of course she knew. But she was dedicated to her marriage and treated me as nothing more than a dear friend."

Nora stood. "Please, don't get up. I shall leave you to discuss the matter privately, for it has no bearing on the case." And a woman who had come to admire her client did not wish to hear a story of unrequited love.

With Sir George's grand house on King Street being a stone's throw from the cathedral, Nora bid Sir George good day and arranged to meet Lord Deville there in half an hour.

The sun was shining brightly. The walk along the narrow cobbled streets proved pleasant. She browsed the shop windows and studied the old Tudor building on Palace Street.

People passed her on the pavement, not giving her a second glance.

So this was what it felt like to be free.

Choosing London as her haven had been a dreadful mistake. Danger lurked on every street corner. Despite her training, she was ill-equipped to deal with cutthroats and murderers. Why had she not come to Canterbury, where the air was clean? Or to the coast, where escape was as easy as sneaking aboard the next ship?

Perhaps when she had solved the case she should go abroad. The valet had found work in France, and the esteemed Reverend Wild would never venture to where men did not speak God's language. The sheer ignorance of the man beggared belief.

Lost in thought, she had not realised how far she had walked until the huge Gothic cathedral burst into view. Crashing to a halt, she gasped in awe while gazing upon the sheer majesty of the building.

A shiver ran through her, the tingle of her soul awakening. Then she remembered one must never judge anything on first impressions. The Reverend Wild appeared the most charitable of men when, in truth, he was selfish and unkind. Lord Deville had the look of a cruel tyrant, yet he was compassionate and caring, passionate and tender.

Recalling just how passionate, Nora pressed her fingers to her lips yet felt nothing. How was it his mouth sparked an inner inferno? The sea should have doused the flames, cleansed her of her sins. Yet when she clung to him as the water lapped their shoulders, she had longed to kiss him deeply again.

"Miss Wild?"

Nora blinked herself awake from her trance, expecting to see the handsome figure of the man she had come to revere. It took her a moment to register the identity of the golden-haired gentleman standing mere feet away.

"Good heavens! It is you. I can scarce believe it."

Nora's world crashed to a halt. "Mr Paisley?"

Sickness twisted in her gut.

Merciful Lord! She had feared meeting someone she knew in London. Never imagined she would meet her father's conspirator in Canterbury. Oh, how she wished the ground would open and swallow her whole.

The gentleman slapped his hand to his mouth and stared as if witnessing a miracle. What lies had her father weaved? What story had he told the man he'd demanded she marry?

She swallowed past a lump in her throat. "What are you doing here, Mr Paisley? Have you relocated to Canterbury?"

Of all the rotten luck.

"Move from Chipping Norton?" he mocked.

"You might have sought another position. You might have grown weary of being my father's curate. He is not the easiest of men. Indeed, he can be wicked and cruel."

"Wicked and cruel?" Mr Paisley's golden brows snapped together in alarm. "Then what he says is true. Upon my heart, you are suffering from your mother's ailment. The strange irritability that turns a Christian woman into a heathen."

"I beg your pardon?"

"The terrible illness that makes a woman have immoral thoughts."

Nora might have demanded he explain himself, but Mr Paisley turned to a group of men lingering some feet away and told them he would follow along shortly.

"I'm in Canterbury on an educational trip," he explained to Nora. "When I expressed concerns over your lengthy absence, your father thought further studies might occupy my mind."

"How considerate of him."

A tense silence ensued.

"It's so good to see you, Miss Wild." Mr Paisley looked

left and right and frowned. "What of your chaperone? Surely you're not allowed to leave without one?"

"Leave? Leave where?"

"Dr Chatham's hospital for the weak-minded."

Fear gave way to her temper. "Mr Paisley, what exactly did my father tell you? Did he mention I ran away because he demanded I marry you?"

Mr Paisley cast a pitying smile. "He told me everything, my dear. Explained you lacked the strength needed to commit to a life in the service of our Lord. That you took the brave step to seek help." He patted her arm like one might pet a helpless dog. "He assured me we would marry once you're well. Although I thought the hospital was in Gloucester."

Nora might have throttled the curate, but he was not to blame for her father's lies. "Mr Paisley, you have been deceived. Dr Chatham's hospital is a figment of my father's imagination. I ran away to escape him, my tormentor. I have no intention of returning to Chipping Norton or marrying you."

Mr Paisley grew suddenly nervous. His breath came quick, and he looked about the cathedral grounds as if seeking assistance.

"Well, I must be going. Good day to you, sir." Nora turned to leave, desperate to flee, but Mr Paisley grabbed her wrist.

"I cannot let you go, Miss Wild, not without a chaperone. I shall escort you back to the hospital, where you—"

"There is no hospital! Let go of me!"

Mr Paisley firmed his grip. "You need help."

A commanding voice cut through the chaos. "Unhand the lady before I slam my fist down your throat. Unhand her now!"

Nora locked gazes with Lord Deville and almost crumpled in relief. "Thank goodness! This is Mr Paisley, my father's curate."

Mr Paisley flinched at the sight of Lord Deville's scar and recovered only to make the wrong assumption. "Dr Chatham, I assure you I have your patient's interests at heart. She should not be allowed to wander the streets without supervision. Not until she's well, at any rate."

"Do I look like a doctor?" the lord mocked before Nora could convince him to lie. "I am Lord Deville. A dear friend of the lady you are presently assaulting."

Dear friend, not client?

Mr Paisley's fingers dug into her arm. "And I am her betrothed, my lord."

Nora thought she might scream, but that would surely see her carted away to the nearest asylum. "Mr Paisley is the man the Reverend Wild wants me to marry. He is in Canterbury on a pilgrimage of sorts."

"I see." Lord Deville squared his shoulders and loomed over the curate. "Mr Paisley, I wonder if you might take a message to the Reverend Wild. Tell him that if he ever attempts to contact his daughter again, I shall burn his wicked soul in the fiery pits of hell."

Mr Paisley clutched his chest, though the fear in his eyes stemmed from more than the threat. "Bless the Lord! Where is Dr Chatham? Does he know you keep company with rakish men? Does he not realise you're susceptible to all sorts of wicked proposals?"

Frustrated to the point of despair, Nora faced Lord Deville and explained the reason for Mr Paisley's odd ramblings. "Let us go now before he makes a scene."

"Yes, before I'm forced to murder one of God's emissaries on consecrated ground." Lord Deville captured her elbow, but Mr Paisley refused to relinquish her, and a tug of war ensued.

"I'll not let her go with you."

"Release her, you buffoon, before I summon a damn constable."

"Mr Paisley!" she cried. People were staring. "Search your

heart for the truth. The Lord surely speaks to you there. My father has tricked you."

"Enough of this!" Lord Deville lost his temper. He shoved Mr Paisley, and the curate went tumbling backwards. "I'm a peer of the realm," he shouted when people gasped and recoiled in horror. "Woe betide anyone who prevents us from leaving."

Nora addressed the crowd while pointing to the curate. "This man is attempting to abduct me. Please. Do not let him follow." And with that, she gripped Lord Deville's hand as if it were the only thing saving her from a life of untold misery.

They hurried away, aware of the commotion behind, of Mr Paisley's pleas and protests, but did not look back.

Indeed, Nora did not draw a full breath until Lord Deville's carriage turned onto the country road mere miles from Highcliffe.

With shaky fingers, she removed her bonnet and placed it on the seat. Then fear gave way to tears, and she buried her face in her hands and wept.

Lord Deville crossed the carriage, moved her bonnet and sat beside her. He gathered her to his chest. "I wanted to throttle the curate after a few minutes. Lord knows how you've dealt with him for years."

Nora wrapped her arm around the lord's waist, welcoming the feel of his hard body, relishing the sensual scent of his cologne.

"Your father is a fool if he thinks you and Paisley would make a good match. You need someone strong enough to nurture your independence. Paisley is a damn milksop."

Nora glanced up and met eyes so warm they would sustain her through the harshest winter. "My father demands obedience from his daughter and his curate. He doesn't care if two people are suited. Mr Paisley is so in awe of him, he is oblivious to his machinations."

"No doubt the encounter will stir the hornet's nest."

Alas, the Reverend Wild knew where to hunt for her now. "A reunion is inevitable. I pray I am strong enough to put up a good fight."

How had her mother managed to hide all these years?

Or had she departed this evil world long ago?

"You won't have to tackle him alone." Lord Deville pressed a gentle kiss to her forehead. "You're here because of me. I'll not forsake you." He dashed tears from her cheek, used the same thumb to stroke her bottom lip.

She stared at his mouth, the confounding ache for him tightening like a coil inside. "Mr Paisley was right about one thing." She inhaled the essence of maleness. For the first time in her life, she wasn't afraid of a man. "When in your company, my thoughts are wholly immoral."

Lord Deville lowered his head a fraction. The anticipation of whether he might kiss her proved unbearable. "Paisley was right about me. What I'm about to do might be described as downright rakish."

Her pulse soared. "But you're always a gentleman with your clothes on. Do you not need to remove your cravat before doing something wicked?"

"It seems you have the power to penetrate my armour, Miss Wild."

His mouth came crashing down on hers. Hot. Demanding.

Despite the urgency to taste him, to drive deep into his mouth, despite lust burning in her veins, every muscle in her body relaxed.

This felt like home.

The only place she belonged.

She was but a slave to his sensual lips, to the tongue tangling rampantly with hers, to the strong hands stroking away her fears.

Despite his ability to turn her insides molten, to make her knees weak, her nipples so hard they ached, it was the gentle way he cupped her head, the caring way he cradled her close that left her breathless.

Such passion might make a woman misplace her morals.

Such tenderness might make a woman lose her heart.

Perhaps that was why she kissed him wildly and moaned into his mouth. Why she gathered her skirts and found herself astride the lord's lap. Why she didn't care that his hands gripped her bare thighs, drew her back and forth over his erection.

Nora knew what it was to be hungry, to starve until her stomach cramped in pain. But the urge to feel Lord Deville's naked body covering hers left her ravenous.

Only vaguely aware of the vehicle charging over High-cliffe's stone bridge, it was the violent rattle of carriage wheels on the gatehouse cobblestones that brought her crashing to her senses.

On a gasp, Nora tore her mouth from his.

What madness!

She glanced down at the hands caressing her thighs.

"We've reached Highcliffe," was all she could say as she scooted off his lap and tried to right her skirts. Heavens! Her heart thumped so fast it might burst from her chest. "I fear my fragile emotions played havoc with my ability to resist you."

His lips curled into a sensual grin. "While attempting to foil Daventry's plan, we miscalculated the power of desire." The gentleman tugged at his placket, attempting to disguise the hard rod bulging in his breeches. "See what you do to me, Miss Wild. I may need a few minutes to compose myself before alighting."

The bond between them was impossible to deny. Had Mr Daventry known she would find the lord irresistible? She feared the inevitable might have happened had there been a few miles left to go.

They were forced to alight when Mrs Egan came dashing

into the courtyard, frantically waving her hands and gesturing to the house.

"All is well, my lord! All is well!" the housekeeper cried as soon as their feet touched the ground. This newfound enthusiasm seemed out of character. "We found Blanche hiding in the pantry. There's no need for concern."

Hiding in the pantry?

"Where is Blanche now?" Nora asked, focusing on the problem and not her bruised lips and pulsing sex. Lord Deville's scent clung to her skin, a heady mix of shaving soap and virile male. Heaven knows how she would keep her hands to herself on the journey to London.

"Resting in her bed," Mrs Egan said in a tone devoid of malice. The housekeeper had mellowed since Lord Deville's threat to dismiss her. Or was this all a ruse? "Blanche became frantic, mentioned being caught in the storm. I gave her a large dose of laudanum to settle her nerves."

Or to render the maid mute and unable to say what was really going on at Highcliffe. Indeed, it was too convenient.

"I want to speak to Blanche before we leave for London." Lord Deville's commanding voice had the housekeeper shuffling nervously. "To reassure myself all is as you say, Mrs Egan."

After a moment's hesitation, she asked they follow her to the maids' chambers located below stairs, though walked like she was on her way to the gallows.

Blanche was sleeping peacefully in her bed. Her face looked pasty, her lips dry, but her hands and arms were free of bruises and blemishes. Nora checked the maid's pulse. It thumped as steady as the mantel clock.

Lord Deville attempted to rouse the maid, but she remained listless and unresponsive. An hour passed before her eyes sprang wide and panic took control of her senses. Poor Blanche ducked under the bedsheets and complained the ghost of Johanna Deville haunted the corridors.

"Give her more laudanum if needed," his lordship barked. "Have someone ride to Hoath and fetch Dr Price. Blanche is clearly delirious and may have caught a chill."

"There's no need to fetch the doctor," Mrs Egan said, wringing her hands. "She will be fine after a good night's rest."

Tired of his deceitful servants, Lord Deville lost his temper. "You're paid to follow instructions, Mrs Egan, not question my authority. When I say fetch the damn doctor, I mean fetch the damn doctor."

"Y-yes, my lord. I shall see to it at once."

Nora cupped Lord Deville's elbow and guided him into the servants' corridor. "We can't leave for London," she whispered. "We can't leave Blanche here." And yet she had exhausted all avenues of enquiry.

The staff were unlikely to confess. And how could she take Blanche at her word when she seemed unstable?

The air at Highcliffe was worse than the noxious fog rising from the Thames. It obscured one's vision, made it impossible to breathe, let alone think logically.

Hope came in the form of the magistrate.

This time, Lord Rutherfield kept his arrogance on a tight leash. "I'll not have Peel think me incompetent. And so I thought to question your staff, Deville, see what they know about the missing maid."

Lord Deville was forced to swallow his embarrassment as quickly as Blanche had downed the laudanum. "Blanche has returned. She dislikes the storms. Mrs Egan has given the maid a tincture to help her sleep."

"Then I've had a wasted journey," Lord Rutherfield snapped.

So why did his shoulders sag in relief?

"Not completely wasted," Nora said, a plan forming in her mind. The magistrate could interview Whittle and Mrs Egan. They could hardly murder the maid in his lordship's absence knowing suspicion would fall at their door. "We have important business in London. But will feel better leaving once you've spoken to the housekeeper and heard her tale."

Lord Rutherfield looked like he would rather dig a seed corn from his sole than question those below stairs. "If you feel it's necessary. I would hate to be considered unhelpful."

As it happened, Lord Rutherfield was extremely helpful. Mrs Egan stuttered through her story as if terrified he would cart her off to gaol.

Nora felt much better about leaving Highcliffe, not so much about spending hours in a carriage with a man whose touch awakened every wicked desire.

CHAPTER 12

The office of the Order
Hart Street, Covent Garden
London

Lucius Daventry sat on the sofa in the Order's plush drawing room, listening intently while Miss Wild explained all that had occurred at Highcliffe during the last few days.

Thankfully, she omitted to mention sharing passionate kisses with her client, or that her client had spent the nine-hour journey suppressing every urge to kiss her again. Indeed, after suffering a sleepless night alone at the Musgrove, Sylvester was acutely aware of just how much he craved Miss Wild's company.

Finlay Cole, one of Daventry's male agents, absorbed the information from the comfort of his fireside chair. It soon became apparent he had been tasked with assisting in the case.

"You say Blanche was unable to answer any questions?" Cole studied Sylvester intently. With hair as black as Satan's heart and wearing a stern expression, the agent was intimidating without the need of a scar. "The maid's timely reappearance is highly suspicious."

"We thought so, too," Miss Wild said eagerly. "Mrs Egan had given Blanche a hearty dose of laudanum to calm her nerves. We waited for an hour, but she woke only to panic about ghosts again. When questioned, the servants told the same story. They found Blanche cowering inside the pantry, but she could not recall how she got there."

Sylvester cleared his throat. "The magistrate agreed to wait for the doctor. As my servants are all suffering from a permanent state of amnesia, we decided to return to town and pursue other lines of enquiry."

"And to lead the servants into a false sense of security," Miss Wild added. "We will return to Highcliffe tomorrow night, much earlier than expected. I have arranged to meet Mr Bower at the old cottage once occupied by Lord Deville's mother. Hopefully, he will have discovered something in our absence."

Like a schoolmaster weighing up a child's tale, Daventry narrowed his gaze. "If you spent the night together in the cave, how did you both keep warm?"

"How did we keep warm?" Sylvester repeated, pushing aside the delightful memory of Miss Wild's arms wrapped around him while she lay nestled in his lap.

Indeed, bells of alarm rang. Not because he was averse to marrying Miss Wild. On the contrary, theirs would make for a passionate union, where every day proved more exciting than the last. No, Sylvester merely disliked being a pawn in Daventry's matrimonial game.

"We made a fire out of the broken barrels," Miss Wild blurted.

Sylvester inwardly groaned.

"You found a usable tinderbox in a damp cave?" Daventry said.

"Yes, thank heavens, wrapped in an old sack at the bottom of a barrel." Miss Wild gave a light laugh to mask the lie. "It saved us having to venture back through the tunnels, and I was able to return Lord Deville's coat."

"How fortuitous." Daventry appeared to find her tale amusing. "And what other lines of enquiry do you hope to pursue in town?"

Miss Wild flipped to a page in her notebook. "If we're to believe Felix Deville was murdered, we must look for reasons why. I doubt it was over a debt. Felix had the means to sell other valuable items to pay his creditors."

"During my own failed quest to find the truth, I visited every gaming hell in London." Sylvester had found nothing but a few old wagers placed in the book at White's, which had since been crossed through. "This is not about a gaming debt, I assure you."

"Few villains will travel sixty miles to push a man off a cliff," Cole said. "It seems such a cowardly way to kill a man."

"Which is why I wish to focus on learning more about Johanna," Miss Wild agreed. "In her courtesan days, she may have made enemies."

"Then you should start by questioning Madame Matisse. She knows every courtesan in London." Daventry gestured to Sylvester. "Take Lord Deville with you. You're not to go there alone."

It was a strange thing to say. Hadn't Miss Wild lived at the Pleasure Parlour for a month? Equally strange was the lady's response.

Life drained from her face. Her hands shook, and she dropped her notebook. "Sir, should Mr Cole not question Madame Matisse?"

Sylvester retrieved the book and returned it to her, though fought the urge to take hold of her trembling hands and offer every reassurance.

"Cole will visit Monroe's bookshop and gather more information about Mr Gifford," Daventry said, unperturbed by her odd reaction. "You will speak to Minette. She trusts you and will tell you anything you need to know."

"But, sir—"

Daventry raised a silencing hand. "Cole will also visit the Servants' Registry and other employment agencies. To see if he can discover why people are fearful of working at Highcliffe. Let's hope gossip travels this far afield."

Cole scanned his own written notes. "How long have you had problems employing staff? How long have the staff at Highcliffe been acting strangely?"

Sylvester recalled the night he returned from Italy to find Felix had replaced most of the servants. Never had he felt more like a stranger in his family home.

"During the three years I spent in Italy, I received numerous letters from my mother." She had written about the weather, local news, disclosed nothing of Highcliffe's secrets. He came to wonder if someone had taken to vetting her missives. "She never mentioned staffing problems. After her death, I came home to find the place much changed."

"Only fifteen servants remain at Highcliffe," Miss Wild said, the health returning to her cheeks. "The rest left suddenly the day Felix Deville died. Those employed there now were all working at Highcliffe when his lordship's mother died eighteen months ago."

"To answer your questions, Cole, I've had problems since inheriting."

Lucius Daventry turned to Cole and informed him of the gossip that had made Sylvester an outcast. "It may explain their hostility. Being illegitimate, I experienced something similar from my father's servants."

The housekeeper arrived with tea. Miss Wild took the opportunity to invite her employer into the hall for a private conversation.

"Tell me about the fisherman's statement," Cole said while

they waited. "Did he say anything to convince you he was lying?"

"I never spoke to the fisherman." No, he would have throttled the truth from the devil's lips. "The magistrate took his statement. He was summoned by the coroner to testify but failed to appear at the inquest. No one has been able to locate him."

"Who is the magistrate?"

"Lord Rutherfield." He didn't mention the man was haughty and overbearing or that they shared a distinct dislike of one another.

"You agree. The fisherman's account seems implausible."

"Nothing about it rings true."

Miss Wild returned, deep furrows lining her brow. Daventry touched her briefly on the arm and whispered something to lift her spirits.

"So, Miss Wild told you about the distressing incident in Canterbury," Sylvester said, making the obvious assumption. He knew she feared a confrontation with her father and prayed Daventry had agreed to offer his protection.

Daventry narrowed his gaze. "No, she did not." He faced his agent. "Miss Wild? Have you something to tell me?"

Her sad sigh tore at Sylvester's heart. "Sir, it was a personal matter and has no bearing on the case. Mr Paisley, my father's curate, saw me near the cathedral and made a frightful scene. Thankfully, Lord Deville was on hand to offer assistance."

He had done more than help her flee the crazed curate. He had dried her tears, held her close, kissed her so deeply concerns of Paisley had melted away.

"We keep no secrets here, Miss Wild," Daventry admonished, though his dark eyes flashed with empathy. "You will tell me what happened, so I may judge for myself."

With some reluctance, she gave a recount of events, her brittle tone revealing the depth of her fears. "My father will learn of it soon enough. Being but nine miles from Highcliffe, I imagine most notable people in Canterbury know of Lord Deville. I doubt the Reverend Wild will make pastoral visits while his daughter embarrasses him before his peers. He will seek vengeance."

Daventry remained silent for a time. "You said the curate drew similarities between you and your mother. That he thought you were in Gloucester."

"Yes, he said I was suffering from my mother's disease —immorality."

"Interesting." Daventry scribbled something in his note-book. "I shall send a man to Chipping Norton today. Have him monitor your father's movements."

Miss Wild exhaled in relief. "Thank you, sir."

"You must focus on the case, Miss Wild. Lord Deville deserves your undivided attention." Daventry took a piece of paper from the low table and handed it to Sylvester. "I had Cole delve into your brother's background. He interviewed his known associates at White's, which led to an interesting discovery."

Sylvester read the letter signed by his brother and written to Monsieur Pierre Badeau, an engineer with an office in Charles Street. Felix had enquired about the cost of having a steel door erected at the entrance to the tunnels.

"Your brother wished to prevent anyone from entering the cave and gaining access to the house," Cole said. "Felix met with Badeau a week before his death. Again, one suspects it is not a coincidence. You might want to meet with him. He lives above his office."

Sylvester struggled with the sudden rush of euphoria. The clue implied all was not well at Highcliffe. The clue confirmed his fears were not baseless.

"Felix made no mention of his plans." He felt a slither of regret over their fractured relationship. "But my brother would not spend money he could ill afford, not unless it was necessary."

"Smugglers may be using the cave," Miss Wild offered. "It would certainly account for Mrs Egan's orders to refrain from going into the tunnels."

Daventry thought for a moment. "Let's see what we can uncover during the next twenty-four hours. Some smuggling gangs run their operations here in town. I shall speak to a few contacts while you question Minette. Then I suggest you return to Highcliffe and continue your investigation there."

Being a man with precious little time, Daventry suggested they leave for the Pleasure Parlour at once, for he had pressing business in Whitechapel.

Sylvester waited until they were settled in his carriage and journeying the short distance to Villiers Street before apologising to Miss Wild for his faux pas.

"Forgive me. When you spoke to Daventry privately, I presumed you were informing him of what happened with the curate."

Miss Wild's faint smile failed to put him at ease. "Pay it no mind. I planned to tell him once we had solved the case. You only spoke out of concern."

Concern and an affection that deepened by the day.

Curiosity burned inside. Her secret conversation with Lucius Daventry had left her shoulders tense, her brow littered with worry lines.

He scrambled to find a reason why. "Are you embarrassed to take me to the Pleasure Parlour? Ever since Daventry mentioned it, you've not been yourself."

She swallowed as if her throat pained her. "Minette took care of me, and I shall be forever grateful, but I saw a side of life I would rather forget."

Intrigued, he pressed her further. "You speak of depraved men's appetites."

"I don't want to speak about it at all," she said, her tone a little panicked.

A man did not need the skill of an enquiry agent to know something terrible had happened at the Pleasure Parlour.

Indeed, as the carriage rolled to a halt in Villiers Street, Miss Wild closed her eyes and prayed for the Lord's protection. "You've forsaken me before," came her heartfelt murmur. "Do not forsake me again."

Every muscle in her body was strung as tight as a bow. Nora couldn't move. She couldn't find the strength to shuffle off the carriage seat. The thought of entering the iniquitous den brought bile to her throat.

Lord Deville sat opposite, silent, still.

His mind was surely conjuring a reason for her hesitance. Had someone touched her inappropriately? Was she haunted by vivid scenes of violence or debauchery? Was it shame? Why would any woman spend her days cleaning up after whores?

"Shall I ask Madame Matisse to come to the carriage?" came the kind voice she trusted, regarded with such fondness. "Shall I go inside and speak to her on your behalf?"

Nora found the courage to look at him. She wanted to throw herself into his arms, have him devour her mouth with his wicked kisses. Make her forget the harrowing event that had taken place in a house of pleasure.

"No. Mr Daventry said I must confront my fears."

She offered no further explanation. How could she without telling him she had killed a man?

"We made an agreement." His weary sigh left her longing to put his mind at ease. "An agreement to speak honestly. You trusted me to save your life. Can you not trust me with this?"

Tell him he'd hired a criminal?

Tell him everything he believed about her was a lie?

"I have come to hold you in high regard." Her heart had never ached for another. Her body had never burned for a man's touch. "You will think badly of me. The thought hurts more than you know."

He sat forward. "If you were forced to do something to survive, I'll not judge you for that. I'm no saint, Honora."

She gasped at the use of her given name. Not because it implied a lack of propriety, but because it reminded her of every intimacy they had shared.

"We'll discuss it later, not now."

"When? I have come to hope—" He paused, looked a little uncomfortable. "I have never met a woman like you. I hoped we might remain *friends* once this is all over."

Friends? He meant lovers. She had seen enough at the Pleasure Parlour to know when a man wished to sate a physical need.

"Speak honestly, so I may understand your meaning. You want more from this relationship than a friend. You want me to share your bed."

He held up his hands. "I want more than that, Honora."

Nora jerked back. Good Lord! Had Mr Daventry put a tincture in his tea? Had he drugged them both into believing in fairytale fantasies?

The lord would change his mind when he learnt the truth.

A knock on the carriage door stole Nora's attention. Harbord, Minette's burly footman and man-of-all-work, gestured for her to lower the window.

"Minette wonders if you're paying a house call, Miss Wild," Harbord said in his broad London accent. "She noticed you from her upper window and asked me to remind you she likes to keep the road clear for patrons."

The last comment brought a smile to Nora's lips.

Minette pandered to her patrons' every desire. Though it

was but two o'clock in the afternoon, most of the rooms would be occupied by paying gentlemen.

"Won't you help me down, Harbord?" Nora opened the door and offered the footman her hand. Standing almost seven feet tall, Harbord was a mountain of a man. "I have brought a friend." Her soon to be lover if Mr Daventry was the magician her colleagues proclaimed.

Lord Deville alighted. His curious gaze swept over Harbord before taking in the impressive facade of one of the most expensive brothels in London.

From her watchtower window, Minette beckoned them inside.

Nora braced herself. She had not crossed the threshold since the night Mr Daventry spirited her away under cover of darkness. Minette had dealt with the constable and coroner. They had not spoken since, only corresponding twice by letter.

"I'll need to frisk the gentleman," Harbord said when they came to a halt in the marble-tiled hallway. He was unaffected by the choking scent of perfume in the air. "It's standard procedure. You know the rules."

Nora turned to the lord, who seemed so intrigued by his surroundings she suspected this was his first time at the Parlour. "Harbord must check for weapons and tinctures."

"Tinctures?"

"Anything that might rob a lady of her right to say no."

Lord Deville raised his arms. He let Harbord search his pockets and pat his muscular thighs.

Minette appeared at the top of the grand staircase, dressed like a duchess in sumptuous red silk, her ebony hair fashioned in a coiffure, her ruby earrings catching the light.

"Harbord, there is no need for formalities," Minette said in her soft French purr. "Show our guests to my private drawing room and have Melisandre fetch a tea tray."

Harbord obeyed his mistress and escorted them to the

rear of the house, to a quaint room with paintings of vine-yards and pretty stone houses set amid lavender fields. Minette was far from home, but in England, she could adopt any persona.

Heat rose to Nora's cheeks when Harbord left them alone, and the sounds of couples at their pleasure invaded the silence.

"You get used to the noise," was all she could think to say as the boards creaked to strained groans and pained cries of release. "I merely think of it as a celebration of love."

"Hardly," he mocked, the growl of a vile obscenity reaching their ears. "Men come here to satisfy their appetites, not to make love to women they admire." He paused, concern marring his brow. "Tell me you don't think what happened between us is in any way similar to this."

Nora had watched Minette's ladies go about their work. Over breakfast, they shared ways to satisfy their clients quickly. They gave the men horrid names, none of them repeatable.

In comparison, she had listened to her colleague, Eliza, discussing how desperately she loved Lord Roxburgh. Their midnight liaisons had been sensual, romantic, and she had confessed to never wanting to leave his bed.

"Kissing you was nothing like this," she dared confess.

The air between them crackled, the way it always did when they were alone of late. Another kiss was inevitable. Indeed, she longed to feel his touch again.

Minette entered, closing the door behind her.

All the worries Nora had suppressed these last seven months burst forth like liquor from a broken cask. She raced into Minette's arms, hugged her tightly and mumbled an apology.

"There now, *cherie*," Minette whispered. She rubbed Nora's back with a mother's soothing strokes. "I have missed you, too, Honora."

"I'm sorry I've left it so long to visit," Nora muttered against the shoulder of Minette's expensive gown. "I was scared to come." Scared someone might blame her for something that wasn't her fault.

"I know. Best say no more about it while we've company."

They hugged for a few silent seconds before Minette straightened and dashed away Nora's tears. "All is well, though Daventry tells me you've been given your first case. As you're here with your client, all is probably not well."

A disturbing thought entered her mind. "You know Lord Deville?"

"It is my business to know prominent men, but I have never made his acquaintance." Minette looked at the peer and inclined her head gracefully. "Forgive me, my lord, but your scar, it confirms your identity."

"No doubt you've heard I'm the Horror of Highcliffe." His sarcasm failed to disguise the fact the moniker pained him. "But I can assure you, Miss Wild is safe in my care."

Minette gave a light laugh. "Daventry trusts you, else you would not be standing here. And his faith, it is good enough for me." She gestured to the sofa. "Please sit. Tell me, how might I assist you?"

Nora sat next to Lord Deville while Minette relaxed in the wing chair with worn leather arms. She had the funds to purchase a replacement but kept it to remind her material possessions were not something one could rely on.

"Mr Daventry suggested we call," Nora said, silently fighting against the memory of her last night at the Parlour. She explained the circumstances surrounding the deaths of Felix and Johanna Deville. "Lord Deville fears his sister-in-law may be alive, may have murdered his brother."

"You are right to be concerned, my lord. Johanna Moore is a devious creature out to further her own ends."

"So you do know Johanna." Lord Deville sat forward, seemingly pleased someone had faith in his suspicions.

"Until I see her rotting corpse, I refuse to believe she's dead."

"Did Johanna ever work at the Parlour?" Nora asked, clinging to the fact she was here in a professional capacity so she might forget her ordeal.

"*Oui*, many years ago."

"How many?"

Minette shrugged. "Almost five. She was one of the first girls I took in after Lord Mottershead died and left me this house. But she lied and stole from my clients. It would be no surprise to find her embroiled in wickedness."

"Did she make any enemies while here?"

Minette chuckled. "Johanna made enemies wherever she went. Lydia was forever playing peacemaker. In the end, she grew tired of being cast in her sister's shadow and eventually abandoned Johanna like everyone else."

"Johanna had a sister?" Nora straightened upon hearing the news. Was this the clue they had been searching for? "Do you know where we might find her? Does she still live and work in London?"

"Johanna never mentioned a sister," Lord Deville interjected. "I guarantee that's where she's hiding."

"Lydia remained in London for a time, though I have not seen or heard from her in years. One of her clients likely made her a permanent offer, somewhere far from here. I would know her direction had she remained in town."

A knock on the door brought Melisandre (whose real name was Janet) with the tea tray. She was dressed like an elegant lady, not a harlot. Her eyes widened upon seeing Nora again. Those thirsty blue jewels drank in Lord Deville's countenance, for she found wounded men more than appealing.

"Put the tray down before it slips from your hands." Minette gestured to the low table. "And close your mouth, Melisandre. Lord Deville is not a client."

Jealousy writhed in Nora's veins. Melisandre had a

goddess' allure, although men paid her to insult them and inflict the worst kind of pain. Perhaps she thought a man with a scar enjoyed the whip of a birch on his back.

"I've heard tales of your wickedness, my lord." Melisandre looked ready to rip Lord Deville's shirt from his muscular torso and add to his list of disfigurements.

"I hate to disappoint, but they're all lies."

Melisandre's predatory gaze shifted to Nora. "I hear you're an enquiry agent now, Nora. Perhaps I should hire you to find out what happened to McGowan."

Guilt made it hard to swallow, but Nora forced herself to remember McGowan deserved his fate.

"We know what happened to McGowan," she said, feigning confidence. "He tumbled down the stairs. We all smelled gin on his breath, and Josephine said he had downed more than a bottle that night."

No one had seen McGowan sneak into her room.

No one had seen her hit him with a coffee pot.

Minette intervened. "Melisandre, the comte will arrive shortly. You should make yourself presentable. Have Harbord prepare the ointments."

Melisandre seemed suddenly excited by the prospect of an hour spent torturing the Frenchman. She left the room, but not before casting a suspicious glance at Nora.

Minette stood and closed the door behind Melisandre. "Perhaps we will leave tea until next time." She meant Nora should make a quick exit before others questioned why she had disappeared the night McGowan died. "Is there anything else I can help you with?"

"Do you happen to have details of the men Johanna entertained here?" Nora wondered if one of them might still be her lover, assuming she was alive. "Or those who bedded Lydia Moore?"

Minette glanced at the door. "You know I cannot reveal confidential information. My success here, it is based on my loyalty to my clients." She lowered her voice to a whisper and addressed Lord Deville. "Leave your direction. Daventry will not permit me to visit Howland Street."

"I'm staying at the Musgrove," Lord Deville mouthed.

"Go now. I shall come as soon as I can."

CHAPTER 13

"Do you want to tell me what happened to McGowan?" Sylvester had repeated the question numerous times in his mind, but he waited until his carriage turned out of Villiers Street before voicing it aloud.

Miss Wild bit down on her bottom lip. She closed her eyes and released a sigh that reached across the carriage and tugged on his heartstrings.

"Honora?" he said, believing he had earned the right to use her given name. "While I despise secrets, that's not why I am asking. Let me help you."

The silence stretched for uncomfortable seconds.

She opened her eyes. "We're playing a dangerous game."

"Dangerous?" He saw nothing dangerous about caring for someone and putting their needs first.

"Like a lame woman does a crutch, I'm getting used to leaning on you, Sylvester."

"Friends depend on each other. It's to our mutual benefit." He felt compelled to play her protector. "I would hardly consider that dangerous."

"Your kindness is more a drug than an ointment."

"A drug you can't do without?"

"A drug that will resort in foolish behaviour if we do not control our addiction." She looked out of the window. "I know how to deal with cruel men. I'm out of my depth with you."

It was his turn to fall silent. Not because he didn't know how to respond, but these feelings filling in his chest were so powerful they stole his voice.

The carriage turned off the Strand onto Newcastle Street.

"We're about to stop at the Musgrove. You must decide what you want to do, Honora. Will you take a room while we wait for Madame Matisse? Shall I wait alone and have Sykes ferry you to Howland Street?"

Her eyes met his. Need at war with logic. "I'm your agent. I must wait with you until Minette arrives. Is renting a room not an unnecessary expense? Might we not sit and enjoy a meal together?"

Though he longed for a private moment to untie the ribbons on her bonnet, smooth his hands through her silky hair and set his mouth to her sumptuous lips, he had to respect her wishes.

"Whatever you think is best."

She gave an uncertain nod. "We shall order tea and see if the Musgrove has a table for dinner this evening."

He did not press for a confession or demand to know what had happened to McGowan. Nor did he inform her that he only ever ate in the privacy of his hotel room.

The reason for the latter became evident as they walked through the lobby. People stumbled over themselves at the sight of his scar. The gasps and sly mutters hit like barbed arrows. Humiliation gave way to anger. It slithered through his veins and coiled serpent-like around every muscle.

He might have razed the place to the ground, but Miss Wild clutched his arm and whispered, "I've changed my mind. I would prefer to rent a room and take tea there. If it's not too much trouble."

He swallowed a sigh of relief. "I can tolerate their igno-rance if you can."

"You should be able to take tea without people staring."

"They'll grow tired of looking, eventually." Though in busy places, there was no respite. "And I sense you fear being in a room with me."

"Yes, because I don't trust myself to behave," she teased. She drew him to the polished mahogany counter where Johnson stood in his pristine grey tailcoat, looking officious. "No doubt you will want to know more about the incident with McGowan."

"Only if you want to tell me. I shan't be offended if you want to take tea alone, Honora." She needed to know she was in control of her destiny. "I shall inform you when your friend arrives." Though he suspected Minette would come under cover of darkness.

He asked Johnson for the key to room 8, aware Miss Wild's gaze lingered on his face. He turned and explained he always rented the rooms on either side of his own to limit any disturbances.

"As I knew I would be returning to town, I kept my account open."

Johnson handed him the key, his silver gaze daring to drift towards Miss Wild. Sylvester might have lied about their rela-tionship, presented her as a cousin from the country, but he had given up explaining his actions.

"We're meeting a friend this evening, Johnson. Send a boy to my room when she arrives, regardless of the time. She will ask for me by name."

"Certainly, my lord."

Sylvester ordered tea for both rooms, then escorted Miss Wild up the large sweeping staircase. They strolled silently along the elegant hallway, the plush red carpet cushioning their footsteps.

Slipping her room key into the lock, Sylvester opened the

door but remained outside. "I shall be next door should you wish to discuss the case. I suggest you rest. It could be a long night."

Disliking the barrier she had placed between them, he moved to walk away, feeling more lonesome than he had during those few years in Italy.

"Sylvester," Miss Wild called softly, the sound as encouraging as morning birdsong. "Sylvester, wait."

He stopped and faced her, the ache in his chest easing somewhat.

She struggled to know what to say, but he couldn't help her.

His confession swirled in the air between them.

You want me to share your bed.

I want more than that, Honora.

She swallowed as if freeing her voice from its shackles. "Stay. Take tea with me. Keep me company while we wait for Minette. I don't want to be alone."

He knew what would happen if he crossed the threshold and they were the only people in a room with a bed. But he could no more deny himself than he could deny his lungs air.

"Are you certain, Honora? There's a chance we might share more than tea."

"Mr Daventry is a master sorcerer. This spell leaves me desperate to further our friendship. Doubtless, when I've told you about Mr McGowan, I shall seek some mode of distraction."

He wanted to be more than someone who helped pass the time.

"Daventry has no hold over me. It's your warm smile, your kind heart and unwavering loyalty that leaves me enchanted." And the way she drank from his lips, as if he was the only life force she needed.

She glanced at the carpet before finding the courage to meet his gaze. "I only blame Mr Daventry because I'm frightened to admit how I feel. I was wrong about your heart. It's not scarred. Despite all you have suffered, it is good and true and calls to mine whenever we're alone together."

Indeed, his heart was pounding now. It ached for hers, as his body ached to know her intimately. "Let us continue this conversation in the privacy of your room."

When a man cared for a woman, simple things carried great significance. She didn't move when he crossed the threshold but let him squeeze past, relishing the closeness. She shut the door slowly, a sensual prelude to their lovemaking. When the lock clicked, she caught her breath as if anticipating his first thrust home.

Unsure what to expect, he stood there, watching her, waiting. The air crackled with the force of something he had never experienced and could not explain.

All he knew was he might die if he didn't have her.

He had never been this hard from anticipation alone.

"I'm not as formidable as I look," he dared to say as she unbuttoned her pelisse. "I haven't the strength to fight this, Honora, no matter how hard I try. I want you. I need you."

"I know," she breathed, setting the garment on the chair. "I would be a terrible enquiry agent if I were oblivious to the signs."

"Then send me away."

"Why, when this is inevitable?" She untied the satin ribbons and removed her bonnet, placing it on the console table. "As I reminded you when we took coffee at McGinty's, I'm four and twenty, not a slip of a girl. I have suffered greatly for my independence, and I would gladly suffer again if it left me free to follow my heart." She closed the gap between them and cupped his scarred cheek. "I want you, too, Sylvester. Since our kiss in the carriage, I have thought of little else."

His tongue felt thick in his throat.

Lust, longing and something infinitely more than admiration teased every nerve to life. Perhaps he *was* a bastard. He was nothing like his father, a man who had spent forever feeling nothing.

She pushed his coat off his shoulders, began untying his cravat. "Once I've removed this, there'll be no time for conversation. Be assured I consent to this union. I just ask that you make allowances for my inexperience."

He stilled her hand before she dragged the silk from around his neck. "Let me remind you, I want more than a lover."

Indeed, she was the one person he couldn't live without.

More than a lover? Surely he meant mistress, not wife!

Perhaps the case had clouded his perception. Perhaps lust was such a powerful emotion it led a person to have impossible dreams.

In the wake of the desperate need to feel close to him, she had ceased listening to the reasons why this was a mistake. The moment he walked away, and her heart stopped, and a cloud of loneliness choked her throat, she decided to take a leap of faith.

"Let's not make any promises," she said, wearing the words like a talisman to protect her from falling too deeply.

"Maybe I want to make promises to you." His voice was low, seductive, firing the blood in her veins. "I'm a man of my word. You know it to be true."

Not wanting to admit he was everything she had ever desired in a man, or that she would likely spend an eternity desperately wanting him, she brought all conversation to an abrupt end and kissed him.

It was a kiss unlike all others.

Yes, when his mouth opened over hers and their tongues

touched for the first time, they both moaned from the pleasure. The hunger writhing in her veins was just as wild and ferocious. Every inch of her body burned.

But this kiss was slow and deep. Hypnotic. Intense. His essence weaved wisp-like over her tongue, down her throat, to tease her heart, her soul, her sex.

They breathed heavily, their lips still locked while he unbuttoned his waistcoat and divested himself of the garment. With a pant, he broke contact only to drag his shirt over his head and throw it to the floor.

"You can't know how much I want you, Honora."

And then he was on her again, his guttural groan filling her mouth, kissing her until she could no longer rouse a rational thought.

Eager to touch him, she ran her palms over the hard planes of his chest. Traced the trail of hair disappearing below the waistband of his breeches, felt every sweet shiver ripple through him. The heat of his skin was intoxicating. The smell of leather and soap and unadulterated male acted like a potent aphrodisiac.

Like a sensual unwrapping, he stripped her bare, distracted her by giving compliments that would make any woman feel like a goddess.

"You're so beautiful," he uttered against her neck, his breath hot on her skin. "Know that you own me, Honora. I am yours to command."

And yet he held the power. She was a slave to the hands smoothing over every valley and curve. To the mouth branding every sensitive spot on her neck, searing her with his mark.

At some point, he must have removed his breeches.

"Say you want me, love," he whispered against her ear, his erection pressing against her buttocks like a hot iron rod. "It's not too late to change your mind."

Change her mind?

Her body ached for this intimacy, ached for him.

"I want you," she panted, turning to face him.

"Do you want to feel every inch of me throbbing inside you?" His wicked words stoked the fire between her thighs. "That's what you're agreeing to, Honora. Me, taking the only treasure you possess."

"You're not taking it. I am giving it freely." Nothing in her whole life had ever felt as right as this. "And if it proves a disappointment, we can put certain parameters in place to prevent it happening again."

It was a foolish thing to say. He might be a thousand miles away, and still her soul would call to his.

A sinful smile played on his lips. "Just like our first kiss, I anticipate our lovemaking will be spectacular." Gripping her buttocks, he crushed her against his body, against his hard shaft.

"You'll need to tell me what to do."

"Listen to your body, love. What do you want to do?"

She wanted to slip beneath his skin, let his essence consume her completely. She wanted to feel safe in his arms. Lose herself beneath the weight of his body. To feel so full with him, she might forget the crippling emptiness.

"I want to kiss you, let you know how much I hunger for your touch, how much I desire you, Sylvester." She reached up and pressed her mouth to his in a slow, sensual caress. "I want to hold your hand and never let go."

"Then come to bed, love." He reached down between their naked bodies and threaded his fingers with hers.

"Yes." She would go anywhere with him.

He drew her to the bed and pulled back the sheets, although she couldn't help but stare at his powerful shoulders, at every sculpted muscle, at his bronzed, blemish-free skin.

"Don't be afraid. I'll not hurt you, Honora."

She looked at his jutting erection and swallowed.

"Just say the word," he assured, "and we can stop."

"I trust you, Sylvester." She gripped his hand—it was more than a habit now. "Show me what to do. Show me how to please you," she said, overwhelmed by the desire to make him happy.

"Just being with you leaves me satisfied beyond measure. And I told you, I'm not a selfish man and will see to your pleasure first."

"What do you mean to do?" She had some idea.

"Kiss you." He brushed his mouth over hers. "Everywhere." He dipped his head to her breast, stroked his tongue over her nipple, drove her near mad with desire.

She arched her back, thrust her hands into his hair. Like a wanton, she encouraged him to take her nipple deeper into his mouth, to suck, suck hard.

"Don't stop," she breathed when he gently lowered her down to the bed. "I like what you do to me."

"You'll like this, too," he promised, moving above her to trail hot kisses down to her abdomen. "Open your legs, love. Trust me. Relax."

Nora's cheeks flamed at the shocking intimacy. She had never been so exposed. But when he stroked her inner thigh, touched his fingers to her sex, she welcomed him between her legs.

She sang his praises as his tongue slipped back and forth over her aching bud. "Oh, you're good at this." She writhed like a wicked wanton beneath his mouth. Never had she known such pleasure. "I—I've never felt anything so ... so divine."

"Then you're in for another treat." He came up on his knees, rubbed her sex with his thumb while pushing two fingers slowly in and out of her sheath.

"Sylvester!" Nora gripped the bedsheets and rocked against him.

The bed creaked.

She shuddered and came apart, her body clamping around him as she moaned in ecstasy.

"Hush, love. When we're at Highcliffe, you can make as much noise as you please. You're more than ready to take all of me. Say you want me, Honora."

She looked at him through glazed eyes, smiled and beckoned him forward. "I have never wanted anything more."

"Wrap your legs around me, love." He positioned himself at her entrance, his erection as solid as steel. "I'll move slowly."

She braced herself, but was captivated by the sudden tenderness in his gaze, by the gentle way he nudged inside her.

A deep, guttural moan escaped him. "You're so warm and wet, so tight you hug me like a glove."

Sylvester rolled his hips and pushed deeper, stretching her wide. The size of him didn't pain her. How could it when they were made to fit together?

"After the next thrust, there'll be no going back."

She settled her hands on his buttocks, looked deeply into his eyes and urged him to fill her full. "Take me. Make me yours."

When he plunged to the hilt, she drank in every detail. She watched his eyes glaze with pleasure, then sweep over her in a loving caress. She watched his mouth part on a pant, then a sensual smile form.

"It's not at all painful," she said, reassuring him.

As he moved in and out of her, as their moans mingled in the air between them, as he pumped at just the right angle to make her climax, Nora wondered what he saw in her eyes.

Could he see she wasn't afraid to give all of herself?

Could he see that she was besotted?

See the deep, abiding depth of her love?

CHAPTER 14

They spent an hour lounging in bed, a hot tangle of limbs, Honora's head resting on his chest. Sylvester had never known such peace. His heart felt light for the first time in years. He had no regrets. From the way Honora pressed her naked body to his and drifted in and out of slumber, she seemed content, too.

"Are you hungry, love?" Overcome with a crippling tenderness, he stroked a wisp of hair from her face, pressed a lingering kiss to her forehead. "I can dress quickly. Order a cold collation for the room. Perhaps wine, if it pleases you."

He'd thought making love to her might ease his craving.

The urge to have her again confirmed he was wrong.

She raised her head and looked at him through sleepy eyes. "Ordinarily, I would have you tug the bell pull and order a sumptuous feast. But the thought of us moving leaves me bereft."

He admired her honesty.

As always, their thoughts were aligned.

"There's little point fetching the tea tray," he said. When the footman knocked and failed to receive a reply, the rattle of china said he had left it on the floor outside the room. "The beverage will be cold now."

She pursed her lips. "I suppose I should get dressed. I need to send word to Miss Trimble. She is expecting me in Howland Street tonight."

He glanced at the window. Sunset was two hours away.

"Minette might not come until dawn." They could not make love again so soon, yet he relished the prospect of sleeping next to her tonight. "She might not come at all."

"Minette always keeps her word."

They fell silent, and his conscience tugged at his heartstrings. "I know what you said about not making promises, Honora, but we need to discuss—"

"Let's not talk about it now. We must try to focus on the case." She sat up, her arm covering her breasts and asked he look away while she hunted for her shift.

He laughed. "There's no need to hide from me. I've had my mouth on every inch of your naked flesh. I could sketch every curve from memory." The thought sent blood racing to his loins.

A blush stained her cheeks. "Yes, but I was delirious then."

They had both been consumed by their passions.

"I'll close my eyes." He propped himself up against the pillows, folded his arms behind his head, squeezed his eyes shut. "You can trust me not to look."

When she slipped from the bed, he pictured her naked form. Skin, creamy white, sweet smelling like rose blooms in summer. Hair, a rich chestnut brown, silky tendrils cascading down her back. He imagined the woman who would be his wife if she could just learn to love him.

He was in love with her.

He'd suspected it since seeing her with the curate. The second the man introduced himself as her betrothed, he'd wanted to rip Paisley's head from his shoulders. And he couldn't stop looking at her, thinking about her, wanting her.

"What if Minette called and we failed to hear her knocking?" Honora said, after informing him he could open his eyes. "Would Johnson not have sent word to room 9?"

"Potentially. We *were* distracted." Sylvester grinned as he considered her standing in her shift and stays. If she wore a hemp sack, he would find her enchanting. "I'll dress quickly, go downstairs and speak to Johnson."

He threw back the bedsheets and strode to the pile of discarded clothes. A man with a hideous scar was not embarrassed about a woman seeing him in a state of semi-arousal.

Honora failed to divert her gaze but disguised the fact with a quick change of subject. "I—I need to ask you a few questions when you return. They came to mind yesterday while at the Hart Street office."

"Then ask me while we're dressing."

"Very well. In reference to the coroner's report, do you recall what injuries your brother sustained in the fall?"

Sylvester felt the heat of her gaze as he dragged on his breeches. "What you would expect when falling from a great height: snapped neck, broken hips and ribs and a punctured lung."

"Any head trauma?"

"A cracked skull."

"Might it point to another cause of death?"

"The coroner said not."

She sat on the chair and slipped her foot into her white stocking. "Might I ask you a personal question about Sir George?"

"Honora, we've just made love," he said, his mouth dry as he watched her smooth the garment up to her thigh and tie the pink ribbon. "You can ask me whatever you please."

Another blush rose to her cheeks. "Did you believe Sir

George when he said your mother was faithful to your father?"

Discovering Sir George's secret had left him shocked. But it also accounted for Felix's dislike of the man. "I've spent a lifetime trying to determine the truth. Before I left for Italy, my mother assured me she had always remained devoted to her marriage."

Honora picked up her dress and tried to shake out the creases. "Have you considered your godfather may have punished Felix for mistreating your mother?"

Had they been speaking about any other man, Sylvester would be suspicious. "I trust Sir George implicitly. Yes, he had cause to kill Felix. Particularly when Felix barred him from attending Mother's funeral."

Honora frowned. "Who did attend the funeral?"

Sylvester experienced the usual stab of guilt for his absence. "Felix and Johanna, and a few notable people, including Lord Rutherfield. She was laid to rest in the private chapel at Highcliffe." As he pulled on his shirt, he recalled something Felix had said. "Oh, and her old friend made the trip from London. My mother had no other family."

Honora dressed in silence, though he could almost hear the whirring of cogs as her mind assembled the information.

After making himself presentable, Sylvester ventured downstairs to speak to Johnson, order dinner and wine.

"An extremely tall gentleman called and left two letters, my lord." Johnson reached into a drawer beneath the counter and produced the missives. A whiff of French perfume reached Sylvester's nostrils. Yes, they were definitely from Minette. "One is addressed to you, my lord. One to your companion."

Sylvester took the letters and noted the feminine script. He might have scolded Johnson for not informing him sooner, but he wouldn't have dragged himself from Honora's arms even if a boy had knocked.

"As you said you were expecting a lady, my lord," Johnson added, sensing his irritation, "I saw no need to disturb you."

Sylvester thanked him and took to the stairs, for he was itching to read the contents in the hope it provided another clue to the mystery.

Honora stared at the green wax pressed into her missive. She did not break the seal but hurried to the escritoire and wrote a note. Snatching her reticule, she said she would return shortly.

While waiting, he turned his letter over in his hand. It was also sealed with the same colour wax used to secure Johanna's monthly epistles.

Honora returned, a little breathless. "I sent a penny boy to the Parlour. To ask Minette why she'd used green wax and if it was one favoured by Johanna."

"Shall I open my letter now?" He waited for her nod of approval before breaking the seal and scanning the first of two lists. "Johanna had four regular clients at the Parlour." Disappointment flared as he revealed names that bore no relevance to the case. "Felix is listed as the fifth. Minette notes that Johanna left the Parlour within weeks of meeting my brother."

"What about Lydia Moore, Johanna's sister?"

Sylvester's gaze drifted down the page. His eyes bulged when he spotted a familiar name. "Damn the conniving devil! Lydia Moore entertained Lord Rutherfield at the Parlour."

"Lord Rutherfield!" Shaking her head, Honora dropped slowly into the chair. "It cannot be a coincidence. Though what can the magistrate have to do with your brother's death?"

Sylvester fell silent, his mind in turmoil.

He understood why Rutherfield failed to mention the connection. But not once had Felix or Johanna spoken about Lydia, or said the local magistrate knew them from the Parlour.

"Mrs Egan looked ready to expire when the magistrate asked to question her." Honora's worried tone echoed Sylvester's worst fear. "What if she knows something that might incriminate him in the murder? What if she feared him not the threat of gaol?"

Anger twisted in Sylvester's gut. "We should head back to Highcliffe tonight. Perhaps interview Mrs Egan and fool her into thinking we know about Rutherfield."

Honora covered her mouth briefly with her hand. "Sylvester, what if the magistrate killed Felix and hired someone to play the role of the fisherman? What if people are scared to work at Highcliffe because they know of the magistrate's evil plot?"

Sylvester released a weary sigh. A servant wouldn't dare cross someone as influential as Rutherfield. The man could manufacture evidence and see an innocent person hanged from the gallows.

"I agree we should leave for Highcliffe," he said, wishing he could snap his fingers and be but a mile from home. "But I must visit Pierre Badeau and discover if Felix mentioned his reason for erecting a door in the tunnel."

Honora gave a curious hum. "You said your mother's friend hails from London. Do you know where we might find her? I wish to ask if she noticed anything unusual on the day of the funeral."

"Mrs Goddard lives in Great Queen Street. Not far from here."

"Excellent. We'll leave as soon as the penny boy returns from the Parlour. It will give me time to write and inform Mr Daventry of our plans."

Sylvester noted there was no sign or mention of the letter she had received. "Have you read your letter from Minette?"

She waved in dismissal. "It was nothing important."

He imagined her tearing it open and absorbing the words while dashing downstairs. After all they had shared this afternoon, and with him pinning his hopes on furthering their alliance, he prayed she would confide in him soon.

As Sylvester's carriage trundled along the busy thoroughfare en route to Great Queen Street, Nora sat silently, her clasped hands resting in her lap. Her disquiet had nothing to do with Minette confirming all the girls at the Parlour used green wax. It had everything to do with the letter.

She had read it quickly.

Minette's reassuring words had failed to bring lasting relief. Everyone believed McGowan had tripped, then tumbled down the stairs. That he had earned the deep gash to his head in the fall. Nora should put the past behind her now. It was a secret she should hug tight to her chest. Take with her to the grave.

And therein lay her dilemma.

She should tell Sylvester the truth. She hadn't meant to hit the oaf who had taken liberties. It had been the only means of saving her virtue. The virtue she had given freely this afternoon to a man who made her soul sing.

She was in love with Sylvester Deville.

The fear of losing him increased by the day. It left her more terrified than any inevitable encounter with the Reverend Wild. She thought love was the cure to all ailments, yet it left her sickening for something she could not explain.

Sylvester valued honesty. Was trust not the foundation of any lasting relationship? And so she swallowed down her nerves. Decided to reveal her damning secret.

"As you can imagine, life at the Parlour was not without its problems."

He jerked when her voice broke the silence. "In that

174

regard, I fear my imagination runs riot. I cannot bear the thought of you suffering, Honora."

"Minette advised I forget what happened on my last night there. That I bury my secret in the hope it is never discovered."

He straightened. "Yet I sense your reluctance to heed her advice."

"How can I forget when it haunts me night and day?" She often lay awake, imagining the hangman's noose squeezing her windpipe. "How can I forget when you deserve to know the truth?"

"You have a duty to yourself, Honora. Do what is right for you, not for me."

A heavy silence descended.

He could demand to know. He hated lies and secrets. And yet he had put her needs first.

"After what we have shared today, I want to share this with you." She inhaled deeply and pushed aside her pain. "For a naive country virgin, living at the Parlour was as dangerous as living on the streets. Minette made me keep to the shadows. She feared her clients would start a bidding war and demand to make use of the new girl."

Sylvester cursed beneath his breath. "I'll call out anyone who touched you inappropriately."

She managed a weak smile. "While Minette kept me hidden, she did not consider the morals of those men who worked for her." McGowan's lecherous grin flashed into her mind, sending a shiver down her spine. "One of her men entered my room while I slept. He was drunk and attacked me in the vilest manner."

Sylvester's eyes blazed, his rage evident. "You'll tell me where I can find McGowan. I assure you, he will never lay a hand on you again."

Nora steeled herself. "He's in St Martin's Burial Ground."

"He's dead!"

"I killed him." Tears fell, splattering like raindrops on her cheeks, though her voice didn't break. "I hit him with the coffee pot I left on my nightstand. Minette forbade me from leaving my room after dark."

"You killed him with a coffee pot?"

"No. Dazed and drunk, McGowan stumbled out into the hall. He fell down the stairs and snapped his neck." Nora said a silent prayer, begging the Lord for forgiveness. "Minette alerted Mr Daventry before summoning a constable. I was spirited away while she gave false evidence."

Magistrates and judges used the Pleasure Parlour.

None would wish to see its proprietor prosecuted.

Sylvester shook his head. "McGowan deserved his fate. You did not kill him, Honora. You were merely protecting yourself."

She snorted. "Do you know how many maids are hung for crimes they didn't commit? Ask Mr Daventry, and he will give you the numbers."

"What I mean is, you shouldn't blame yourself."

"I will always blame myself." She tried to blink her tears away. "It's a secret I had sworn to keep. I should have told you before ... before inviting you into my bed."

The carriage drew to a sudden stop in Great Queen Street.

Sylvester sat forward, wiped her tears and clasped her hands. "Love, the man would still be alive had he kept to his quarters. McGowan killed himself. Daventry agrees else he would not have hired you or sent you to the Parlour today."

"I care what you think, not Mr Daventry."

He brought her hand to his lips and kissed her knuckles. "I think you're the most courageous woman I have ever known. I understand your reluctance to speak about your trauma, but I know you would never hurt anyone intentionally."

Relief washed through her. "After McGowan's death, two

other girls complained about him. Because of the nature of their work, they felt they deserved his unwelcome advances." Minette was furious no one had mentioned McGowan's tendencies sooner. "You don't think any less of me?"

He gave an incredulous snort. "How could I? You're the person I admire most in the world."

Grateful he had not forsaken her, she pressed a lingering kiss to his palm. "I'm glad I told you now and not while we were at the Musgrove. I doubt I would have stopped kissing you then."

"Tell me again when we reach Highcliffe." His dark gaze dropped to her lips, his voice turning husky. "When you've entered my chamber through the adjoining door and slipped into my bed."

Never had anything sounded so appealing. In his arms, she had found her own heaven. But danger lurked in the shadows. She sensed her life was about to take another tragic turn. Happiness always eluded her.

Unable to voice her fears, Nora kissed his palm again. "Then let us focus on achieving our tasks quickly tonight in the hope we may reach Highcliffe in the morning."

He released her, and after explaining that Mrs Goddard was often a little eccentric, they alighted and knocked on the townhouse door.

The butler led them into a comfortable drawing room where a white Pomeranian lay sleeping on a red velvet chaise. Mrs Goddard appeared wearing a pink dress with excessive flounces, having applied a dab of rouge to her cheeks. She seemed thrilled the son of her old friend had decided to call.

The dog was not so pleased by the lady's misplaced attention and barked until a footman came to offer the animal a biscuit treat.

"Ignore Basil. He refuses to share his mamma with anyone. Have no fear. He has only ever bit the vicar." Suddenly realising she had not seen Sylvester since his mother's passing, Mrs Goddard swept forward and clasped his hands. "Please accept my condolences. Elisabeth was my dearest friend. There's not a day goes by that I don't think about her sweet smile."

Sylvester inclined his head. "The house is much changed without her."

The Pomeranian barked again, and Mrs Goddard was forced to sit and let the ball of fluff jump onto her lap. She gestured for them to sit on the sofa, her bright blue gaze lingering on Nora for longer than necessary.

"Tell me you bring good news, Sylvester," the lady said, making the natural assumption. "Elisabeth hated you being so far away in Italy and prayed you would return home and marry."

Sylvester made the introductions, referring to Nora as his agent, not his lover, and explained he was merely ensuring the coroner and magistrate had conducted a thorough investigation into the nature of his brother's death.

"We come because Miss Wild wishes to ask you a few questions."

"Oh!" Mrs Goddard's disappointment was palpable. She glanced between them. "How odd. There is a definite spark in the air, and I am rarely wrong about such matters." She turned to the dog and pouted. "Tell them, Basil. Mamma is never wrong in matters of the heart. Is she? No!"

Nora cleared her throat. "Mrs Goddard, how might you describe Felix and Johanna Deville's relationship?"

Mrs Goddard stroked her dog. "I can tell you there wasn't the same spark I am witnessing here. No, I wouldn't be surprised to find they despised each other to the marrow of their bones."

"Did you notice anything specific?"

"One can smell when a relationship is rancid." Mrs Goddard reached for her monocle and considered Nora through one wide eye. "You seem of genteel upbringing, Miss Wild. What happened to your parents?"

"My parents?" Nora suddenly wished she had the power of invisibility. "My parents died some time ago." It was not a complete lie. Both were dead to her. And she was unlikely to meet this lady again. "My father was a vicar, madam."

"A vicar! Good gracious!" Mrs Goddard covered the dog's ears. Basil growled. "He dislikes men who preach. Don't you, dear? Yes, you do." She kissed the dog. "You know, I married below my station, Miss Wild. Society will forgive anything if it's a love match. We can discuss it during dinner. You will stay?"

Nora's stomach growled at the mention of food.

"Dorothea, we're to travel to Highcliffe this evening," Sylvester said but asked if she might like to visit his home when the weather improved. He explained that they must leave once she had answered their questions. "Did you notice anything amiss at my mother's funeral?"

Dorothea's mouth puckered with annoyance. "I only wish I had, but that devil had buried her before I received word my dear Elisabeth was dead."

Sylvester jerked his head. "Felix told me you attended the funeral."

"Then he lied," Dorothea said, full of indignation. "Make no mistake, that boy was his father's son. Heartless. As cold as a crypt."

Nora shared a glance with Sylvester. The worry lines on his brow said their thoughts were aligned. Did anyone attend the funeral? Had Felix buried his mother before someone raised their suspicions? Before the coroner could consider another cause of death?

Murder!

CHAPTER 15

The glow of candlelight in Pierre Badeau's office window confirmed someone was working late. No one answered the door, despite Sylvester hammering the iron knocker.

"Monsieur Badeau!" Sylvester cupped his eyes and peered through the dusty pane. He saw the outline of a figure and so rapped on the glass, determined to rouse the fellow.

Dorothea's revelation had left him restless. Like a fool, he had thought his brother above murdering his own mother. The fact no one could find her maid should have raised Sylvester's suspicions.

Honora touched his arm gently. He longed to pull her into an embrace, to kiss her so deeply he would forget his failings.

"If Felix killed her, I will dig up his bones and feed them to the dogs." Beneath his breath, Sylvester cursed his brother to Hades. "I should never have left her alone in that godforsaken place."

"You're concocting a story. We know nothing for certain."

"Then why the hell did Felix lie about the funeral?"

"Perhaps he wished to hurt you." Honora's shrug said she didn't know what to believe. "Perhaps he was playing the dutiful son to punish you for your absence."

He shot her a sharp look. "I came as soon as I could."

"I am merely trying to understand his motive."

Sylvester scrubbed his face, though it failed to stop the muscle in his jaw twitching. He kicked the door and shouted to Badeau. "I know you're in there!"

"One moment, please," came a man's irate voice.

The bolt scraped against metal. The lock clicked. The door opened a mere fraction. A man with olive skin and a mop of thick black hair peered through the narrow gap.

"It is late, monsieur. The office, it is closed for the day."

"Are you Pierre Badeau?"

His gaze shifted between them. "Who is asking?"

Sylvester presented his calling card and waited while the man studied the script in the muted light. "You met with my brother Felix Deville. I wish to discuss the reason he hired you."

"Then you might explain why he never paid me," the Frenchman scoffed.

Sensing the man's reluctance to invite them into his office after hours, Sylvester modified his tone. "Please." He was not averse to begging. "We must leave for the coast tonight, but I need to ask you a few questions about my brother's plans for Highcliffe. I shall pay any debt owed to you."

The last comment softened the deep furrows between the man's brows. He stepped back and opened the door wide. "Come in out of the cold, monsieur." He inclined his head to Honora. "Madame."

They entered Badeau's office, a room with a small seating area and a large oak desk littered with measuring instruments. Bookcases lined every wall, the volumes thick and old. Iron bookends held a rolled map open on the desk.

"Surely you heard us knocking." Sylvester caught a whiff of garlic and rosemary and wondered if he had disturbed the man's meal. "I hammered loud enough to wake the dead."

Badeau gripped a pair of brass tongs and stoked the fire.

"When working, I have learnt to ignore the din of the city."
He gestured to the sofa, to the well-worn seats. "Sit, if you
please."

Sylvester waited for Honora to sit before settling beside
her. Having her close brought immense comfort. He reached
between them and held her hand.

"Can you tell me why Felix Deville hired you?" Sylvester
watched Badeau rummage through a box of files he had
lugged to his desk. "We were told he wanted you to erect a
steel door between the tunnel and cave at Highcliffe."

Badeau pulled out a file, removed the contents, and rifled
through the papers. "Your brother, he kept many secrets. He
would tell me nothing of his plans. He hired me to work in
the dungeon. Paid the required deposit but never settled his
account."

"What sort of work?" Sylvester said.

Felix always kept Sylvester in the dark. But Mrs Egan had
mentioned the old iron door blocking the entrance to the
cave had been removed due to damage. It was yet another
reason why she warned about venturing below ground.

"*Mais oui*! Here it is." Badeau crossed the room and
handed Sylvester a plan of the subterranean passageways. "I
visited Highcliffe to reinforce the door in the hidden room
and to change the locking mechanism."

"I beg your pardon?" While the Frenchman had an excellent grasp of the English language, Sylvester feared he had
misheard. "Did you say hidden room?"

"Indeed."

Sylvester shivered from a sudden chill.

"The secret room opposite the dungeons," Badeau said, as
if it were common knowledge. "Your ancestor, he hid there
during an invasion many centuries ago, *non*?"

"Yes, I know the story, but my father assured me it was
just that—a tale invented by Samuel Deville to deter others
from raiding his home." According to family legend, his

ancestor had mounted covert attacks on the rogues who had invaded the castle. Samuel hid in the room by day. Slaughtered the enemy by night.

Badeau's eyes widened. "It is not a tale. I have seen the room and carried out the necessary structural work on the door." He stabbed his finger at a particular point on the plan. "Your brother, he asked me to erect another door, but I said I would do so once he had settled his account."

"But then Felix died."

"I wrote to you. To ask if you wished me to carry out the work and to beg you to settle your brother's debt."

Sylvester frowned. "I never received your letter."

"That explains why you did not pay. Yet it is most odd."

When Badeau returned to root through his desk, Honora whispered, "Why would your brother reinforce the door to a secret room? Do you suspect he locked Johanna in there? It may account for why her body was never found."

Fear held Sylvester's heart in an icy grip. Would they enter the room to find Johanna's corpse? Was Mrs Egan an accomplice in the crime? It would certainly explain her odd behaviour.

He firmed his grip of her hand, appreciating the softness of her skin, the warmth of her touch. "We must proceed with caution."

If he lost her, he would never recover.

"We should return to the cottage, not the house. See if Mr Bower has discovered anything in our absence." She brushed her thumb over his, and he recognised his own compelling need to prolong every intimacy. "Only then can we decide the best course of action."

Had he been wrong about Johanna?

Was she the victim, not the perpetrator?

Had Felix killed her and thrown himself off the cliff in despair?

And who had he been arguing with? Mrs Egan?

He tried to make sense of the chaos in his mind, but Badeau returned with a letter. "Then you did not send this missive, *non*?"

Sylvester took the proffered letter, noticing it bore a broken Deville seal. He scanned the instructions written by a man's hand. The signature was like his but lacked the aristocratic flourish.

Honora leaned closer. "What does it say?"

The scent of her rose perfume calmed his rising temper.

"It's a request written two months ago, supposedly from me. Asking for a spare key to the new mechanism Monsieur Badeau fitted to the door in the secret room." He firmed his jaw as alarm and anger knotted in his stomach. "The forger enclosed the sum of ten pounds as payment."

"That is what seemed odd," Badeau said.

"Despite the debt my brother owed, did you send the key to Highcliffe?"

Badeau slapped his hand to his heart. "But of course. I took the key there myself. No one could survive for more than a few days trapped in that room. The image, it haunted me day and night."

And yet Sylvester had not been there to welcome the Frenchman. He had been out hunting for his mother's heirlooms. "Who took receipt of the key?"

"A woman." Badeau shivered. "A woman with eyes as cold as the gorgon Medusa. She was most distraught I had taken the trouble to call and did not offer refreshment or to reimburse me for the stage."

"But you gave her the key?"

"She snatched it from my hand. Shooed me away as if I were a peasant with the plague. Slammed the door in my face."

"Was her name Mrs Egan?"

The Frenchman shrugged. "She never gave her name. But I am certain she said she was the housekeeper."

CHAPTER 16

Monsieur Badeau's revelation meant delaying their departure by an hour. Honora insisted on delivering a note to the Hart Street office, alerting Mr Daventry of the secret room in Highcliffe's dungeons. Fearing Mrs Egan planned to lock them inside and throw away the key, she begged her employer to rescue them if they failed to return in three days.

With Sykes' skilled driving and the wind at their back, it was a little after daybreak when the coachman steered Sylvester's carriage onto the narrow dirt track leading to the cottage.

Dawn did not bring hope for a new day.

Dark clouds hung over Highcliffe. Mist crept along the ground like ghosts slithering from their graves. The air was so damp it chilled a man's bones.

"Drive to Whitstable, not Herne Bay," Sylvester told Sykes. "Purchase provisions. Coal or wood. Food and candles. Tallow will do. Under no circumstances are you to visit Highcliffe."

"Aye, milord." Sykes removed his hat and stood feeding the rim through his stubby fingers. He waited until Honora entered the cottage before gathering the courage to speak.

"Begging your pardon, milord, but there's something you should know. It might be nothing. But a man gets an itch between his shoulders when something don't feel right."

Sylvester had suffered from the same damnable itch for a year. Hence why he had taken the brace of pistols from beneath the carriage seat.

"Speak freely," he said, clutching the mahogany box.

Sykes glanced briefly over his shoulder. "It's Mrs Egan, milord. She ain't got a good word to say about me. Reckon it's because I've seen her sneaking about late at night, up to no good, I expect."

Yes, probably dancing around bonfires and sacrificing the villagers' firstborns. "Perhaps her duties keep her up after hours."

"She hides things in the outhouse, blankets and candles, and she's the only one with a key. A man might force the lock, but she's the sort what invents spiteful stories. Given a chance, she'd have me out of Highcliffe quick as a wink."

Sylvester silently damned Mrs Egan to Hades.

"Have you mentioned your concerns to anyone else?"

Sykes' eyes widened. "On my honour, milord. I'd never speak out of turn and shouldn't have mentioned it now, not without proof. But Mrs Egan is up to something. I expect the magistrate thinks so, too."

"The magistrate? You speak of Lord Rutherfield?"

"Aye, milord. Myrtle said he often visits the house when you're away. It slipped out accidentally, and she begged me not to blab. A man might think there's wickedness afoot."

Rutherfield had been snooping about the damn house?

Sylvester's anger was no longer a raging inferno.

It was a cold, dark fury.

"Let's speak of it no more until we find proof." He had faith in his coachman, though a niggling doubt said he should be wary. "But I thank you for bringing the matter to my attention."

Sykes apologised for being the bearer of bad news, then he left to fetch provisions.

Sylvester entered the cottage to find Honora alone. He placed the mahogany box on the old oak table and scanned the room. The place was cold, the hearth littered with leaves, the wood basket empty.

"Is Daventry's man not here?"

"No. The door was open, but there's no evidence to suggest Mr Bower slept here last night." Honora gestured to the copper kettle hanging by the grate. "He never starts the day without a hot cup of tea."

"It appears no one has been here for more than a year." Sad memories of his mother invaded Sylvester's mind. He couldn't help but picture her sprawled on the stone floor. Helpless. Dying. He imagined his brother's hands wrapped around her neck, throttling the last breath from her lungs.

Guilt was an ever-present hollowness in his chest.

Only cowards ran away.

"I know what you meant when we spoke at the coffee-house," he said, past regrets sitting like a ton weight on his shoulders.

Honora appeared confused. "Spoke about what, exactly?"

"You called yourself a coward because you left the vicarage rather than face your problems." He gave a sad sigh. "I'm a coward for leaving Highcliffe."

During those restless hours when he couldn't sleep, he often regretted his decision. Now, as he stood before the love of his life, he couldn't help but be grateful for his choice.

"My mother did not deserve to end her days in this hovel."

Honora glanced around the cottage. "I find it rather quaint. There's an air of peacefulness, a luxury one does not find at Highcliffe. Perhaps your mother loved it here."

Sylvester considered the cottage again through fresh eyes.

His mind roused a vision of a couple in love, sipping wine before a roaring fire, away from life's disturbances.

"And you're mistaken in your assumption," she continued. "I'm a coward for not leaving the vicarage sooner. And for hiding behind a disguise when I should have had the strength of my convictions."

He realised he hadn't seen her spectacles in days.

"I have spent the last year wishing things were different. Meeting you changed everything." He would suffer a decade of heartache to experience the love he felt now.

"Perhaps it was always meant to be."

The cloud of sadness lifted, and he smiled. He reached for Honora's hand and drew her close. "When this is over, I shall make you a gift of this cottage." He hoped it would be a wedding present. "A place you may invite me to, when the mood takes you. A place where happy memories will make the sad ones bearable."

He lowered his head and settled his mouth on hers.

She slipped her tongue over his in a slow, teasing caress, his cock growing instantly hard from the sensation. She possessed the power to make him feel like any normal man in love, happy, untroubled.

"Perhaps we should lock the door," he whispered.

"Mr Bower might be back shortly." She stroked his cheek as if she loved the feel of marred skin. "And we've much to do today. Perhaps tonight we might meet for an illicit liaison."

Sylvester kissed her once more, accepting her enticing invitation.

He pulled away, masculine pride filling his chest when he noticed Honora was breathless. Then he realised her gasp was triggered by something she had witnessed through the window.

"What in heaven's name?" She moved past him to stare outside. "Here's Mr Bower now, hurrying across the open field with three women." She pressed her nose to the glass.

"One must be injured because Mr Bower is supporting her weight. Perhaps Blanche is still unwell. Quickly. They're heading for the cottage."

Sylvester joined her at the window and observed the group. Yes, one woman lacked the strength to walk. "The one striding ahead looks to be Mrs Egan."

His housekeeper's willowy frame was instantly recognisable. But as they trudged closer, Sylvester questioned if his eyes were deceiving him.

"What the devil!" He gripped the window sill. "That's not Blanche."

Honora faced him. "Who is it?"

Shock forced him to draw a ragged breath.

The power of speech abandoned him.

"Sylvester? Are you well?" Honora stroked his back. "It cannot be Johanna, either." Confused, she gazed out of the window. "The woman looks too old to be Blanche, or your brother's wife."

"It's not Johanna."

Good grief! He could barely believe his eyes.

"Then who is it?"

"It's ... it's my mother."

How could it be? He was undoubtedly asleep in his carriage and would wake when they bounced through the next rut in the road.

"Your mother!"

Suddenly, his muscles spurred him into action. He darted out of the cottage and raced through the overgrown garden, charged out into the open field, almost taking the gate off its hinges.

"Mother!"

"Sylvester!" His mother clutched her heart when their gazes collided. She almost dropped to her knees, but Bower gripped her waist and urged them all to keep moving.

"Now's not the time for questions, my lord," Daventry's

man said, glancing nervously over his shoulder. "Quickly. We need to get them into the cottage. Happen, we can talk then."

Sylvester followed behind, his mind a cloud of confusion.

How could his mother be alive?

Where had she been for the last eighteen months?

Why the hell had Felix lied?

Honora appeared in the doorway. She gripped the frame, looking equally shocked by this new development.

"Come inside," she beckoned. "I shall light the fire."

"No!" Bower shouted. "No one must know we're here. Not until her ladyship and Edith are safely out of harm's way."

The next few minutes passed in a blur. With his mother being unsteady on her feet, Sylvester helped her into the fireside chair. Her face was pale, much thinner than he remembered. She complained of aching muscles and stiff joints. And though he hadn't laid eyes on her in four years, she looked to have aged ten.

By God, she was alive!

It beggared belief.

Honora appeared with a blanket, wrapping it gently around his mother's shoulders. "This should keep you warm, my lady. The coachman will be back in an hour or two with provisions."

His mother smiled at Honora. "Th-thank you, Miss Wild. Mrs Egan told me you've come to Highcliffe to help my son solve a mystery."

Solve a mystery? She had saved him from himself. She had given him hope. A future. A reason to live. She had healed his scarred heart.

"Lord Deville hired me to discover who was sending him monthly missives. He believed your daughter-in-law might be responsible."

"There is much to tell you, my dear, but I am so tired."

His mother gestured to his housekeeper. "Mrs Egan will explain. Edith may help with the story, too." Glancing up at Sylvester, she gasped as if only just noticing his scar. "Bless my heart, it is true. Your wicked brother sliced your face, left you disfigured."

"Yes. It's true." He glanced at Honora. His heart was so full of love it might burst from his chest. "Although I have stopped seeing it as a hindrance."

"Mrs Egan said you're much changed of late." His mother cast her watery gaze over Honora. "I believe I have you to thank for that, Miss Wild."

"Lord Deville needed a confidante. Mrs Egan has made his life unbearable this last year, and he did not know who to trust."

Sylvester knew who to trust now.

Mrs Egan gave a whimper. "They would have killed us all had his lordship discovered the truth." She paced back and forth, wringing her hands, only stopping to peer out of the window. "They're sure to find us here. I know you were trying to help, Miss Wild, but you've made matters a lot worse. We were lucky to escape with our lives."

"We've been cowards long enough," his mother said.

Sylvester absorbed the information, but one question burst to the fore.

"Mother, please explain how you're alive when I have wept over your gravestone." He scrambled to think of an explanation. Monsieur Badeau's underground plans flashed into his mind, along with the demand for a spare key to the secret room. "Blessed Mother and all the saints! Tell me you haven't been living beneath Highcliffe."

Perhaps unused to breathing clean air, his mother inhaled deeply. "When I threatened to report Felix for smuggling, he locked me in a hidden room in the dungeons and refused to let me leave."

"But Felix died a year ago!"

"And I have been kept locked in there ever since."

"By whom?" He whirled round to face Mrs Egan. "Damn it, woman. You had better explain yourself."

"It's not Mrs Egan's fault. She has done her best." A little distraught, his mother waved a limp hand at his housekeeper. "Please explain the story to my son, from the beginning."

Mrs Egan kept her frantic gaze on the window while she began the incredulous tale. "It all started after your brother married his mistress. Her sister read the announcement. She appeared on the doorstep clutching her carpet bag, giving a sad story about needing somewhere to stay."

"We know her as Lydia Moore," Honora said.

"Oh, that devil goes by many names." Mrs Egan's mouth twisted in disdain. "When his lordship's debts started mounting, Miss Moore suggested a little venture. A harmless bit of trading, she said."

Having seen the broken barrels, an imbecile could decipher what that meant. "They let smugglers use the cave for a share of the booty." Sylvester silently cursed Felix for his damn stupidity.

Mrs Egan nodded. "Just a couple of times. That's what they agreed. But Miss Moore and her debt-ridden lover needed money and so blackmailed the master into letting the smugglers use the cave monthly."

"Her lover Lord Rutherfield?" Honora tried to ascertain.

Terror flashed in Mrs Egan's eyes. "Oh, the magistrate is the spawn of Satan, that's for sure. He had the servants move the goods. Said it was his insurance against them squealing." Tears welled. "He threatened us with the noose if we so much as breathed a word."

Edith spoke up. With her gaunt face and sallow skin, she looked as weary as his mother. "One footman refused to help them. He fled the house but was arrested soon after for sheep rustling. Despite pleading his innocence, they hanged him in Blean Woods without a trial."

That explained Mrs Egan's sudden panic when the magistrate arrived to enquire about the missing maid. Most people cowered when Rutherfield wielded arrogance like a steely blade.

"You don't need to worry about Rutherfield anymore," Sylvester assured her. "Influential people in London already know of his connection to Lydia Moore. He'll be the only one hanged from the gallows."

Mrs Egan dared to leave her post. "There's one more shipment coming in tomorrow night, then they're leaving England. There can be no witnesses. I heard them say they planned to torch Highcliffe and all those inside. Then the authorities will be none the wiser."

Torch his family home!

Over his dead body!

Sylvester would throttle Rutherfield before he could strike the flint. "Them? Are you telling me Lydia Moore visits Highcliffe in my absence?"

"Lydia Moore works at Highcliffe," Honora said. "To keep the staff silent, she must be a threatening presence in the house."

Sylvester straightened. Among the staff, there was only one woman pretty enough to snare Rutherfield in her trap. "Blanche?"

"Her nervous disposition is all an act."

"She's a devious one, that's for sure," Mrs Egan confirmed.

Sylvester scratched his head. "But she carved the word *help* into the bed canopy. She arranged to meet us outside the castle walls and reveal all."

"Doubtless, Blanche would have lied," Honora said. "She would have lured us away from Highcliffe. Perhaps told us Johanna was alive and living in London. In our absence, she could continue her nefarious deeds without fear of being caught."

Bower cleared his throat. "I investigated the tunnels and

the cave, like you said, Miss Wild. That's when I saw Mrs Egan bringing a basket down into the dungeons. I watched her enter a secret room and followed her inside."

"You certainly gave us a fright, Mr Bower," Sylvester's mother said before turning to Honora. "When you showed Lord Rutherfield the letter from Peel, he panicked. When you reported the maid missing, he thought Blanche had betrayed him. That's why he came to Highcliffe."

So Blanche's manic episode had been an act, too.

A chill slithered through Sylvester. He had left Rutherfield at Highcliffe, unaware he was Blanche's partner in crime. The question now was, had the couple conspired to murder a peer?

"Who killed Felix?" Not that he cared. Not after his brother's bare-faced lies. Not after the rogue had kept his own mother prisoner in the dungeons.

"Blanche killed Felix." His mother retrieved a lace handkerchief from her sleeve and dabbed tears from her eyes. "She pushed him off the cliff when he tried to end their partnership."

Who would have believed the timid maid could be so callous and cruel? Yet she had been running her criminal activities from the house for more than a year. If only one courageous person had spoken up. No wonder Rutherfield had made no attempt to find the killer. He was an accomplice to the crime.

"We knew, but were powerless to act." Mrs Egan darted back to the window. "They kept her ladyship alive in case they had to blackmail you, my lord. What could we do but try to keep her safe?"

"You're not to blame, Mrs Egan," his mother reiterated. "Few would have coped under the strain you've suffered these last few years."

"Where is Blanche now?" Sylvester would simply take her

into custody. Keep her locked in the secret room while he hunted for Rutherfield.

"She left Highcliffe with the magistrate," Mrs Egan said. "We've not seen her since, but she will return tomorrow and play at being the maid while waiting for the shipment."

Bower cleared his throat. "Her ladyship's testimony will be vital to the prosecution. And we couldn't risk Blanche doing away with the witnesses before the shipment arrived. That's why we decided to move your mother before Blanche returns. I sent a letter informing Mr Daventry, rode to Whitstable yesterday to make the mail coach."

Silence ensued while Sylvester processed the information.

It was all too much to take in.

Honora asked Mrs Egan about Pierre Badeau. The housekeeper confirmed Blanche had the only key to the secret room. That she feared the inevitable might happen and so sought a way to rescue her mistress if need be.

Sylvester gave a growl of frustration. "You should have released her the moment Badeau delivered the key."

"They would have killed her." Mrs Egan's harried voice carried the depth of her fear. "Besides, the magistrate said he had evidence to convict you for the murders, my lord. That you've no alibi for the night in question. That he has a letter proving you had a motive. Her ladyship didn't want that."

That bloody letter! He knew better than to put threats in writing. But what else could a man do when a thousand miles from home?

"Rutherfield can't prove a damn thing," Sylvester snapped, but then caught himself. "Murders? You know Johanna is dead."

His mother sighed. "Fearing they would kill her, too, Johanna escaped through the tunnels. They found her body in the cave. It was dark. She must have fallen from the steps."

"Or someone pushed her," Mrs Egan added. "They buried her in an unmarked grave, my lord."

Johanna was dead.

And yet he had been convinced she was alive.

"Then who gave the missing tome to Mr Gifford?" If that really was the lackey's name. "Who wrote to me each month to lure me away from Highcliffe?" The answer seemed obvious now. "Blanche wrote them. She wanted me to believe Johanna was alive, to lead me on a wild goose chase."

"They were biding time, my lord, before doing away with the witnesses." Bower's solemn tone reflected the gravity of the situation. "There's money to be made on the black market. Blanche and Rutherfield must have been desperate to receive the last few consignments."

Sylvester fell silent, contemplating what the devil to do now.

He locked gazes with Honora. Her confident smile said she knew exactly what to do. Indeed, he was overcome with a sudden sense all would be well.

Honora cleared her throat. "Assuming Lord Deville is in agreement, I have a plan." She paused, waiting for everyone's undivided attention. "Sykes will take Lady Deville and Edith to Canterbury to stay with Sir George. While there, they will document all that has occurred so far. Sykes will continue to London and ensure Mr Daventry knows of Rutherfield's scheme. I shall give him a note."

"Sir George!" his mother gasped. "The poor man thinks I'm dead."

"Seeing you alive will be the highlight of his life." Sylvester went on to explain that under no circumstances was Sir George to visit Highcliffe and play the hero.

"Forgive me, Mrs Egan," Honora continued, "but I must ask that you return to the house and resume your duties."

The housekeeper turned a deathly shade of pale. She clutched her throat. "What if I'm not back before Blanche returns? What if she's checked the dungeon room and found her ladyship missing?"

"Then we will apprehend her and fool Lord Rutherfield into accepting the shipment on his own." Honora thought for a moment. "Are the other servants trustworthy? Are any in cahoots with Blanche and Lord Rutherfield?"

"No, they're all scared the magistrate will hang them for aiding the smugglers. Whittle thinks we're all damned. That his lordship should abandon Highcliffe before he suffers his brother's fate."

With no choice but to trust the housekeeper's word, Honora revealed the next part of her plan. "Blanche must believe we're still in London. She must feel confident enough to accept the shipment of contraband tomorrow."

Silence ensued.

"With the cottage being two miles from the house, we cannot remain here," Sylvester said. It would take a servant half an hour to cover the distance. "Mrs Egan won't have time to alert us should they change their strategy."

Honora raised a brow in obvious challenge. "There is somewhere close we might stay. Somewhere Blanche won't think to look."

He trawled his mind but could think of nowhere.

"A place close to the house and the cave," she added.

Recognition dawned. "You mean we hide in the secret room?"

The idea posed some problems. Though the thought of spending time alone with Honora banished all concerns. He would take the brace of pistols to use for protection. And Honora carried a dagger in her reticule.

"We can receive regular updates from Mrs Egan."

"It will mean being locked in the small space," he said. Had Honora's experiences at the vicarage not left her dreading the prospect?

She swallowed deeply. "I shall manage."

Having fled Highcliffe once before, Sylvester had no intention of doing so again. His ancestor had hidden in the secret room. During midnight assaults, he had claimed back the castle. Maybe history was about to repeat itself.

"I can't promise it will be comfortable." It was probably cold and dank, but at least they would be together. Lord knows how his mother had survived this past year.

"Your brother may have been a cold-hearted blackguard," his mother said weakly, "but he afforded me certain luxuries." She glanced at Honora but said nothing about the impropriety of them sharing the room.

Bower agreed to monitor the shore and watch for approaching boats. Said he would fend for himself, but they could trust him to appear when the time was right.

"It's settled then. We will remain in the secret room and wait for Mrs Egan to raise the alarm." Honora's tone lacked the excitement he felt coursing through his veins. "She will rouse the staff into action."

Sylvester nodded. "Together, we'll rid Highcliffe of this evil blight."

CHAPTER 17

One would think entering a hidden room in a dungeon would be like stepping into the mouth of a beast: dark, damp, terrifying. Escape should be the primary goal as the threat of death loomed large.

Yet with scarlet material cascading from the ceiling and propped up in the corners with posts, the small chamber resembled a royal tent. A luxurious retreat where one might forget the scourge of war. A place where a lady might succumb to all temptation.

Sylvester gazed around the room. "It's not what I expected."

Nora noted the carved mahogany bed, big enough for one, the thick fur throws, and the truckle that had been Edith's resting place for over a year. The room boasted a bookcase lined with leather-bound volumes. An ornate washstand and porcelain bowl. An armoire. A needlework frame. Candle lamps galore.

Mrs Egan had lit the lamps—and reminded them not to cover the ventilation grate in the floor—before locking them inside the space that carried the piquant scent of dried herbs and frankincense.

"I could happily spend a week in here." Nora tried to ignore the wrench of fear in her gut that had nothing to do with feeling trapped. Elisabeth Deville was alive. Everything would be different now. "Though I would go out of my mind if forced to stay for months."

"My mother said Blanche took her out into the garden while I was away purchasing family heirlooms. She let her bathe and fetch clean clothes. Warned her they would kill me, too, if she made any attempt to flee."

The prospect of leaving must have proved daunting. Elisabeth Deville had lost one son and couldn't cope with the thought of losing another.

"Fear is like a heavy chain around one's neck." Nora had spent years plucking up the courage to leave the vicarage. Had her father threatened to kill someone she loved, she would have suffered the abuse. "The servants believe they're accomplices to kidnap and murder. So you can see why they've kept you in the dark this last year."

Sylvester took a book from the nightstand and flicked absently through the pages. "Still, you must think me a complete fool for not knowing my mother was alive. Is that why you're quiet, distant? Why you barely said two words to me on the walk here?"

His weary sigh squeezed her heart.

"We're all in shock," she said.

It wasn't a lie. Nor was it the reason for her silence.

How could she tell him she had come to believe in fairy-tales? That she had allowed herself to hope such an esteemed gentleman might marry an enquiry agent? That she loved him? Was so dreadfully scared of losing him?

"That's a gross understatement. Never in my wildest dreams had I believed such a thing possible." His downturned mouth curled into a grin. It was a wonderful sight to behold. "My mother is alive."

She forced a smile. "I'm happy for you, Sylvester. Truly, I am."

"But it makes you think of your mother." He placed the book down and closed the gap between them. When he took her hand, she thought she might cry. "Together, we will find out what happened to her. We'll trawl the length and breadth of the land. Leave no stone unturned."

Together?

There would be no together now.

The knowledge left her insides cramping in pain.

A tear slipped down her cheek.

As always, he was there to wipe it away.

"Once Blanche and Lord Rutherfield are in custody, I must return to London." Nora anticipated his response before continuing. His life had been nothing but complications. She would not be the cause of a conflict with his mother. "Mr Daventry mentioned a new client, and I am excited to take another case. I shall have little time to spare. No doubt you will be busy, too."

The lie left her nauseous.

She would rather feel the whip of her father's tongue, rather tolerate McGowan's drunken assault than let Sylvester believe she didn't care.

A muscle in his cheek twitched. "You mean to live your life without me?" He released her hand abruptly. "Forgive me. Foolishly, I assumed we would discuss any future plans once this was over. Now I understand your reason for insisting I make no promises."

The room seemed suddenly smaller. As if the walls were closing in. Restricting the flow of air. Squeezing the last breath from her lungs.

"That's not—"

"Clearly, what happened at the Musgrove hotel meant nothing to you," he snapped while she stood there, the truth burning a hole in her heart. "Had I known that to be true, I would have left you to your tea."

Hating that she'd hurt him, she appealed to his common sense. "Your mother will want you to take a wife, not pander to your mistress. You're the last Deville. You need to marry well and sire an heir."

"Ah, you use my mother and title as an excuse to reject me." He stepped closer. "Have I not told you on numerous occasions that I want more than a lover? Have I given any indication of being so weak-minded I would bow to society's rigorous expectations?"

Nora shuffled back.

His nearness left her weak.

"You led me to believe you cared for me," he said, forcing her to retreat until her back hit the wall and there was nowhere left to go. "For all the terrible things people have done to me, that is by far the cruellest of all."

Oh, she didn't want him to go through life believing a lie.

"I'm in love with you," she blurted, unable to contain the upsurge of emotion. "I love you more with each breath, with each passing day. I don't want you to suffer, Sylvester. We're from different worlds. What would people say if you took an enquiry agent for your wife? Your mother would not survive the embarrassment."

For three heartbeats, he remained silent, still.

"You're in love with me?" he said, a smile forming.

"Deeply so."

He reached out, tenderly stroking her cheek with the backs of his fingers. "I am so in love with you, I doubt I could ever explain it in words." He gestured to his scar. "This. This is the second-best thing that has ever happened to me."

Nora frowned. "You can't possibly mean that." Yet his scar was as much a part of him as his teasing grin.

"It's made me appreciate what's important. It led me to you." He touched his forehead to hers and inhaled deeply.

"Had I lost you, I would never have left this room. I truly would become the Horror of Highcliffe."

His mouth found hers, and he kissed away her fears.

"Marry me, Honora. Help me rid this house of lies and deceit. Let our love break the curse." He drew back, fixing her with his arresting gaze. "Say you'll consent to be my wife."

His wife!

"Sylvester, are you sure you—"

"I don't want to spend another day without you."

The thought of returning to London and him staying behind left her bereft. He held her heart in his hands. In spite of all the terrible things that had happened within Highcliffe's walls, it felt like home. He felt like home.

"Pinch me." Her laugh rang with pure happiness.

"Is that something you learned at the Pleasure Parlour?"

"No. Tell me this is real and not a wonderful dream."

He curled his fingers around her nape, breathed a whisper of a kiss against her lips. "Let me show you this is not a figment of your imagination. Let me make love to you again, Honora." He pressed his solid body to hers, moving against her in an arousing rhythm. "Let me pleasure you, make you come so hard you'll feel the depth of my love."

She swallowed, the muscles in her core clenching in anticipation. "Mr Paisley was right. I find I am easily swayed by your illicit proposals."

"Well, you will keep company with rakish men."

While he had the power to make her forget her woes, the notion of making love in the secret room dampened her ardour.

"Sylvester, I cannot writhe naked with you in your mother's bed, nor in Edith's truckle bed, for that matter."

He glanced briefly around the room. "We might improvise." A slow smile formed, one wicked and dangerously sinful. "How adventurous are you, Miss Wild?"

"How adventurous?" she said in a teasing purr. "Why, I

slept all night in a damp cave despite a steely rod digging into my hip. I risked death by drowning just to be close to a man I admire. I think that makes me bold and daring."

He shrugged out of his coat and threw it to the floor. "Then I see no reason to move from here. I can easily support your weight."

After her education at the Parlour, Nora understood his meaning. And she knew he had the strength to hold her. She could recall every toned muscle in his impressive physique.

"We'll keep our clothes on ... in case Mrs Egan appears." His voice was low and husky. "But if you're willing, I shall pleasure you first, love."

Willing? She was near mindless with love and lust.

She smoothed her hands up over his shoulders and pressed her open mouth to his. This would be a quick mating, she suspected. Indeed, he slipped his hand beneath her skirts, promised to worship her for hours in his Jacobean bed.

Lust quickened in her belly as his fingers moved slowly over her sex. She was so wet they slipped easily back and forth in a sensual rhythm. Hypnotised by every sweet caress, she opened for him—opened her legs wide so he could push his fingers inside her, opened her mouth to take every desperate drive of his tongue.

"Don't stop," she panted as his lips blazed a trail of fire down her neck. She took every deep thrust of his fingers.

The need for release built in a maddening crescendo.

"You're so hungry for me, love."

She had never been so ravenous. She needed his fingers rubbing her bud, his hard shaft pushing inside her. "Hurry. I need to feel you. All of you."

Like the brazen ladies at the Parlour, she reached down between their bodies and cupped the solid length of his arousal.

"Stroke me again," he growled, fumbling with the placket

of his breeches. He freed himself, hissed when she wrapped her fingers around his shaft.

Touching him proved addictive.

He was so hot and hard. She liked hearing his groans of pleasure, liked that his breath came quick, that he was so aroused yet continued playing her like a maestro.

Her knees buckled as she came apart, still gripping his throbbing erection, her pleasure rippling through her, him swallowing her keen cries.

Both mindless with desire, he gathered her skirts, lifted her clean off the floor and urged her to wrap her legs around his hips.

And then he was pushing inside her, thrusting upwards, letting her feel every inch of his love. "God, you feel so good."

His breath hitched when she kissed his scar. He stopped mid-thrust and looked her keenly in the eyes. The look of gratitude almost made her weep.

"I love you," she said, the truth of it thrumming in the air between them.

"Then say you'll be my wife. Marry me."

"Yes," she breathed as he filled her to the hilt. "There's nothing I want more in this world than to spend a lifetime with you."

CHAPTER 18

Exhausted from the long journey and their lovemaking, Sylvester gathered Honora into his arms and dozed for a few hours. When they woke, they talked about their plans for the future. How they might catch two smugglers and still live to tell the tale.

Sometime later, Mrs Egan arrived with a basket. The housekeeper glanced at Sylvester, at Honora's mussed hair and the small bed, and quickly distracted herself by discussing the dinner menu.

"There's venison stew, asparagus and waffle potatoes." Mrs Egan placed the basket and a bottle of claret on the small table. "I know how you love Cook's desserts, Miss Wild, so I managed to steal an extra portion of rhubarb tart. You'll need your strength for what lies ahead."

It was a desperate bid to make amends.

To enable them to creep into the tunnel unnoticed, Mrs Egan had called a meeting to distract the servants. And so Cook presumed the meal was for his mother and Edith.

"Did my mother drink claret nightly?" Sylvester teased.

"I managed to sneak into the wine seller and slip it into the basket, my lord," she said, trying to appease him.

"Of course you did. You're a master of deception, Mrs Egan."

The woman's cheeks flamed.

"Has Blanche returned?" Honora said quickly.

Sylvester smiled. The mere sound of her voice roused a merciless hunger. He wanted to climb Gabriel's Tower and shout from the rooftops, tell everyone Honora was to be his wife.

"Not yet. She usually rides to Hoath the night before a shipment. Happen she'll return in the morning, ready to whip us all into shape."

As Blanche knew nothing about the spare key, her actions struck him as odd. "If Blanche believes she has the only key to this room, how did you tend to my mother in her absence?"

Mrs Egan looked uncomfortable. "Normally, she leaves after I've served dinner. She's always back the next morning."

Honora offered a reason for the change. "Blanche left two days ago. That tells me she no longer cares if Lady Deville lives or dies. I doubt she has left England already, not when there are so many witnesses to her crimes."

"Then she plans to return before the shipment." Unease slithered down Sylvester's spine. He had never had so much to lose. "She plans to watch Highcliffe burn tomorrow night."

A heavy silence settled between them. No matter how prepared a man might be, one could never predict the workings of a wicked mind.

He touched Honora gently on the back, for no reason other than physical contact soothed his spirit. It was hard to remain objective when they had both suffered from a gross injustice. It was hard not to believe they would suffer again.

"You're certain none of the servants know we're hiding down here?" Sylvester attempted to confirm before his morbid mood consumed him. Was he a fool to trust his housekeeper? "Not even Whittle?"

The pair were close. He had seen them whispering in the shadows. On the walk back to Highcliffe, Mrs Egan confessed that the butler had forged Sylvester's signature to obtain the spare key from Pierre Badeau.

"No, my lord. But they think something is amiss. They were up with the cock's crow and thought Blanche had murdered me when they found my bed empty."

"What explanation did you give?"

"That you want to lease the cottage to a new tenant. That with us being short-staffed, I'd gone there early to make a list of repairs. It explained the mud on my hem."

Despite her reassurance, he offered a warning.

"You've been fooling me for a year, Mrs Egan. Yet I have no choice but to believe you now." Sylvester firmed his jaw. "Miss Wild's colleagues in London are aware of the situation. Be sure to choose the winning side."

In a move that shocked him, Mrs Egan dropped to her knees and grabbed his hands. "My lord, I swear on my mother's grave, I would never have let them hurt her ladyship."

"Yet you held her prisoner in this damn room."

"We're simple folk, my lord, forced to do the master's bidding. It was your brother who first made us load the chests and barrels. He paid us handsomely by way of a bribe. When the magistrate took over, he threatened us with the noose."

Rutherfield had taken leave of his senses. Sylvester couldn't wait to catch him in the act and witness his arrogance crumble beneath the weight of his guilt.

"You must have known the truth would come to light eventually," Honora said with a touch of sympathy.

Mrs Egan's teary gaze flitted between them. "They were going to kill her ladyship and Edith. Said they would let us live if we kept quiet. If we took the secret to the grave."

"Had you come to me and confessed, I would have devised a plan to trap Rutherfield." He had always known there was something unsavoury about the devil. Men often used arrogance to hide major flaws.

"With all due respect," Honora said, touching him gently on the arm, "your brother betrayed their trust. How were they to know they could trust you? Mrs Egan might have fled with the others. Those servants who stayed did so to protect your mother."

"Please, my lord!" Mrs Egan implored. "We were all so scared. Make an example of me, but I beg you to spare the others the noose."

The comment left Sylvester more hurt than angry. "The fact you think I would see you hang for my brother's mistake says you know nothing about my character."

"Catching the criminals is all that matters." Honora spoke with the calm voice of reason. "We must work together to rid ourselves of the threat." She helped Mrs Egan to her feet. "If we're to keep our wits, we must forget about the past."

Mrs Egan managed a weak smile.

"It will all be over soon." Honora clutched Sylvester's hand, held Mrs Egan's in a gesture of camaraderie. "But be prepared. Blanche and Lord Rutherfield will not give up without a fight."

No, they had killed once before.

They would have no qualms killing again.

The following morning, Mrs Egan failed to arrive with the breakfast basket. While Honora's stomach growled in frustration, apprehension clawed at Sylvester's shoulders.

"She will come," Honora reassured him when he started pacing.

He stopped and watched her attempt to pin her hair in the muted light. All negative feelings dispersed, leaving his heart full of love. Another part of his anatomy proved equally heavy, and he wondered if there was time to make love to her again.

Another hour passed.

Honora took a volume from the bookcase. "Read to me." She spoke in a soft, soothing voice, lay on the bed and beckoned him to squeeze in beside her.

While he prayed it was an invitation to do more than recite a few lines, he knew she meant to distract him. Despite his misgivings over Mrs Egan's loyalty, he could not deny himself the opportunity to draw her close, kiss her, love her.

Sylvester settled his head on the plump pillow, gathered Honora to his chest and read from the book of sonnets. Oddly, the first line of Robert Herrick's poem conveyed the change in him since meeting Honora.

"*How love came in I do not know,*" he read, stopping to brush his mouth against her hair, taking a moment to acknowledge love had crept slowly into his heart, catching him unawares.

The poet questioned if his love transcended the physical world, if it had always lived deep in his soul. That was Sylvester's interpretation. It did feel as though he had loved Honora long before they'd met.

Typically, it ended with the mention of a lover departing. It drew his mind back to the daunting task ahead. All that was at stake.

As if aware of his shifting moods, Mrs Egan arrived to restore his faith in humanity. She glanced over her shoulder before speaking in a hushed voice. "Blanche has returned. She's none the wiser."

"Does she think you're bringing food to Lady Deville?" Honora whispered, delving into the breakfast basket and snatching a slice of honey cake.

Mrs Egan nodded, though she became agitated. "I feared she would come down to speak to her ladyship, but she's ransacking the rooms, taking valuables small enough to store in her carpet bag. I'm powerless to stop her, my lord."

Sylvester silently cursed. Blanche had the Devil's cheek.

She'd likely stolen his mother's diamond parure.

"Possessions can be replaced," he assured his housekeeper. "At no point must you risk your life by attempting to confront her."

Honora swallowed a mouthful of cake. "Did she mention Lord Rutherfield? Did she give any indication when we might expect him? Surely, he will have to come through the tunnels to access the cave."

A pompous oaf like Rutherfield wouldn't climb into a rowboat.

"He comes on horseback under cover of darkness. We know to expect him long after sunset. The lugger anchors a mile out at sea while the rowboat enters the cave. They'll come ashore at high tide, between two and three in the morning."

They had a long wait ahead of them.

Anything could happen in the meantime.

"Should Blanche come down to speak to my mother, we will have no choice but to detain her." Blanche had killed a man. She was unhinged, unpredictable. "In which case, we will have to devise another way to get Rutherfield into the cave."

Keen to keep a watchful eye on Blanche, Mrs Egan left them to their meal. She returned to bring an early dinner basket and to inform Sylvester the maid had cleared his dressing room of cufflinks and stickpins.

Later, around midnight, she came to inform them Rutherfield had arrived. That Blanche was currently up to her usual antics with him in Sylvester's bedchamber.

"Rutherfield tups the damn maid in my bed?" Although Blanche wasn't actually his maid, just a murdering, thieving strumpet.

Mrs Egan's cheeks flamed. "Forgive me, my lord, but—"

"You're powerless to act. Do you bring other news?"

"I heard the magistrate say they should leave Highcliffe before the shipment arrives. That it's too great a risk to wait. But Blanche always uses her womanly wiles to subdue him, and the man is besotted."

Rutherfield and Felix had much in common.

Mrs Egan returned for the last time at two o'clock in the morning. "I've sighted the lugger off the coast, my lord," she whispered, rubbing the back of her neck though it did nothing to banish the tension. "And the magistrate came through the tunnels. He's waiting in the cave for the rowboat."

"Is Blanche with him?" Honora said. After hours spent trying to stay awake, the news gave her a boost of energy.

"No one has seen Blanche for an hour, ma'am. There's no telling if she went down to the cave or if she's signalling to the lugger from the clifftop."

Sylvester looked at Honora and attempted to keep his voice even. "We should take a pistol each and head to the cave." His earlier suggestion about going alone had fallen on deaf ears. And he would rather have Honora beside him than waiting in the hidden room like a sitting duck.

"Agreed." She turned to Mrs Egan. "Arm yourself with a weapon. Tell those servants you trust what has transpired. Assure them they will not be punished for Lord Rutherfield's crimes. Then keep to your room until this is all over."

Though her brow had more furrows than a farmer's field, Mrs Egan managed a smile. "Good luck, Miss Wild. May I say I've never met a woman so brave?"

Honora touched the housekeeper affectionately on the arm. "Love gives a coward courage, Mrs Egan. Be assured, we have love in abundance."

They couldn't risk bringing a lit lantern into the tunnels, which made carrying a loaded pistol all the more dangerous. With Honora gripping the back of Sylvester's coat, they padded slowly through the blackness until they reached the circular chamber.

Amidst the gloom, Sylvester stopped and listened to get his bearings. The erratic thumping of his heart, their heavy breathing and the gentle *whoosh* of the sea were the only discernible sounds.

Then, like the guiding hand of God, a rush of wind upon his face directed him to the tunnel leading down to the cave.

"Are you all right to continue?" he whispered.

"Yes. But if we die tonight, know that I love you."

Overcome with a sense of dread, Sylvester turned around. He found her mouth in the darkness, drank her kiss like a potent elixir, as if it might give him the strength to defeat their enemies.

"I love you," he whispered against her temple when they embraced. "All those dark days mean something now. Without them, I would never have found you."

"This is the beginning, not the end. We must remember that when we confront Blanche and Lord Rutherfield."

They kissed again, with a hunger that might never be sated, but the sudden stomp of footsteps and the glow of candlelight caught them by surprise. With nowhere to hide, Sylvester shielded Honora and aimed his pistol at the approaching figure.

"Stop, else I shall put a lead ball between your brows." He kept his voice low, menacing. "Raise your lantern. Let me see your damn face."

"Don't shoot, my lord. I beg you."

Sylvester recognised the voice instantly. "Whittle?"

"I came to the hidden room to find you, my lord. Mrs Egan told me of your plan. I hoped to be of some assistance." Whittle held the lantern aloft and stepped closer. "The magistrate said I'm to come to the cave to help unload the rowboat. Thomson is already down there."

Damnation!

Sylvester firmed his tone. "For your sake, I hope you speak the truth. Rest assured. If you're lying, I shall shoot you in the ballocks."

Whittle whimpered. "On my oath, I've been forced to help those devils. Follow me down to the cave, and I shall prove it, my lord."

Honora stepped aside. "Do you know what happens to the barrels once you have unloaded them?"

Sylvester hadn't considered how Rutherfield disposed of his ill-gotten gains. It was not as though he could make house calls asking if anyone wanted a cheap pound of tea.

"We wait for the other boat to arrive. We transfer the goods, and the magistrate takes payment."

The other boat?

"What does Rutherfield earn per shipment?" Sylvester estimated it could be no more than a hundred pounds. "Who is he selling the contraband to?"

Whittle glanced back over his shoulder. "I know he took receipt of a thousand pounds on the last run, my lord. The smugglers bring in stolen goods, too, expensive jewellery and silver from abroad. The items are sold in and around London." Whittle shrugged. "As to who the people are, I couldn't rightly say."

It all made more sense now. With the recent reduction on imports, Rutherfield wouldn't risk his neck for a pittance.

Sylvester fell silent while considering how Whittle might fit into their plan. "Proceed as normal. I shall count on your support when I reach the cave and need to overpower Rutherfield. Until then, let him believe you're on his side."

Whittle nodded. "We hoped they'd be gone soon, my lord. That we could free her ladyship and forget this terrible business. But Mrs Egan said they mean to kill us all."

"They'll be gone tonight. Arrested, drowned or shot, it makes no odds to me." He cast Honora a sidelong glance. "This will be a happy home." Though he couldn't quite shake a sense of foreboding. "Should anything untoward happen tonight, you're to give my mother a message."

Whittle nodded.

"Miss Wild is my betrothed. Should anything happen to me, she is to be cared for accordingly. Do you understand?"

Whittle seemed unsurprised by the request. "I shall inform her ladyship if it proves necessary, my lord." The butler straightened and said he should head to the cave before Rutherfield became suspicious.

Honora waited until Whittle had disappeared into the tunnel before throwing herself into Sylvester's arms. "Nothing will happen to you tonight," she whispered, yet fear choked her voice. "Tell me we'll prevail."

"We must prevail." Their lives depended upon it.

On that sobering note, he kissed Honora one last time. They waited for a few minutes before creeping along the dark tunnel. Sylvester reminded Honora she was to remain hidden in the passage and keep watch for Blanche.

"Good God, man, look!" Rutherfield's arrogant bark echoed from the depths of the cave. "Can you see the damn rowboat or not?"

"My eyes aren't what they used to be," Whittle said.

"Then you should have a care. A man might easily fall from these steps and break his neck. He might tumble into the water and drown."

"Or he might hang for no reason at all."

"Impudent fool." Rutherfield gave an angry growl. "And you will address me with the respect my position dictates."

"Yes, my lord," Whittle mocked.

Sylvester edged closer to the steps and peered into the cave. Lantern light and the glow from a lit brazier made it easier to navigate the stairs.

"Be careful," Honora whispered.

"I will, love."

Whittle happened to glance up as Sylvester appeared from the tunnel, and set about distracting Rutherfield.

"Is that the rowboat, my lord?" Whittle pointed through the cave mouth to the never-ending stretch of sea. "There, in the distance. I know they don't light the lamps, but I'm sure I saw a spark."

While Rutherfield peered out into the night, Sylvester clung to the wall and descended another five steps.

"Swing your damn lantern," Rutherfield told Thomson.

The footman obeyed. The men kept their gazes seaward, waiting for the signal. It came. A quick spark amid the blackness. Then another.

"There! Did you see it? A flash!" Rutherfield sounded panicked and pleased. He pulled his watch and inspected the time. "They're late. They should be unloading now."

"What if a Navy cutter has apprehended the lugger?" Whittle said. "What if the Customs officers have captured the smugglers, and it's a trap? What—"

"Enough!" Agitated to the point his heart might give out, Rutherfield dragged his hand through his hair. "Everything will go according to plan. This is the last shipment. Then we can forget about the smugglers and live the rest of our days in peace."

"One imagines you won't have many days left," Sylvester said, stepping off the stairs. He cocked his pistol and aimed it at Rutherfield. "One imagines you'll swing from the scaffold with your smuggling friends before the month is out."

Wide-eyed, Rutherfield swung around. His mouth gaped open, and it took him a few seconds to recover. Then he leant on his aristocratic crutch and spoke with haughty arrogance.

"Must you persist in being a thorn in my side, Deville? Surely, even a man with your poor intellect can assess the situation and see I'm here in a professional capacity. Of course, when I arrest you, you will need to explain why you've been taking money from smugglers and letting them use your cave."

Sylvester kept control of his temper.

The peer was a liar and as crooked as a lover's sixpence.

"Where is Blanche?" Sylvester glanced about the cave. "Mrs Egan said she cleared the house of valuables and fled into the night."

Rutherfield's chin quivered. "Why should I care about the fate of your maid? Find her yourself. I am in the process of dealing with a more serious crime."

The magistrate would protest his innocence until he dropped through the trap door and his neck snapped in two.

"How strange. Blanche left a letter naming you the one who pushed Felix off the cliff. She named you the ringleader of the smuggling operation. As the person who kept my mother prisoner in a secret room for more than a year."

Rutherfield froze. The sea breeze blew a lock of hair over his brow, but he remained statue-still.

"No doubt you thought my mother was still locked in her dank cell." It wasn't so dank. Sylvester had loved every minute spent in there. "By now she's in London, dining with Peel, telling him how Lydia Moore corrupted her son and the local magistrate. How you met at the Pleasure Parlour during your frequent visits to town."

Rutherfield managed a sneer. "You tell a good story, Deville. I shall give you that. But I shall tell Peel your brother was in cahoots with the maid. That I have been conducting a secret investigation, trying to catch Blanche and her cronies in the act." He gestured to Thomson and Whittle though they hardly looked like professional thieves.

"Then you will have to murder us all, *my lord*," Whittle

said, every syllable dripping with disdain. "Everyone in this house will testify against you."

The magistrate looked like he might whip Whittle with his tongue, but then Thomson cried, "The rowboat is here!"

A small boat laden with wooden chests and barrels appeared from around the bay. Two men pulled on the oars while one sat nestled amid the cargo.

Sylvester considered his predicament. The smugglers were undoubtedly armed. If they came ashore, he would be outnumbered. Rutherfield was neck-deep in the mire and would murder Sylvester before being apprehended.

Forced to make a quick decision, Sylvester kept his pistol trained on Rutherfield and shouted to the smugglers, "Turn around! The Customs officers are here! It's a trap! Leave now!"

Rutherfield firmed his jaw. He shifted on the spot, clearly torn between calling his friends back and maintaining his ridiculous charade.

The smugglers stopped rowing. One stood, the vessel rocking beneath him while he tried to discern what was happening in the cave.

Whittle took up the gauntlet, waving his hand and shaking his lantern, pointing and shouting for the devils to leave.

The rogues suddenly turned in their seats. In a blind panic, they took to rowing in the opposite direction.

Rutherfield's breathing quickened.

He had no hope of making an escape.

"One would think a man of your intellect would have armed himself with a pistol," Sylvester mocked. "As God is my witness, you'll hang for this."

"Not necessarily." The magistrate stripped off his coat and placed it to the ground as if he meant to fight. "Sometimes one has to improvise," he said, hurling something in Sylvester's direction.

The stone hit Sylvester's scarred cheek. The shock knocked him backwards, leaving him no choice but to drop the pistol and use his hands to break his fall.

He expected Rutherfield to scramble about the ground, keen to be the first to retrieve the weapon. But the conceited fool jumped from the rocks and plunged into the sea.

"Stone the crows!" Whittle cried. "He's sure to drown!"

Rutherfield heaved a breath and thrashed about as the cold penetrated every muscle. He took a few weak strokes, and managed to swim fifty yards towards the rowboat, stopping to tread water, wave and shout at his comrades.

The men in the boat rowed towards the lugger waiting about a mile out at sea. Then two Navy cutters came into view, their vast white sails a symbol of hope on the horizon, and a speedy chase ensued.

Smaller boats appeared from the bay, surrounding the rowboat. Shots rang out, sparks of orange in the darkness.

Sylvester saw Rutherfield duck below the surface, attempting to avoid detection. He emerged from the inky depths once, though floundered as the flurry of vessels displaced the water, and he was suddenly swamped by a wave.

Rutherfield did not surface again.

"Well, the magistrate must answer to his maker now," Whittle said, his mood sad, resigned. "No doubt we'll be meeting him soon, Thomson. The Customs officers will want to take us into custody."

"I shall make sure they know you were protecting my mother. That you were forced to assist Rutherfield in his crimes." Sylvester refused to let his staff pay for the magistrate's greed.

Whittle sighed. "Blanche will lie and take us all to the scaffold. That's if she's not ten miles from here by now."

Sylvester hoped that wasn't the case.

He did not want to spend his life looking over his shoulder.

He turned to the steep flight of steps. If Honora had seen Rutherfield take to the water, why had she not made an appearance?

"Honora!" he called but received no reply.

When she failed to answer for the third time, a jittery feeling in his stomach forced him to mount the stairs. By the time he burst into the tunnel, his heart was in his throat.

And for good reason.

The tunnel was empty.

CHAPTER 19

The moment Lord Rutherfield jumped from the rocks into the sea, and Nora knew Sylvester was safe, her thoughts had turned to Blanche.

Why had she not come down to the cave?

Would she not wish to inspect the contraband?

Two answers presented themselves. One left her frustrated enough to creep back through the dark tunnels, to climb the worn steps and enter the house. If Blanche had fled Highcliffe, Nora would track her down. Make her pay for all the terrible things she had done. It was the only way to bring Sylvester lasting peace.

The other answer proved terrifying. So terrifying, Nora kept her pistol raised as she moved stealthily through the servants' corridor.

What if Blanche had prepared a bonfire?

What if the magistrate had planned to leave the cave by boat, and it was Blanche's job to destroy the evidence of their crimes?

But where on earth was she?

Nora stopped outside Mrs Egan's private sitting room and

knocked lightly on the door. It took the housekeeper some time to answer.

"Miss Wild!" she said in a stunned whisper. "We're all hiding in here as you instructed." She peered through the narrow gap as if Highcliffe's toxic air might escape into the room and choke them.

"Have you seen Blanche? She's not in the cave."

"She might be in the old armoury. The magistrate said the daggers on the wall date back to the fourteenth century. That she should pack them into her carpet bag for they would sell for a hefty price across the water."

Rutherfield's greed knew no bounds. Better was a poor man who walked in his integrity, her father often preached. While Nora hated thinking about his biblical quotes, that one seemed rather apt.

"You don't need to worry about the magistrate anymore." Nora doubted he would survive a few minutes in the depths of a volatile sea. "Close the door and keep it locked."

Mrs Egan frowned. "Are you alone?"

"Don't worry about me, Mrs Egan. Lock the door."

Nora didn't wait for her response. She crept along the dimly lit corridor and climbed the stone stairs to the ground floor. The door creaked as she entered the hall. Thankfully, it was deserted.

Remembering the route they had taken the night of the tour, she clung to the shadows and slipped through the passage to the armoury. A shuffling noise reached her ears, along with the patter of footsteps.

She peered into the armoury. A pale stream of moonlight caught the steel swords lining the wall opposite the window. The fan of daggers on the circular wooden shield said Blanche hadn't stolen them yet.

Where was she?

The door leading to the watchtower banged in the wind.

Sylvester always kept it locked. The battlements had been poorly repaired many years ago. Crumbling mortar made the stone walls unstable. No one was allowed to go up there.

And yet someone had.

It was obvious who.

Nora took a deep breath and opened the door carefully. Keeping her back pressed to the wall, she climbed the circular staircase. By the time she reached the top, she'd convinced herself Blanche was lurking in the darkness. Indeed, she saw the devious maid leaning against the battlements, staring out to sea, her golden hair blowing in the wind.

"Blanche? What are you doing out here?" Nora hid the pistol behind her back and took to play-acting to buy herself time. "Are you well? Mrs Egan couldn't find you."

Blanche struggled to tear her gaze away from the array of rowboats and ships involved in a sea battle some distance from the shore. She flinched at the sound of gunfire. When she did turn around, she did so slowly.

"Miss Wild? I thought you were in London," she said in a nervous tone that was as fake as her name. She no longer wore her maid's garb but a blue dress pretty enough to entice any man at the Parlour. "I heard gunfire and feared we were at war."

Nora glanced at Blanche's hands, relieved to see no sign of a weapon. "We returned early because we found Mr Gifford. The man who sold the book of Greek tales."

It was a lie, but Blanche had to know the man. How else had he come by the tome? Why else would she write the note directing Sylvester to Monroe's bookshop?

Blanche inhaled a sharp breath. "Mr Gifford? What did he say?"

She made no mention of the book. Did not praise them for their excellent work or ask how they had found the man.

"He confessed to being part of a smuggling operation." All

things considered, it was a logical assumption, and Nora was tired of playing games. "The Customs officers are out in force tonight. Mr Gifford turned traitor and named his accomplices."

Who *had* alerted the Customs officers?

Was it a coincidence? Had Mr Daventry received Mr Bower's letter and spent the last two days mounting an attack?

Blanche remained silent.

"Lord Rutherfield had his suspicions. Lord Deville found the magistrate waiting in the cave." The Almighty would likely strike Nora down for all the lies she'd told today. "They arrested the smugglers when they came ashore."

Blanche struggled to maintain her angelic facade. Her throat worked tirelessly as the wicked woman hiding beneath made her first appearance.

"You really are a pathetic creature, Miss Wild." Blanche wrinkled her nose in disdain. "I've seen the way you look at Deville. You fool yourself into thinking men like intelligent women. It's rather pitiful, truth be told."

"You're fooling yourself if you think all men are like the degenerates you entertained at the Pleasure Parlour."

Blanche blinked, evidently shocked Nora knew so much. "Men need women to suck away their petty fears," she said as if she had suppressed her crude nature for far too long. "Men are too cowardly to punish the world for their misgivings. Hence why they make women spread their legs and take a pounding."

Having spent a month at the Parlour, Nora wasn't shocked or offended by the lewd terms. "When Minette spoke of you, she described a woman overshadowed by her wicked sister. And yet you're every bit as evil. You killed Felix Deville because he refused to play your games."

Blanche's face twisted with contempt. "I killed a coward. Trust me. The world is a better place without him."

"And what of the servants? What of Sylvester Deville? You planned to kill us all and sail away into the night with your lover."

Blanche's eyes widened. "Gifford told you we were lovers?"

"Gifford? I speak of the magistrate."

Blanche clutched her belly and laughed. "Rutherfield? A man so weak he would sell his soul for a quick tupping? I'll grant you, none of this would have been possible without him. But I used him, as he did me when I worked at the Parlour."

A tense silence ensued.

Blanche glanced over her shoulder. She saw the lugger surrounded, captured, and knew her only option now was to flee.

"Step aside, Miss Wild. No doubt you've had a miserable life, too, else you wouldn't be working as an agent, and you certainly wouldn't know Minette."

Nora raised her pistol and cocked the hammer. "You know I must take you into custody. You must pay the price for your crimes."

Blanche gestured for Nora to lower the weapon. "You've been kind to me. I have no desire to hurt you, and so you will let me leave."

Nora stared, lost in a memory.

The Reverend Wild had shown a slither of kindness on occasion. Only to chain her to the bedpost the second she lowered her guard. He said there was no worse evil than a bad woman. Indeed, Blanche would likely push Nora over the battlements when she turned her back.

"We are alike in one way." Nora kept a defensive stance, kept her voice firm as she had been taught to do. "We're both prepared to fight for what we want, what we believe."

Blanche laughed. "You won't shoot me, Miss Wild. You

haven't the heart for murder. Put the weapon down and let me pass."

No, Nora couldn't pull the trigger even if provoked. "My intention would be to maim, not murder." Lies were often the first form of self-defence. "You'll come with me, else I shall be forced to shoot you in the leg and drag you down the stairs."

Blanche's confidence faltered.

Fear danced briefly in her eyes.

When she held out her arms, palms up, as if surrendering to the shackles, Nora knew she planned to escape.

Blanche came two steps closer and offered her wrists again.

It was a ploy. A distraction.

She released a beast of a growl and darted forward.

In the panic, Nora did fire, nicking the woman's arm when she had only meant to frighten her into surrendering. Blanche's scream rent the night air, while Nora was left wrestling with her conscience.

But the injury only fuelled Blanche's determination to flee. She charged at Nora, taking them both down to the flagstones.

The pistol went skittering across the floor.

Each grappled for supremacy.

Blanche tried to reach for the weapon, perhaps intending to use it as a club. "I'd rather die here than hang!"

"I mean to hand you to the authorities alive!" Nora grabbed Blanche's arm, blood coating her fingers as she squeezed the wound.

"Argh!"

Somehow, they ended up on their feet.

Blanche hurled Nora into the solid battlement wall. The stones moved. The mortar crumbled. The tower shook beneath them, and two merlons crashed to the ground below.

"We will both fall to our deaths!" Nora cried, struggling to escape Blanche's hold of her arm, but the woman was like a demon possessed.

The patter of hurried footsteps brought Mrs Egan.

The housekeeper's eyes widened at the sight of the missing merlons. Wielding a rolling pin, she hurried forward, grabbed Blanche's dress and yanked her back.

"You've made our lives a misery," Mrs Egan snarled, sounding as mean and as menacing as when Nora first arrived. "We intend to make you suffer."

The thud of booted footsteps brought Sylvester. Blood trickled from a cut on his cheek. He gaped at the sight of the damaged battlement and quickly beckoned her forward.

"Honora, step away from the edge. Quickly." Sylvester reached out as if it were his life at stake. "All the stones are unstable. One push, and they'll topple."

Nora took a steady step forward, but Blanche broke free of Mrs Egan's grasp and captured her wrist.

"Leave, else I shall drag your precious Miss Wild over the edge with me." Blanche shuffled backwards, gripping the back of Nora's dress with her other hand.

"Please! Don't!" Sylvester stood rigid, his face ghostly pale. "Doubtless, my brother deserved his fate. Miss Wild has done nothing to warrant such cruelty."

"Perhaps I enjoy stealing from the nobility. Call it vengeance for the nabob who stole my virginity all those years ago."

Like Melisandre, Blanche had found an outlet for her hatred.

Nora dared to look over the edge into the never-ending darkness. No one could survive the fall. "We've all lost something, Blanche. We've all suffered. Lord Deville must bear a permanent scar for his brother's mistakes."

Blanche gave a mocking snort. "If I wore a scar for every day I've suffered, it would make for a hideous sight." She glanced out at the Navy ships waging war on the smugglers.

"Perhaps in the next life I might be born a man, and then I shall seek vengeance."

From her resigned tone, it was evident she meant to jump.

Sylvester thought so, too. "If you want to play the martyr, then release Miss Wild." He didn't wait for a response, but dashed forward, grabbed Honora's other wrist and refused to let go.

A tug of war ensued.

Another stone fell from the battlements.

Blanche laughed, the sound like a crazed cackle. "Perhaps the tower will collapse, and we'll all die tonight."

Nora's life hung in the balance. Like the night at the Parlour when she fought with McGowan, she had a choice to make. Save herself, or let Blanche hurl them both over the edge.

Choosing to live, Nora stamped hard on Blanche's foot.

"Argh!" Blanche cried for the umpteenth time tonight. She relinquished her grip as she lost her footing.

Sylvester pulled Nora to safety as more loose stones tumbled from the battlements.

Blanche realised she was about to plummet two hundred feet and accepted her fate with calm serenity. She closed her eyes and opened her arms. Then she fell back gracefully, plunging to her doom.

Sylvester entered the drawing room to find Honora seated on the sofa with Myrtle, reassuring the weeping maid all would be well. Most women would have taken to their beds having suffered such an ordeal. But the house was in chaos. His staff had flown into a state of panic when they learned the Customs officers had entered the cave.

Honora cast him a loving smile when he came to warm his

hands by the fire. He needed to hold her, feel the heat of her body, kiss her, bask in the knowledge they had both survived.

Clearly bound by the same intense need, she dismissed Myrtle. "Try to get a few hours' sleep. It will be dawn soon. No doubt we will have much to concern ourselves with tomorrow."

"Yes, ma'am." Myrtle dabbed tears from her eyes. She thanked Honora and dipped a curtsy as she passed Sylvester.

Honora was on her feet and in his arms as soon as Myrtle closed the door. "I have never been as scared as I was tonight."

Sylvester stroked her hair from her face to calm his racing pulse. When he thought of Blanche nearly dragging Honora over the battlements, he could barely catch his breath.

"What possessed you to climb the tower on your own? Blanche was as crazed as the damn curate. You might have been killed."

"Let's not worry about what might have been. We're alive. That's all that matters." She came up on her toes and kissed him open-mouthed. "Fate has other plans for us, wonderful plans."

"Fate is currently taking command of the situation in the cave." When she looked bemused, he added. "Daventry is with Bower and the Customs officers. They've brought the smugglers ashore and bound them in chains."

Her eyes widened. "Mr Daventry has come to Highcliffe?"

"After receiving Bower's letter, he visited Peel's office and the Custom House. He hasn't slept for two nights while organising the capture of the smugglers." Sylvester smiled to himself. Daventry still managed to look wide awake and immaculate. "He will be up to see you shortly. He's staying here tonight."

Disappointment swept over her face.

He, too, had hoped to spend an intimate few hours alone.

"Have you told him our good news?" she said, smoothing

her hands over his chest and kissing him so deeply, he contemplated barricading the door.

"He was preoccupied. We can tell him together."

They decided not to take advantage of the moment. While Sylvester longed to demonstrate how much he loved the woman who would be his wife, he would not risk Daventry catching them in a clinch.

Indeed, they were sitting in opposite chairs when Daventry strode into the drawing room. "I'll not refuse a stiff drink, Deville."

The request was the only indication Daventry had found the last few hours taxing. Sylvester invited him to sit on the sofa, then moved to fill a crystal goblet with brandy.

"Are the Customs officers still in the cave?" Sylvester said, offering Daventry the glass. "I expect they will want to take statements from the servants. Will want to hear from my mother."

Daventry downed a mouthful of liquor and hissed to cool the burn. "I hope you have no objection, but I told your coachman to travel to Canterbury at dawn to fetch her ladyship and Edith. Mr Heyburn is in charge of the operation and needs a complete account of all that occurred here."

"He does know the servants were forced to act as they did?" Honora said, her concern for his staff evident. "Lord Rutherfield threatened to hang them all as accomplices if they failed to assist him."

Daventry bemoaned the scourge of dishonest men. "When I informed Peel of Rutherfield's duplicity, he assured me the servants have nothing to fear. Providing none of them profited from the venture."

"They were forced to take money." Sylvester could hardly believe he was defending the people he had been ready to dismiss.

"As long as they can repay the Treasury, there should be no

issue." Daventry glanced at Sylvester over the rim of his glass. "I'm sure you will settle any debt on their behalf."

Mrs Egan appeared and asked if they required refreshment or a light repast, though Sylvester sensed it was an excuse for her to assess the situation.

They all declined her offer.

"Go to bed, Mrs Egan," Honora said, taking charge. "We can fend for ourselves if need be. We don't expect the staff to rise with the lark. Household chores can wait."

Like a bloodhound sniffing a scent, Daventry waited for Mrs Egan to leave before saying, "You sound like the mistress of the house, Miss Wild. Strange that you never thought to consult Deville."

Honora's cheeks flushed when she realised her mistake.

"We're to be married," Sylvester said, coming to her aid. "As my betrothed, she can do what she pleases. And after all that's happened here, the staff regard her with the utmost respect."

A glimmer of a smile played on Daventry's lips. "Then permit me to offer my sincere felicitations. And your mother approves?"

Sylvester shrugged. "I'm sure she will when we tell her. What's not to love about Miss Wild?"

"Indeed. I assume you're leaving the Order, Miss Wild. Highcliffe is a fair distance from London."

"I find I rather like living by the sea, sir."

"You and Deville have that in common."

"Yes, besides other things." Honora glanced at Sylvester. "Sir, we've come to the conclusion you're the most successful matchmaker in London." Honora gave a light laugh. "When I marry Lord Deville, all of your protégés will have wed their clients."

"Not quite." Daventry failed to hide a secretive smirk.

"You've hired another agent? Oh, Miss Trimble will be delighted." Honora pressed her hand to her heart. "I never mentioned it before, sir, but she's most distraught about losing her position. When I returned to Howland Street before our meeting the other day, I saw her shoving clothes into a valise. When I questioned her, she said one must be prepared for every eventuality."

"Rest assured. Miss Trimble's welfare is my priority." Daventry tossed back the rest of his brandy, then considered Honora. "It's a shame I'm losing you, Miss Wild. Together, you and Deville have caught one of the largest smuggling gangs south of the Thames."

Looking baffled, Honora shook her head. "We assumed Lord Rutherfield was involved in a small, low-key operation."

"Rutherfield was nothing more than Lydia Moore's lackey. One of Monroe's employees provided the clue to catching the man behind it all. He remembered seeing Gifford enter the Craven coffeehouse opposite the bookshop, which presented another line of enquiry."

"But we asked Monroe if his employees had seen anything pertinent," she said defensively. "He said no."

"Cole can be quite persuasive. The lad seemed nervous, and so Cole followed him home. The lad didn't tell Monroe because he thought Gifford might return to set fire to the bookshop. Thankfully, the waiter at the Craven knew Gifford."

Sylvester sat forward. "Gifford used his real name?"

"Apparently, it carries some weight in those parts, which is how Cole found he ran a smuggling operation. The address he gave to Monroe belonged to a printer who used to forge documents for Gifford before he died."

"So, Mr Gifford is head of the smuggling gang," Honora said. "Blanche suggested she was Gifford's lover, so it does make sense."

Daventry explained how they followed Gifford's gang to the docks and watched them board a vessel. They trailed them to the Thames Estuary, down past the Isle of Sheppey to Highcliffe.

"It sounds like a well-planned operation." Sylvester wondered at the extent of Felix's involvement. Like Rutherfield, had he been trying to appease a selfish woman?

He glanced at Honora, aware he was the luckiest man alive. There wasn't a selfish bone in her body. She was not obsessed with power and wealth. If he asked, she would live with him in the ramshackle cottage for the rest of her days.

Daventry placed his empty glass on the side table. "Leaving Bower behind was exactly the right decision, Miss Wild. I'm not sure I would have arrived here in time had his letter missed the mail coach." He glanced at the mantel clock. "Well, we should get some sleep. They're moving the smugglers to a gaol in Canterbury within the hour. Heyburn will return later to conduct the interviews."

They spoke about the arrest of Gifford's gang, and Daventry agreed Minette might know something of the connection between Lydia Moore and the smuggler.

Perhaps it was the mention of Canterbury and memories of Mr Paisley that made Honora ask, "Have you received news from Chipping Norton?"

"Sadly, no. As you can imagine, I've been occupied with other matters these last two days. But I'll visit Canterbury en route to London and find this Paisley fellow myself."

Honora glanced at Sylvester and smiled with relief.

Daventry stood. "I should visit the cave before retiring." He cast an appraising glance around the drawing room. "I was told your brother emptied the house of all valuables. While you've done an excellent job of furnishing this room, Deville, what of the large empty space by the window?"

Having visited Highcliffe previously, Daventry knew what Sylvester planned to put there. "Now that I have kept my end of the bargain and taken excellent care of your agent, does that mean I might purchase my great-grandmother's harp-sichord?"

Daventry looked at Honora and gave a mischievous wink. "As a master matchmaker, it was always my intention to give it to you as a wedding gift."

CHAPTER 20

"Mr Heyburn is a rather stern fellow. I'm surprised he didn't strap me to the rack and turn the crank." Sylvester's mother flopped onto the damask sofa and pressed her lace handkerchief to her brow. "I gave him the written statement, but he insisted I repeat the story three times." Her light laugh was music to his ears. "I sounded like Lady Hanbury's parrot. Do you remember the bird revealed all her husband's secrets?"

Fond memories of a summer spent in Cornwall entered his mind. The summer before his mother made the damning revelation and Sylvester's world took a downward tumble.

He nodded. "I believe they got rid of the bird when it squawked, 'his lordship kisses the footman'."

"Yes, it was a dreadful affair."

A brief silence ensued.

Sylvester glanced out of the drawing room window with a sense of longing. The sun was shining for the first time in months. There wasn't a storm cloud in sight. Honora had taken a picnic down to the beach, and Sylvester was keen to join her once he had informed his mother of his plans to marry.

"Did Heyburn say he was leaving this afternoon?"

"No." His mother sighed. "Doubtless, he will want me to answer more questions. When defrauding the Government of revenue, no allowances are made for one's age or title."

"Heyburn must be certain of the facts, Mother. He found it hard to believe I didn't know you were alive."

A look of guilt passed over her pale face. "Sylvester, Blanche killed your brother. How could I be sure she wouldn't kill you? One loses all sense of perspective when living in a dungeon."

"I know. I was merely explaining Heyburn's motive for being thorough." Again, he glanced at the blue sky, relishing the prospect of spending an afternoon lost in Honora's warm embrace. "Daventry assured me Heyburn and his men will return to London tonight."

He needed to venture to London, too.

He would not wait for the banns to marry Honora.

"Sylvester, you seem preoccupied, rather tense." She patted the seat next to her. "Sit down. I wish to talk to you while we have a quiet moment to ourselves."

He obliged, keen to seize the opportunity to reveal his own news. "There's something important I must tell you first."

His mother reached for his hand and clasped it tightly. "You can tell me anything, but first, let me convey my sincere apologies. I have had a lot of time to reflect. I know my foolish mistake hurt you deeply."

Hurt him? It had crushed his soul.

Made him an outcast in his own home.

"It hurt more than you will ever know." The moment demanded the truth. "And yet now that I look back from a state of complete bliss, I find the thought no longer pains me as it once did."

"You're in love with Miss Wild," she stated, keeping a reassuring grip of his hand. "It's plain to see."

"I'm so in love with her, I have asked her to be my wife." Even as he said the words, a warm glow filled his chest.

"One assumes she said yes. Mrs Egan said we would all be doomed had you not hired her to help solve the mystery. When Miss Wild sang your praises this morning, it was evident she admires you, too."

"Yes, we're to marry."

"Wonderful." She tapped his hand affectionately. "There is nothing more important in this world than love. I have learnt that the hard way and hurt those I love in the process."

Sylvester had to ask the question that mattered most. "We've spoken of this before, but I ask again. Am I the legitimate son of Frederick Deville? I must know. Should the truth ever come to light, it would affect my children's marriage prospects."

With a heart-wrenching sigh, his mother cupped his marred cheek. "You are the true heir to Highcliffe. You are a Deville, and I was wrong to suggest otherwise. Marry Miss Wild, sire sons and daughters who will take your legacy and do something worthwhile. Never think of it again."

Relief rippled through him. He raised his mother's hand to his lips and brushed a kiss to her knuckles. "And what of you? Will you remain here?"

She smiled. "As to that, I hope you understand but I am to marry Sir George. We have loved each other for a long time. I must embrace this second chance, must seize the day."

The news did not come as a complete surprise.

"You must follow your heart, for I intend to follow mine." He released her and stood. "Forgive me, but I have a pressing engagement on the beach."

She smiled. "Then you should not keep Miss Wild waiting."

Sylvester made to leave but turned. "If I could ask one thing of you, it's that you're kind to Honora." He raised a hand when she attempted to interrupt. "I know you will be, but I would be lapse in my duty to her if I did not consider all her emotional needs."

"You're an honourable man, Sylvester. Which is just as well, as you need to rid this family of your brother's shame."

His mother's comment stayed with him as he ambled through the herb garden and made his way to the clifftop. For the first time in his life, his heart brimmed with purpose.

Indeed, he stopped at the place where he first captured Honora in his arms, remembering how the world had suddenly felt right. Daring to step closer to the edge, he noticed her on the beach, sitting on a plaid blanket. She was more engrossed in the contents of the basket than the pages of her book.

God, he loved her with every breath.

Perhaps he would have watched her for a few minutes had a man not come striding along the beach in her direction. Sylvester's thundering heart almost burst from his chest when he realised it was that devil Paisley.

The crazed curate walked with purpose.

Like a man on a mission to rid the world of sin.

Honora reached into the basket and retrieved another piece of Cook's asparagus tart. It really was the most delicious thing she had ever tasted. She held a lock of hair off her face, took a bite, and gazed out over a calm sea.

The sudden break in the weather reflected her current state of mind. The case was solved, the smugglers captured. Lord Rutherfield and Blanche would trouble them no more. Soon, Mr Heyburn would return to London and their problems would be a distant memory.

Nora's stomach performed a little flip when she thought about marrying Sylvester. In her wildest dreams, she never imagined she could love a man so deeply. Now she owed Mr Daventry another debt, one she definitely could not repay.

Hearing the crunch of shingle on the deserted beach, she experienced another flutter as she waited for Sylvester to appear. But then she heard someone call her name and realised it wasn't the velvet-edged voice she knew.

Nora turned and saw a man approaching. She recognised Mr Paisley when he stumbled on the shingle, lost his hat and chased it along the beach.

"Miss Wild!" Mr Paisley waved.

Heaven help her!

Nora jumped to her feet, knocking over the basket. She scanned the vicinity, searching for any sign of her father. God forbid he should decide to make the trip from Chipping Norton. But it was a hundred and sixty miles each way. Nigh on impossible for the Reverend Wild to have received a letter and made the journey.

Feeling a little more at ease, Nora straightened. "Mr Paisley. We really should stop meeting like this. Are you taking a tour of the area?"

"Miss Wild." He heaved to catch his breath. "I came to call at the house but saw you heading along the path down to the beach."

Nora raised her chin. "Oh! Then I hope you've come to offer an apology for your appalling behaviour in Canterbury."

Mr Paisley's frown said there would be another scuffle. "On the contrary, I came to rescue you. To explain the situation to Lord Deville. One hopes to appeal to the gentleman's good sense. Make him see that you're ill, and he should not place any value on any promises you've made."

Nora took a step back. "It sounds like you have come to rescue Lord Deville from the clutches of a harlot."

Mr Paisley reached out to her, and she shrugged her arm away. "Miss Wild, please understand. In his absence, I must act in your father's stead. As a Christian man, I feel compelled to ask his lordship to assist in returning you to Chipping Norton."

In an attempt to keep calm, to buy herself time, she pulled another lie from her arsenal and fired it at Mr Paisley.

"As a Christian man, you can rest assured. I married Lord Deville yesterday by special licence. You may address me as Lady Deville or your ladyship. If you visit the house, my husband will confirm my status."

Mr Paisley's eyes widened, but he failed to reply.

"Please inform my father of my good fortune," Nora continued, feeling rather empowered. "Though after the deplorable lies he has told about me, my husband intends to appeal to the Archbishop and have my father removed as vicar of Chipping Norton."

Mr Paisley remained dumbfounded.

"Dr Chatham doesn't exist," she continued, resisting the urge to prod the man's chest. "He is a figment of my father's imagination. There is no hospital for the weak-minded. I ran away because my father is a brute and a bully."

The curate struggled to absorb the information. He scratched his temple. "But I have seen a letter written by Dr Chatham. I mean, I wasn't meant to see it and only caught a glimpse. But he mentioned his patient's illness and requested the yearly fee of forty pounds."

It was Nora's turn to stare in bewilderment. "I assure you, the letter does not relate to me. Perhaps it had something to do with a parishioner. Perhaps my father—" She stopped abruptly as another thought entered her mind. One exciting and terrifying in equal measure. "Did you happen to note the person's name?"

"Yes!" Mr Paisley threw his hands in the air. "That is what I am trying to explain. The letter spoke of a Miss Wild, patient of Dr Chatham in Gloucester. Though when I saw you in Canterbury, I thought I had made a mistake."

Nora scoured her mind to find a rational explanation, but

Sylvester came charging across the shingles. He grabbed Mr Paisley by his floppy cravat and hauled the curate two feet in the air.

"How dare you come to my home and threaten—"

"I explained we married yesterday," Nora interjected.

"Lay a hand on my wife, and it will be the last thing you do."

Legs flailing, Mr Paisley couldn't speak for choking.

"Release him, Sylvester! Mr Paisley admits he made a mistake. He promises to return to Canterbury." She looked at the curate. "I suggest you remain in Canterbury and seek a new position."

Sylvester released Mr Paisley, though grabbed the man by the scruff of his collar when he dropped to his knees. "You're leaving, Paisley. We never wish to lay eyes on you again. Is that understood?"

"My lord, if you—"

"Is that understood?" Sylvester dragged the fellow across the beach while Nora quickly gathered the blanket and basket. Indeed, he hauled Mr Paisley up the steep bank and along the clifftop and did not release him until they reached the stables.

"Sykes!"

The coachman looked up from inspecting the front wheel of Sylvester's carriage. "Aye, milord?"

"Ferry Paisley to Canterbury." Sylvester firmed his jaw and glared at the curate. "Should you cause any problems en route, I shall speak to the Archbishop and see your future prospects reduced to dust."

In the blink of an eye, the curate was bundled away to Canterbury.

Nora explained all that occurred on the beach. "Perhaps my father planned to send me to Dr Chatham's hospital." She clutched her hand to her throat as she considered an alternative fate. "Thank heavens I ran away when I did."

"Perhaps Paisley made a mistake." Sylvester wrapped his arm around her waist and pulled her close. "What say we take a trip, see if this Dr Chatham fellow even exists? Let's see if we can discover what wicked fate your father had planned for you."

"Travel to Gloucester? It's rather a long way." And yet every instinct said she should investigate this hospital for the weak-minded. "You don't suppose—" She stopped abruptly, wondering if the curate had made a mistake and Miss Wild really read Mrs Wild.

"Suppose what?"

"Nothing. Pay it no mind. Being in love leaves one prone to moments of fancy. But it does make me wonder if my father sent my mother to such a place."

A heaviness settled in her chest. Fourteen years was a long time to spend in a hospital. Had her mother suffered from a form of mental instability? Mr Paisley had intimated as much. Though she could only recall her mother being loving and kind and of sound mind.

Sylvester cupped her nape and kissed her tenderly on the forehead. "I'll speak to Heyburn and Daventry, tell them we're leaving for London and Gloucester as soon as Sykes returns."

"What if we have a wasted journey?"

"It won't be wasted. One way or another, we will uncover the truth."

The outskirts of Cranham Woods
Some nine miles from Gloucester

After an exhausting three days spent visiting Doctors' Commons to procure a special licence, suffering the long journey to Gloucester and hunting for the hospital, Nora peered through the wrought-iron gates of Chatham Asylum.

The mansion house looked like a family home, not a dark and miserable place for the insane. Stone steps led past the manicured lawn to an impressive oak door. The day was bright, the sky unburdened by storm clouds. A sweet little robin hopped onto the gate pillar. There was no sign of the black crow of death.

"Honora, we've stood staring for more than five minutes." Sylvester's hand settled on her back. "Would you like me to knock and make the necessary enquiries?"

"Thank you, but no." Nora released the sigh she had held for fourteen years. During their search for Dr Chatham, hope had sparked in her chest, a belief her mother was alive. But what would she find beyond the walls of the welcoming house? "This is unlike any asylum I've heard spoken about."

"What is it you fear? That she left of her own accord?"

Their thoughts were so in tune Sylvester could read her mind. "What if she ran away from both of us? What if I've invented a story to ease the heartache? One about a perfect parent torn away from her only daughter?"

Sylvester captured her hand. Even through her kid glove, she felt the thrum of his life force. "We won't know unless we ask. Either way, I am here as the crutch you've grown accustomed to leaning on."

She managed a smile at the memory of their journey to the Musgrove hotel. It had been impossible to fight the profound feelings. Impossible to deny she had fallen in love with him.

"You're right," she said. "A person is better equipped to deal with facts, not uncertainties."

He arched a brow. "Another of Daventry's insightful quotes?"

"Miss Trimble's, actually."

"I think she likes me," he said, referring to their brief visit to Howland Street. He was the first man Miss Trimble had treated with an ounce of kindness. Although a sudden pressing engagement prevented her from sitting down to take tea with them.

"She seemed to like you, though it may be because she has a scar on her neck. She hides it well and doesn't know I caught a glimpse of the mark."

"So it had nothing to do with my charming smile?"

"Nothing." Nora found her mood suddenly lifted. Indeed, she squared her shoulders, quite prepared to face whatever the day should bring. "Let us enquire after Dr Chatham. The gate is open. Perhaps he knows of a miracle cure to ease a troubled mind."

"Maybe he calls it an asylum to scare away visitors. I might hang the same sign on Highcliffe's gatehouse, then I shall have you all to myself."

Nora tapped him playfully on the arm, thoughts of how they might spend their evening banishing all worries about Rosemary Wild.

She steeled herself for disappointment, opened the iron gate and let Sylvester lead her up to the front door.

It took five minutes for someone to answer. A young, muscular gentleman dressed in shirtsleeves, black trousers and waistcoat opened the door a fraction and asked they state their business.

Sylvester introduced them and presented his calling card.

Presuming the lord had a relative in need of treatment, the fellow led them down an elegant corridor and directed them to wait in Dr Chatham's office. The room was much like any gentleman's study, with mahogany furnishings and wall-to-wall bookcases filled with neat volumes.

Minutes later, the doctor entered. He was a man of fifty,

his dark hair peppered grey. He welcomed them to his hospital, though his gaze lingered on Sylvester's scar.

Sylvester frowned. "You say this is a hospital, yet it clearly states *asylum* on the gate."

The doctor smiled warmly. "The locals demand I post it as a warning. They do not consider an illness of the mind the same as an illness of the heart." He shrugged. "I treat patients regardless of what ails them."

"The gates were unlocked," Nora said, a pain twisting in her stomach at the thought her mother might have left years ago. "Are you not worried your patients will escape?"

The doctor shook his head. "Why would they leave when life is much kinder to them here?" He glanced at the clock on his desk with mild impatience. "Am I to understand you have a relative who needs a diagnosis?"

Nora kept her hands clasped in her lap to stop them shaking. "Might you have a patient here by the name of Rosemary Wild? She may have arrived many years ago, fourteen to be precise."

If not, it meant her father planned to bundle Nora into a hired coach and ferry her to Gloucester in the dead of night.

Dr Chatham's smile faded. "I'm afraid such information is confidential. May I ask why it concerns you?"

Nora explained her fears, said she believed the Reverend Wild paid a yearly sum to keep someone at the hospital. That she had seen written proof.

Dr Chatham stood. "I shall have to check the files. If you will excuse me." And then he left and promised to return shortly.

The next ten minutes proved unbearable. Her heart thundered. Her mouth was so dry she couldn't speak. With her nerves on edge, Nora jumped to her feet when the doctor returned.

"You must prepare yourself for a shock," he said but was

suddenly cut short when a woman wearing a pretty green dress flew into his office.

She took one look at Nora, clutched her chest and burst into tears. "Honora! It is you! I never thought to see you again." Mild panic flashed in eyes Nora barely remembered. "Does your father know you're here?"

Nora failed to find her voice.

Sylvester stood, explained who he was and why they had journeyed to Gloucester.

Nora merely stared.

Rosemary Wild did not look to be suffering from any mental disorder. She looked happy and healthy. Her brown hair was fashioned into a simple chignon. One might get the impression she was the mistress of this grand house.

Resentment spread through Nora's chest. "You're not a patient," she stated, her blunt tone taking them all by surprise. "You've spent fourteen years in this hospital, been cured of your ailments, yet you did not return home."

No one had locked this woman in a dungeon.

"I was a patient," her mother said nervously. "I did suffer a sickness of the mind, brought about by the pressure of being a vicar's wife. Your father was not an easy man to live with."

Anger surfaced. "Yes, he is a brute and a bully and demands his own way. He uses force when necessary, but that is not the worst of it." Tears welled now. "The worst is that he hasn't a loving bone in his miserable body."

"But he wrote to me, assured me you were well."

Sylvester explained that he had come to hire Nora because she worked as an enquiry agent. That they had fallen in love and would marry before the month was out.

Her mother frowned. "But your father said you married his curate six years ago. I presumed you were happy."

Dr Chatham intervened. He explained how it had taken years for Rosemary to regain her health, and she would likely relapse if she returned to Chipping Norton.

"Forgive me, Honora," her mother clutched her hands. "I didn't want you to suffer the shame. People are cruel. I didn't want your husband to know of my illness." She turned her distraught gaze to Dr Chatham. "Can they stay for a few hours? Can I have time to explain things properly to my daughter?"

"Rosemary, this is your home. Take Honora to the sitting room. Take as long as you need."

Nora spent a few emotional hours with her mother while Dr Chatham and Sylvester toured the hospital. When they parted, Nora promised to say nothing to her father, promised to write and visit again, though she wasn't sure she would.

"I'm sorry," Sylvester said once they were settled inside his carriage. "I'm sorry your mother fell short of your expectations."

Nora had dreamed of a different reunion. But that was when she saw life through a child's innocent eyes. One look at the handsome man opposite made her feel grateful she was a woman.

"I'm glad I spent a few hours with her. And I do understand why she cannot return home." She sighed, exhaling years of trapped emotion. "In a weird way, I feel less angry towards my father. Perhaps he was scared of losing me, too. Control is a form of fear."

"Surely you don't condone his behaviour?"

"No, but understanding a possible reason makes it easier to live with." And Miss Trimble was right. When forced to confront a harsh reality, the truth was often not as painful as the story one concocted in one's mind.

"No one's life is perfect," Sylvester said. "Sometimes people don't love us like we want them to. Sometimes our lives are better for it."

Nora smiled at the man who would soon be her husband. "It's probably for the best. My heart is so full of love for you, there's no room to love anyone else. Except for our children."

Sylvester's gaze slipped slowly over her body, and he quirked his brow. "We've got a long journey back to London. Perhaps we should think of a way to pass the time." His sensual smile stoked lust's embers. "These blinds afford every privacy."

Keen to take him into her body and show him just how much she loved him, she lowered her voice to purr. "As you're dressed like a gentleman, perhaps you mean to distract me by reciting poetry."

He took to untying his cravat. "Rest assured. Soon, you'll be alone in a carriage with the most rakish of men."

CHAPTER 21

Highcliffe
Ten days later

"Your romance began the moment you bid on the harpsichord." Rachel Hunter gestured to the cypress instrument near the window in the drawing room, a wedding present from Mr Daventry. "Lord Deville knew the action spoke of loyalty and strength of heart."

Nora glanced at her husband. Despite being deep in conversation with the men, he looked up and offered a smile that heated her blood.

What was the surprise he had planned for their wedding night? Nora looked to the mantel clock and silently wished the next few hours away. If only the cogs would spin faster.

She turned her attention to her colleagues, though only Rachel worked for the Order now. "It's as Mr Daventry always says. The truth speaks to the heart. We grew to trust each other fairly quickly."

"What happened to your spectacles?" Eliza teased.

"Mrs Egan is wearing them. She said they soften the harsh angles of her face, and she's tired of looking like a grump."

They all laughed.

"Your housekeeper is very attentive," Julianna noted.

"She's relieved the dark days are over, that's all."

With the help of extra servants, Mrs Egan had whipped the house into shape for the wedding. Nothing was too much trouble. This morning, she had hugged Nora in the privacy of her sitting room and thanked her for the umpteenth time.

Elisabeth Deville had been equally kind and gracious. After a day spent giving Nora advice on how to run such a vast house, she had taken her upstairs. Carefully moving the tapestry in what was now Nora's chamber, Elisabeth searched for the loose stone only to reveal a box of jewels hidden behind.

"I am the only one who knows it's here," Elisabeth had said. "Sylvester's great-grandmother wrote about it in a diary I found tucked away in the library."

Nora touched the diamond necklace at her throat, part of the parure that had once belonged to Elisabeth's mother.

"What a pity Miss Trimble couldn't come," Julianna said, bringing Nora's attention back to the present. "Mr Daventry said she has taken ill and doesn't have the strength to make the long journey."

"Yes, he assures me she will make a speedy recovery."

It was all rather strange. Miss Trimble had seemed perfectly well a week ago and said she was looking forward to the wedding. But then they decided to marry at Highcliffe, and the lady found herself plagued by a mystery illness.

"I do hope Mr Daventry hires more agents." Eliza sighed. "My heart goes out to Miss Trimble. To find oneself redundant must have been a terrible blow."

"Mr Daventry did suggest he'd not finished playing matchmaker," Nora said, recalling their previous conversation. "But should Miss Trimble find herself alone, perhaps one of us might hire her. I'm told she used to be a governess for a family in Vienna."

Rachel leaned closer. "I hear Mrs D'Angelo is with child."

No one dared look at the lady talking to Mrs Daventry on the sofa. But she did place her hand on her abdomen far too frequently.

"What's this?" Sylvester said, coming to stand behind Nora. "Whispering in the corner? One might think you're a smuggling gang planning your next operation."

He set his hot hand to Nora's waist, sending a delicious shiver down her spine. Oh, how she wished they were alone to indulge in every pleasure.

"We were discussing Miss Trimble." Nora kept her voice even, despite the rogue stroking his thumb back and forth in a secret caress. "And whether one of us might hire her to be our governess."

"Are you sure she was a governess?" he said, joining the conversation and sparking everyone's interest. "I can't shake the thought that she looks familiar. She has the bearing of an aristocrat, though the fact she's highly educated poses a contradiction."

"Few fathers believe knowledgeable ladies make good brides," Julianna agreed. She had spent enough time in noble homes to know. "Perhaps Miss Trimble earned her graceful countenance while working abroad. Perhaps she worked for a wealthy family in Vienna."

Nora found the subject fascinating. Not as fascinating as the man currently playing havoc with her senses.

Aware of her need to spend an intimate moment alone, Sylvester pressed his mouth to her ear and merely whispered, "Come."

The memory of them making love in the cottage last night flitted into her mind. Indeed, she could barely follow her friends' discussion.

"If you will excuse me for a moment," she said before her

breath quickened and she climaxed from mere thought alone. "I should find Mrs Egan and check the preparations for dinner tonight."

"Allow me to play escort," Sylvester said.

No one asked why she didn't just tug the bell pull and summon the housekeeper. No one questioned Lord Deville's need to involve himself in household affairs. Or why the groom's mother didn't take matters in hand on her son's wedding day.

Sylvester suggested they visit his study and ring for Mrs Egan there. Indeed, he drew her into the inherently masculine room and promptly locked the door.

His mouth was on hers in an instant, hot and needy.

"Watch my hair." She tilted her head so he could kiss her neck and growl all the wicked things he would do now away from prying eyes. "What about our guests?"

"They won't notice if we're gone for an hour." A sensual hum escaped him. "And you look divine in pink silk."

"While I'm desperate to push you into that chair and sit astride your thighs, we should rejoin our guests in the drawing room. And I don't want to spoil tonight's surprise."

He looked at her, his lustful smile turning mischievous. "Let's hope we're guaranteed good weather."

It was clear he was struggling to keep the secret. And if she knew what to expect, she might relax and enjoy her wedding day.

"So we'll be outside?" she asked, smoothing her hand over his chest, inducing him to confess. "Won't it be cold?"

"Not with the braziers and the heat of my body warming you."

So, they were not spending the night in the hidden room. He wasn't taking her to Westgate, not when they had guests in the house. Besides, they were going to Cornwall next week to roam the clifftops and walk barefoot along the sandy beaches.

"You're taking me to the cave," she said, making an insightful guess. When he hesitated, she slipped her hand down to cup the evidence of his arousal. "Tell me, so I won't be disappointed."

"Have I ever left you unsatisfied?"

"Never. But you're a romantic at heart, and we shared our first kiss, our first night together in the cave. It makes sense you would want to make love to me there."

He hissed a breath as she took to stroking him. "Perhaps I'm going to strip you naked, love, ready for your first swimming lesson."

"Hmm, you're such a good tutor, my lord. No doubt I will want many lessons. Indeed, marrying me might prove profitable."

Sylvester brushed his mouth over hers. "Love, with you as my wife, I feel as rich as Croesus."

THANK YOU!

I hope you enjoyed reading *Your Scarred Heart.*

What is Miss Trimble's secret?
And what will a woman who despises men think of Mr
Daventry's plan?

Find out in ...

No Life for a Lady
Ladies of the Order - Book 5

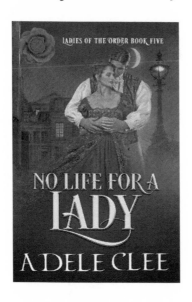

More titles by Adele Clee

Avenging Lords

At Last the Rogue Returns

A Wicked Wager

Valentine's Vow

A Gentleman's Curse

Scandalous Sons

And the Widow Wore Scarlet

The Mark of a Rogue

When Scandal Came to Town

The Mystery of Mr Daventry

Gentlemen of the Order

Dauntless

Raven

Valiant

Dark Angel

Ladies of the Order

The Devereaux Affair

More than a Masquerade

Mine at Midnight

Your Scarred Heart

No Life for a Lady